OXFORD STUDENT TEXTS

Series Editor: Steven Croft

Aphra Behn: The Rover

Aphra Behn
The Rover

Edited by Diane Maybank

Oxford University Press

OXFORD
UNIVERSITY PRESS

Great Clarendon Street, Oxford OX2 6DP

Oxford University Press is a department of the University of Oxford.
It furthers the University's objective of excellence in research, scholarship,
and education by publishing worldwide in

Oxford   New York

Auckland   Cape Town   Dar es Salaam   Hong Kong   Karachi
Kuala Lumpur   Madrid   Melbourne   Mexico City   Nairobi
New Delhi   Shanghai   Taipei   Toronto

With offices in

Argentina   Austria   Brazil   Chile   Czech Republic   France   Greece
Guatemala   Hungary   Italy   Japan   South Korea   Poland   Portugal
Singapore   Switzerland   Thailand   Turkey   Ukraine   Vietnam

Oxford is a registered trade mark of Oxford University Press
in the UK and in certain other countries

British Library Cataloguing in Publication Data
Data available

ISBN: 978-0-19-832573-4

1 3 5 7 9 10 8 6 4 2

Typeset in Goudy Old Style MT
by Palimpsest Book Production Limited, Grangemouth, Stirlingshire

Printed in Great Britain by Cox and Wyman Ltd., Reading

The publishers would like to thank the following for permission to reproduce
photographs: p2: Mary Evans Picture Library; p6: Westminster Abbey;
p8: National Portrait Gallery; p11: Historical Picture Archive/Corbis;
p170: Oxford University Press; p175: The Bridgeman Art Library; p180: Time Life
Pictures/Getty Images; p184: Photostage/Donald Cooper; p187: Chris Harris/Willamette
University, Salem, Oregon; p200: City of London Guildhall Library.

Contents

Acknowledgements

The text of the play is taken from *Aphra Behn: The Rover and Other Plays* edited by Jane Spencer (*Oxford World's Classics*, 1998).

Acknowledgements from Diane Maybank

My thanks go to Steven Croft for his positive encouragement and to Jan Doorly for her friendly, professional advice at all stages of this project. Of the many excellent critical works I have read on Aphra Behn the writing of Janet Todd and Derek Hughes stands out as being particularly rigorous and inspiring. Finally I would like to thank those bright and enthusiastic students with whom it has been a pleasure to spend many a happy hour acting and discussing *The Rover*.

This book is dedicated to my husband Bill Sellicks, with love.

Editors

Steven Croft, the series editor, holds degrees from Leeds and Sheffield universities. He has taught at secondary and tertiary level and is currently head of the Department of English and Humanities in a tertiary college. He has 25 years' examining experience at A level and is currently a Principal Examiner for English. He has written several books on teaching English at A level, and his publications for Oxford University Press include *Literature, Criticism and Style*, *Success in AQA Language and Literature* and *Exploring Language and Literature*.

Diane Maybank attended the universities of Kent, Cambridge and London where she studied English Literature as an undergraduate and Film Studies as a postgraduate. She has been teaching English and Media Studies for over 30 years in schools and colleges in France, New Zealand and the UK. She currently teaches in the English and Media Department at a sixth form college.

Foreword

Oxford Student Texts, under the founding editorship of Victor Lee, have established a reputation for presenting literary texts to students in both a scholarly and an accessible way. The new editions aim to build on this successful approach. They have been written to help students, particularly those studying English literature for AS or A level, to develop an increased understanding of their texts. Each volume in the series, which covers a selection of key poetry and drama texts, consists of four main sections which link together to provide an integrated approach to the study of the text.

The first part provides important background information about the writer, his or her times and the factors that played an important part in shaping the work. This discussion sets the work in context and explores some key contextual factors.

This section is followed by the poetry or play itself. The text is presented without accompanying notes so that students can engage with it on their own terms without the influence of secondary ideas. To encourage this approach, the Notes are placed in the third section, immediately following the text. The Notes provide explanations of particular words, phrases, images, allusions and so forth, to help students gain a full understanding of the text. They also raise questions or highlight particular issues or ideas which are important to consider when arriving at interpretations.

The fourth section, Interpretations, goes on to discuss a range of issues in more detail. This involves an examination of the influence of contextual factors as well as looking at such aspects as language and style, and various critical views or interpretations. A range of activities for students to carry out, together with discussions as to how these might be approached, are integrated into this section.

At the end of each volume there is a selection of Essay Questions, a Further Reading list and, where appropriate, a Glossary.

We hope you enjoy reading this text and working with these supporting materials, and wish you every success in your studies.

Steven Croft *Series Editor*

The Rover in Context

Aphra Behn, successful playwright, poet, novelist and translator, was England's first professional woman writer. So where are her achievements commemorated? The only image of her on display in London's National Portrait Gallery hardly does her justice. A copy by Robert White of a likeness by John Riley, it is a line engraving published some 27 years after Behn's death and measures a scant 9 by 13 centimetres. A stout leather covering protects the image from daylight.

The sense of discretion and propriety here is at odds with the reputation of the feisty lady who loved public life and sought fame in London's court and theatre circles in the 1670s. In the National Portrait Gallery, she needs to be protected from fading away from view altogether. The contrast between the engraving and the richly coloured three-quarter-length portraits of her fellow writers from the later Stuart period is marked. Step into an adjacent gallery and you will exchange bold glances with the many periwigged gentlemen of the Kit-Cat Club – writers like Joseph Addison, William Congreve and John Vanbrugh. These are all men whose portraits speak confidently of values and privileges shared in the clubs and coffee houses of the period. Behn would not have wanted to be among them, as they were supporters of the Whigs (pro-Parliamentarian and Puritan) and she was a radical Tory by temperament and political choice, supporting the Stuart monarchy and traditional institutions.

In the end the image does not matter. Its features are stereotypical rather than individual; it could depict any lady of means in the late seventeenth century. The context tells us more, especially about Behn's status in English literature. She was the author of a body of work that had to be stoutly defended against charges of plagiarism (passing off other people's work as her own) and indecency from the moment it was published. The nondescript engraving is a pointed reminder of her continuing marginalized position in the study of English literature.

There are few clues to Aphra Behn's appearance. This image was first published in 1716

The Rover was and still is Behn's most successful play. It is still occasionally performed; more in America than England, and more on university campuses than in the commercial theatre. When she wrote it she had some seven years' experience of writing for the London stage and was mid-way through her career. She was to go on to write more plays than any of her contemporaries with the exception of John Dryden. The first performance took place at the Duke's Theatre, Dorset Garden, on 24 March 1677, before an enthusiastic audience that included Charles II. Its instant popularity ensured repeat performances and much-needed income. Where had this woman, whose plays attracted royal favour, come from? How had she manoeuvred herself into such an advantageous position? Without husband or patron she succeeded in an art form that, by the late seventeenth century, had become almost exclusively the preserve of aristocratic men.

Open to interpretation: A life of Aphra Behn

There is more documentary evidence of Behn's birthplace, family connections and career than there are surviving portraits. However, scholars disagree about most of it. Bear this in mind as you become familiar with the 'facts' of her life. Placing the word 'probably' or 'perhaps' in front of many of these assertions is the right approach.

Aphra Behn was born at Harbledown, near Canterbury in Kent. Her father, Bartholomew Johnson, was a barber or innkeeper. His wife, Behn's mother Elizabeth, was a wet-nurse. Local baptismal records of around 1640 show the christening of a baby girl born to the couple and named Eaffery or Aphra. Elizabeth Johnson gained very good employment as a wet-nurse to the influential and aristocratic Colepeper family. It was a connection that may have improved Aphra's life chances.

From such humble beginnings as these we can only guess at how Behn acquired the education she would need to pursue a writing career in London. Where did she learn to make easy reference to the classics in her writing? Where did she gain the confidence to contribute to the philosophical, political and scientific debates of her day? Where did she acquire the fluency needed to translate poetry and fiction from French? Somehow the barber's daughter found a privileged education in her youth. One theory is that she may have shared the Colepeper children's private education through her mother's connection as wet-nurse to the family.

Behn's story moves from the south of England to South America. There are claims that in 1663 her father was appointed lieutenant-general to the English colony of Surinam, now Dutch Guiana, and that he died on the outward voyage to the colony. It is said that Behn and her female relatives completed the journey and stayed in Surinam for about two months, living on a plantation. It seems unlikely that her father rose from

3

barber/innkeeper to such a prestigious position; but this does not mean that Behn did not undertake the voyage to Surinam. She could possibly have been employed on a mission there as a government spy.

On her return to England in 1664 she became Mrs Behn. Her husband's surname suggests that he was of Dutch or German origin – a London merchant, perhaps? Or a seaman she met on the voyages she undertook? Did he die of plague in 1665? Whatever the circumstances of this brief marriage, in 1666 Behn was signing her correspondence 'AB' and 'A. Behn', but seems to be widowed. Did a widow's status give Behn the best chance of an independent life in seventeenth-century London?

Records show that in 1666 Behn travelled to Antwerp as a spy in the service of Charles II during the second Dutch war between Holland and England. Her instructions were to obtain military and political information from William Scott, whom she had known in Surinam. She did glean some useful information as Scott warned her of the Dutch fleet's plan to sail up the Thames. However, Behn's spymasters chose to ignore the intelligence she gathered, and even refused to pay her expenses. There were rumours that she was Scott's mistress; a woman in her position would attract notoriety.

This easy defamation of Behn becomes a common theme in her life. Later it was to take the form of undermining her artistic achievements. In 1667 Behn returned to England with debts resulting from her unpaid spying activities, debts which may have landed her in prison. Out of prison and with her debts cleared by 1669, Behn began her writing career and the historical record becomes slightly better documented. *The Forced Marriage*, her first play, was performed by the Duke's Company at Lincoln's Inn Fields in 1670. It achieved a successful six-night run.

Between 1670 and 1689, Behn completed 18 plays. She could turn her hand to both tragicomedy and tragedy, but sex comedy was her strongest genre. Despite her popular success, Behn wrote her first seven plays, including *The Rover*, without dedications to patrons. She remained without the financial security of patronage for an unusually long period of time. Did her gender make her less attractive to patrons from the court circle? As she makes plain to her critics with a mixture of pride and pique, she was a woman 'forced to write for bread and not ashamed to owne it' (preface to *Sir Patient Fancy*, 1678).

Behn was always quick to defend her position as an independent woman playwright. She was especially stung by the slur of immodesty heaped on her by critics unable to view a woman writer who dealt with strong sexual themes as anything better than a whore. The charge of plagiarism also hurt deeply. Her unconventional private life fuelled speculation; by 1674–5 Behn had begun what was to be a long-term relationship with bisexual lawyer John Hoyle. There is no evidence that he supported her financially, and she continued to 'write for bread' with increasing success. Building on the popularity of *The Rover* she produced a sequel in 1680. Although it was well received, however, it failed to achieve the success of its earlier namesake.

Behn turned to writing poetry, translations and fiction during the 1680s. She approached these new genres with relish. Their breadth enabled her to draw on her Tory political convictions, her interest in science, and the materialist philosophy of Thomas Hobbes. Necessity also played a part; towards the end of Charles II's reign political conspiracies emptied the theatres and the demand for new plays fell away. Behn still needed to earn a living by writing, and 1686 marked her return to the theatre with *The Lucky Chance*, followed by the popular farce *The Emperor of the Moon* in 1687. This must have been a difficult year for Behn as it saw the arrest and inconclusive trial of her partner John Hoyle for sodomy.

In 1688, with her health failing, Behn published *Oroonoko*. She drew on her youthful experiences in Surinam for her setting, themes and characters. Some critics view this work as a pioneer novella or short novel. It is remarkable for its representation of colonial subjects; its astute depiction of a black African slave came in a period when few could see the potential of such subjects for sympathetic handling in fiction. Behn continued her writing career with the novel *Love Letters between a Nobleman and his Sister*. It is set during the political upheavals of the end of Charles II's reign and the beginning of James II's. She took the opportunity to satirize the factionalism of the period. As the title suggests, Behn kept to her challenging sexual themes to the end of her life.

Behn died on the 16 April 1689, two months into the reign of William and Mary. Always a loyal supporter of the House of Stuart, she lived to see the dynasty continue, though humbled and wielding much less power. She is said to have penned a guarded eulogy to the new monarchs shortly before her death.

She was buried in Westminster Abbey beneath a black marble slab bearing only her name. The slab bears no reference to father or husband, which is remarkable for a woman's grave at this time.

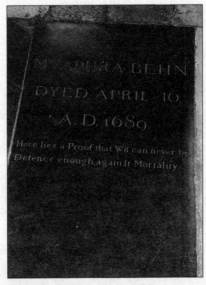

Aphra Behn's gravestone in Westminster Abbey is remarkable for bearing no reference to her father or husband

Opportunities for women? The restoration

Behn lived during one of the most bloody and turbulent periods in English history. England was torn apart by civil war between 1642 and 1651, when the conflict between the Parliamentarians led by Oliver Cromwell and the royalist followers of Charles I set neighbour against neighbour, father against son. This period of national shame, blood-letting and betrayal is far removed from *The Rover*'s sunny Mediterranean setting in 1650s Naples. The play follows the fortunes of a group of royalist Cavaliers in exile following their defeat at the hands of Cromwell.

It is not, though, a nostalgic, myth-making piece whose sole purpose is to celebrate the freewheeling brilliance of the exiled noblemen. It was performed at a time when the restored monarch Charles II was facing considerable domestic and foreign difficulties. He was mired in debt and, unlike the Cavaliers, unable to defy his poverty. The fractious, fragile friendship of the Cavaliers satirizes the in-fighting of Charles's courtiers. Those in the audience paying sufficient attention would find in *The Rover* a warning about a monarchy that was again losing its way. Backtracking a little into the history of this complex period will provide the context you need to understand Behn's use of this retrospective setting.

The main phase of the English Civil War had ended in 1649 when Charles I was beheaded and the Commonwealth was proclaimed. The execution of God's anointed monarch was a deeply scarring event, whichever side of the political divide you stood on. After his defeat at the battle of Worcester in 1651, the heir to the throne, also named Charles, escaped to the Continent and settled in Paris for much of the period – the so-called interregnum. His fellow courtiers lived in Spain, Italy, Germany and the Spanish Netherlands. All awaited the call to arms and the chance to win back the English crown by conquest.

But there was to be no invasion of England in heroic style.

Instead, Charles was invited to return and accept the crown because of the rather complex workings of English politics. He duly returned and was crowned King Charles II in 1661. Supporters of the king were given back some of their confiscated lands.

King Charles II, in a portrait dated about 1680

In 1662 Charles married the Portuguese princess Catherine of Braganza. This marriage failed to produce an heir to secure the Protestant royal line, a failure that contributed to instability and further political upheaval in the late Stuart period.

War had brought both a desire for social change and its opposite, a fear of the disorder that such change might bring. So how might women like Aphra Behn have benefited in a situation of uncertainty and flux? Men and women inhabited very different and separate spheres of activity in seventeenth-century England. Women rarely ventured outside the domestic and family milieu; power at all levels lay in men's hands. Writers in all academic disciplines sought to justify the inferior status of women by citing the analogy between a wife's duty to her husband and a husband's duty to king and country. If things were amiss in the domestic sphere because women were overstepping the mark, there would be unstable government, it was claimed.

But attitudes such as these, hostile to women's interests and aspirations, were being questioned by the mid-seventeenth century. Women had, after all, stepped into their soldier husbands' shoes to manage the family estates during the war. Opportunities had opened up for women to publish their ideas and contribute to the political and religious debates of the age. For a time this was made easier by a weakening of state censorship amid the turmoil of civil unrest. It would be an exaggeration to say that there was any significant move towards sexual equality in the way it is understood today, but there was a moment of opportunity for some women who were well enough placed to take advantage of it. Women had no new rights in law, but they could speak out about what was denied them more loudly and articulately than before. Despite the re-imposition of censorship that occurred at the restoration of the monarchy, women writers like Behn now had more opportunities to publish their work. They received recognition, fame and intense scrutiny as male critics adjusted to the challenge posed by women finding a public voice.

Behn always showed a genuine and consistent loyalty to Toryism and the Stuart monarchy, taking every opportunity to satirize Puritans and Whigs in her plays. Her political allegiances can be understood in the context of the limited choices open to women like her. Behn favoured the atmosphere and values of the Stuart court, where a woman could gain a reputation for intellectual ability and honour without the protection of a husband. There was a sexual freedom for men and woman within the court circle that was not possible in the world at large; some wives and well-placed mistresses could wield considerable

9

political power. Behn was attracted to this exclusive world, feeling that its libertine ways had more to offer clever, witty women than the mercenary values of the marriage market. The coffee houses, inns and country estates where a growing number of middle-class intellectuals were at liberty to exchange ideas and pursue them into print were strictly male only. The court at least valued women, albeit in a rather narrow fashion by today's standards. Behn certainly expressed her admiration for the more powerful mistresses, women like Nell Gwyn, who knew how to use her relationship with the king and courtiers to her advantage. The court circle, despite its apparent openness, was in reality a private coterie in which women could operate competitively. To write for the stage was truly to move into the public sphere.

Setting the scene: Restoration theatre

The Puritans had closed London's theatres in 1642 by Parliamentary decree. They considered it sinful for men, and especially women, to act in public, because to pretend to be someone else was a form of deceit. The new king reversed this decision in 1660 and theatres were soon in business again. Charles's personal interest in plays and the women who acted in them meant that intimate links with the court were soon established; he even lent his coronation robes as a costume for the actor Thomas Betterton in William Davenant's production of *Love and Honour*, written in 1649.

Within just three months of his return, Charles showed his determination to rebuild a theatrical tradition in London by granting royal patents to two of his veteran supporters. These men, Thomas Killigrew and William Davenant, were practising playwrights who had returned from exile with him. The patents gave them powers to establish rival theatre companies and to build new playhouses in the capital. Such was the influence of the king's patronage that it allowed Killigrew and Davenant to operate what was effectively a monopoly on commissioning plays and mounting productions. The patents survive to the present day and are still the legal foundations of the Theatre Royal in Drury Lane and the Royal Opera House, Covent Garden.

The King's Company, established by Killigrew, had a full repertoire from the start because it had inherited the performance rights to many plays of the Elizabethan, Jacobean and Caroline theatres. In 1674 it moved into the Theatre Royal, Drury Lane, built by Sir Christopher Wren. The Duke's Company, established by Davenant, lacked the same performance rights to plays. Davenant's solution was to commission new ones from writers such as Aphra Behn. The company performed in the Dorset Garden Theatre from 1671.

Thomas Killigrew (1612–1683), dramatist and theatre manager, had served Charles I and became a prominent figure at the court of Charles II

Before the Civil War all female parts had been played by male actors, with some exceptions. The Banqueting House in London's Whitehall had been used between 1622 and 1635 to stage spectacular masques in which the queen and her attendant ladies took part. As this was a strictly private pastime and not open to the paying public, the practice was not considered inconsistent with a woman's honour. The male-only rule changed with the new patents, which stipulated that women should play women's parts in public performance. Records show that a woman played the part of Desdemona in William Shakespeare's *Othello* in 1660. This may have been the first time a woman played a female part on the public stage in London.

Royal patronage, new buildings and eager audiences soon created a thriving theatre scene in London. For nearly two decades the companies competed in a very productive atmosphere, until troubled political times relating to the royal succession occasioned a drop in demand for new material. Audiences dwindled, fewer new plays were commissioned and a merger became the only way to ensure survival. In 1682 the two companies renamed themselves the United Company. This company survived until 1695, some six years after Behn's death.

Behn was one of only three professional playwrights to emerge in the first decade following the restoration – most playwrights were aristocrats writing for pleasure rather than for a living. For a woman to penetrate even the margins of the coterie centred on Charles II was an achievement in itself. Behn did more than that, for she established herself as one of the most prolific and successful playwrights of the period.

The Rover

The earliest recorded performance of the play was at the Dorset Garden Theatre on 24 March 1677, with the following cast:

MEN

Don Antonio (the viceroy's son)	Mr Jevon
Don Pedro (a noble Spaniard, his friend)	Mr Medbourne
Belvile (an English colonel in love with Florinda)	Mr Betterton
Willmore (the rover)	Mr Smith
Frederick (an English gentleman, and friend to Belvile and Blunt)	Mr Crosby
Blunt (an English country gentleman)	Mr Underhill
Stephano (servant to Don Pedro)	Mr Richards
Philippo (Lucetta's gallant)	Mr Percival
Sancho (pimp to Lucetta)	Mr John Lee
Biskey, and Sebastian (two bravos to Angellica)	
Officers and Soldiers	
[Diego,] Page (to Don Antonio)	

WOMEN

Florinda (sister to Don Pedro)	Mrs Betterton
Hellena (a gay young woman designed for a nun, and sister to Florinda)	Mrs Barry
Valeria (a kinswoman to Florinda)	Mrs Hughes
Angellica Bianca (a famous courtesan)	Mrs Quin
Moretta (her woman)	Mrs Leigh
Callis (governess to Florinda and Hellena)	Mrs Norris
Lucetta (a jilting wench)	Mrs Gillow
Servants, other Masqueraders (men and women)	

THE SCENE
Naples, in Carnival time

Prologue

Written by a person of quality

Wits, like physicians, never can agree,
When of a different society:
And Rabel's drops were never more cried down
By all the learned doctors of the town,
Than a new play whose author is unknown;   5
Nor can those doctors with more malice sue
(And powerful purses) the dissenting few,
Than those with an insulting pride, do rail
At all who are not of their own cabal.
  If a young poet hit your humour right,   10
You judge him then out of revenge and spite:
So amongst men there are ridiculous elves,
Who monkeys hate for being too like themselves.
So that the reason of the grand debate,
Why wit so oft is damned when good plays take,   15
Is that you censure as you love or hate.
  Thus, like a learned conclave, poets sit,
Catholic judges both of sense and wit,
And damn or save as they themselves think fit.
Yet those who to others' faults are so severe,   20
Are not so perfect but themselves may err.
Some write correct, indeed, but then the whole
(Bating their own dull stuff i'th' play) is stole:
As bees do suck from flowers their honeydew,
So they rob others, striving to please you.   25
  Some write their characters genteel and fine,
But then they do so toil for every line,
That what to you does easy seem, and plain,
Is the hard issue of their labouring brain.

And some th'effects of all their pains we see,   30
Is but to mimic good extempore.
Others, by long converse about the town,
Have wit enough to write a lewd lampoon,
But their chief skill lies in a bawdy song.
In short, the only wit that's now in fashion,   35
Is but the gleanings of good conversation.
As for the author of this coming play,
I asked him what he thought fit I should say
In thanks for your good company today:
He called me fool, and said it was well known,   40
You came not here for our sakes, but your own.
New plays are stuffed with wits, and with debauches,
That crowd and sweat like cits in May-day coaches.

Act I Scene I

A chamber
Enter Florinda and Hellena

FLORINDA What an impertinent thing is a young girl bred in a nunnery! How full of questions! Prithee, no more, Hellena, I have told thee more than thou understand'st already.

HELLENA The more's my grief; I would fain know as much as you, which makes me so inquisitive; nor is't enough I know you're a lover, unless you tell me too who 'tis you sigh for.

FLORINDA When you're a lover, I'll think you fit for a secret of that nature.

HELLENA 'Tis true, I never was a lover yet; but I begin to have a shrewd guess what 'tis to be so, and fancy it very pretty to sigh, and sing, and blush, and wish, and dream and wish, and long and wish to see the man, and when I do, look pale and tremble, just as you did when my brother brought home the fine English colonel to see you – what do you call him? Don Belvile.

FLORINDA Fie, Hellena.

HELLENA That blush betrays you. I am sure 'tis so; or is it Don Antonio, the viceroy's son? Or perhaps the rich old Don Vincentio, whom my father designs you for a husband? Why do you blush again?

FLORINDA With indignation; and how near soever my father thinks I am to marrying that hated object, I shall let him see I understand better what's due to my beauty, birth and fortune, and more to my soul, than to obey those unjust commands.

HELLENA Now hang me, if I don't love thee for that dear

disobedience. I love mischief strangely, as most of our   30
sex do, who are come to love nothing else. But tell me,
dear Florinda, don't you love that fine *Inglese?* For I
vow, next to loving him myself, 'twill please me most
that you do so, for he is so gay and so handsome.

FLORINDA Hellena, a maid designed for a nun ought not   35
to be so curious in a discourse of love.

HELLENA And dost thou think that ever I'll be a nun?
Or at least till I'm so old, I'm fit for nothing else:
faith, no, sister; and that which makes me long to
know whether you love Belvile, is because I hope he   40
has some mad companion or other that will spoil my
devotion. Nay, I'm resolved to provide myself this
Carnival, if there be e'er a handsome proper fellow
of my humour above ground, though I ask first.

FLORINDA Prithee be not so wild.   45

HELLENA Now you have provided yourself of a man,
you take no care for poor me. Prithee tell me, what
dost thou see about me that is unfit for love? Have I
not a world of youth? A humour gay? A beauty passable? A vigour desirable? Well-shaped? Clean-limbed?   50
Sweet-breathed? And sense enough to know how all
these ought to be employed to the best advantage?
Yes, I do, and will; therefore lay aside your hopes of
my fortune by my being a devotee, and tell me how
you came acquainted with this Belvile; for I perceive   55
you knew him before he came to Naples.

FLORINDA Yes, I knew him at the siege of Pamplona:
he was then a colonel of French horse, who, when the
town was ransacked, nobly treated my brother and
myself, preserving us from all insolences; and I must   60
own, besides great obligations, I have I know not what
that pleads kindly for him about my heart, and will
suffer no other to enter. But see, my brother.

Enter Don Pedro, Stephano with a masking habit,
and Callis

PEDRO Good morrow, sister. Pray when saw you your
lover Don Vincentio?   65

FLORINDA I know not, sir – Callis, when was he here? –
for I consider it so little, I know not when it was.

PEDRO I have a command from my father here to tell
you you ought not to despise him, a man of so vast
a fortune, and such a passion for you. – Stephano, my   70
things.

[Don Pedro] puts on his masking habit

FLORINDA A passion for me? 'Tis more than e'er I saw,
or he had a desire should be known. I hate Vincentio,
sir, and I would not have a man so dear to me as my
brother follow the ill customs of our country, and   75
make a slave of his sister; and, sir, my father's will
I'm sure you may divert.

PEDRO I know not how dear I am to you, but I wish
only to be ranked in your esteem equal with the English
colonel Belvile. Why do you frown and blush? Is there   80
any guilt belongs to the name of that cavalier?

FLORINDA I'll not deny I value Belvile. When I was
exposed to such dangers as the licensed lust of
common soldiers threatened, when rage and conquest
flew through the city, then Belvile, this criminal for   85
my sake, threw himself into all dangers to save my
honour: and will you not allow him my esteem?

PEDRO Yes, pay him what you will in honour; but you
must consider Don Vincentio's fortune, and the join-
ture he'll make you.   90

FLORINDA Let him consider my youth, beauty and
fortune, which ought not to be thrown away on his
age and jointure.

PEDRO 'Tis true, he's not so young and fine a gentleman

as that Belvile; but what jewels will that cavalier   95
present you with? Those of his eyes and heart?

HELLENA And are not those better than any Don
Vincentio has brought from the Indies?

PEDRO Why how now! has your nunnery breeding
taught you to understand the value of hearts and eyes?   100

HELLENA Better than to believe Vincentio's deserve
value from any woman: he may perhaps increase her
bags, but not her family.

PEDRO This is fine! Go, up to your devotion: you are
not designed for the conversation of lovers.   105

HELLENA (*aside*) Nor saints, yet awhile, I hope. – Is't not
enough you make a nun of me, but you must cast my
sister away too, exposing her to a worse confinement
than a religious life?

PEDRO The girl's mad! It is a confinement to be carried   110
into the country, to an ancient villa belonging to the
family of the Vincentios these five hundred years, and
have no other prospect than that pleasing one of
seeing all her own that meets her eyes: a fine air, large
fields and gardens, where she may walk and gather   115
flowers!

HELLENA When, by moonlight? For I am sure she dares
not encounter with the heat of the sun; that were a
task only for Don Vincentio and his Indian breeding,
who loves it in the dog days. And if these be her daily   120
divertisements, what are those of the night? To lie in
a wide moth-eaten bedchamber, with furniture in
fashion in the reign of King Sancho the First; the bed,
that which his forefathers lived and died in.

PEDRO Very well.   125

HELLENA This apartment, new furbished and fitted out
for the young wife, he (out of freedom) makes his
dressing room, and being a frugal and a jealous

coxcomb, instead of a valet to uncase his feeble
carcass, he desires you to do that office: signs of 130
favour, I'll assure you, and such as you must not hope
for, unless your woman be out of the way.

PEDRO Have you done yet?

HELLENA That honour being past, the giant stretches
itself, yawns and sighs a belch or two, loud as a musket, 135
throws himself into bed, and expects you in his foul
sheets; and ere you can get yourself undressed, calls
you with a snore or two: and are not these fine blessings to a young lady?

PEDRO Have you done yet? 140

HELLENA And this man you must kiss: nay, you must
kiss none but him, too – and nuzzle through his beard
to find his lips. And this you must submit to for three-
score years, and all for a jointure.

PEDRO For all your character of Don Vincentio, she is 145
as like to marry him as she was before.

HELLENA Marry Don Vincentio! Hang me, such a
wedlock would be worse than adultery with another
man. I had rather see her in the *Hôtel de Dieu*, to waste
her youth there in vows, and be a handmaid to lazars 150
and cripples, than to lose it in such a marriage.

PEDRO [*to Florinda*] You have considered, sister, that
Belvile has no fortune to bring you to; banished his
country, despised at home, and pitied abroad.

HELLENA What then? The viceroy's son is better than 155
that old Sir Fifty. Don Vincentio! Don Indian! He
thinks he's trading to Gambo still, and would barter
himself (that bell and bauble) for your youth and
fortune.

PEDRO Callis, take her hence, and lock her up all this 160
Carnival, and at Lent she shall begin her everlasting
penance in a monastery.

HELLENA I care not; I had rather be a nun than be obliged to marry as you would have me, if I were designed for't.   165

PEDRO Do not fear the blessing of that choice; you shall be a nun.

HELLENA Shall I so? You may chance to be mistaken in my way of devotion. A nun! yes, I am like to make a fine nun! I have an excellent humour for a grate. (*Aside*) 170 No, I'll have a saint of my own to pray to shortly, if I like any that dares venture on me.

PEDRO Callis, make it your business to watch this wildcat. – As for you, Florinda, I've only tried you all this while, and urged my father's will; but mine is, 175 that you would love Antonio: he is brave and young, and all that can complete the happiness of a gallant maid. This absence of my father will give us opportunity to free you from Vincentio by marrying here, which you must do tomorrow.   180

FLORINDA Tomorrow!

PEDRO Tomorrow, or 'twill be too late. 'Tis not my friendship to Antonio which makes me urge this, but love to thee, and hatred to Vincentio; therefore resolve upon tomorrow.   185

FLORINDA Sir, I shall strive to do as shall become your sister.

PEDRO I'll both believe and trust you. Adieu.
      Exeunt Pedro and Stephano

HELLENA As becomes his sister! That is, to be as resolved your way as he is his.   190
      Hellena goes to Callis

FLORINDA [*aside*] I ne'er till now perceived my ruin near;
      I've no defence against Antonio's love,
      For he has all the advantages of nature,
      The moving arguments of youth and fortune.

HELLENA But hark you, Callis, you will not be so cruel 195
to lock me up indeed, will you?

CALLIS I must obey the commands I have; besides, do
you consider what a life you are going to lead?

HELLENA Yes, Callis, that of a nun: and till then I'll be
indebted a world of prayers to you, if you'll let me 200
now see, what I never did, the divertisements of a
Carnival.

CALLIS What, go in masquerade? 'Twill be a fine farewell
to the world, I take it; pray, what would you do there?

HELLENA That which all the world does, as I am told: 205
be as mad as the rest, and take all innocent freedoms.
Sister, you'll go too, will you not? Come, prithee be
not sad. We'll outwit twenty brothers, if you'll be
ruled by me. Come, put off this dull humour with
your clothes, and assume one as gay, and as fantastic, 210
as the dress my cousin Valeria and I have provided,
and let's ramble.

FLORINDA Callis, will you give us leave to go?

CALLIS (*aside*) I have a youthful itch of going myself. –
Madam, if I thought your brother might not know 215
it, and I might wait on you; for by my troth, I'll not
trust young girls alone.

FLORINDA Thou seest my brother's gone already, and
thou shalt attend and watch us.
        Enter Stephano

STEPHANO Madam, the habits are come, and your 220
cousin Valeria is dressed and stays for you.

FLORINDA 'Tis well. I'll write a note, and if I chance to
see Belvile, and want an opportunity to speak to him,
that shall let him know what I've resolved in favour
of him. 225

HELLENA Come, let's in and dress us.
        Exeunt

Act I Scene II

A long street
Enter Belvile melancholy, Blunt, and Frederick

FREDERICK Why, what the devil ails the colonel, in a
time when all the world is gay, to look like mere Lent
thus? Hadst thou been long enough in Naples to have
been in love, I should have sworn some such judgement had befallen thee.   5

BELVILE No, I have made no new amours since I came
to Naples.

FREDERICK You have left none behind you in Paris?

BELVILE Neither.

FREDERICK I cannot divine the cause then, unless the   10
old cause, the want of money.

BLUNT And another old cause, the want of a wench;
would not that revive you?

BELVILE You are mistaken, Ned.

BLUNT Nay, 'adsheartlikins, then thou'rt past cure.   15

FREDERICK I have found it out: thou hast renewed thy
acquaintance with the lady that cost thee so many
sighs at the siege of Pamplona; pox on't, what d'ye
call her – her brother's a noble Spaniard, nephew to
the dead general – Florinda. Aye, Florinda: and will   20
nothing serve thy turn but that damned virtuous
woman? Whom on my conscience thou lovest in spite,
too, because thou seest little or no possibility of
gaining her.

BELVILE Thou art mistaken, I have interest enough in   25
that lovely virgin's heart to make me proud and vain,
were it not abated by the severity of a brother, who
perceiving my happiness –

FREDERICK Has civilly forbid thee the house?

BELVILE 'Tis so, to make way for a powerful rival, the   30
  viceroy's son, who has the advantage of me in being
  a man of fortune, a Spaniard, and her brother's friend;
  which gives him liberty to make his court, whilst I
  have recourse only to letters, and distant looks from
  her window, which are as soft and kind   35
    As those which heaven sends down on penitents.
BLUNT Heyday! 'Adsheartlikins, simile! By this light the
  man is quite spoiled. – Fred, what the devil are we
  made of, that we cannot be thus concerned for a
  wench? 'Adsheartlikins, our cupids are like the cooks   40
  of the camp: they can roast or boil a woman, but they
  have none of the fine tricks to set 'em off, no hogoes
  to make the sauce pleasant and the stomach sharp.
FREDERICK I dare swear I have had a hundred as young,
  kind and handsome as this Florinda; and dogs eat me   45
  if they were not as troublesome to me i'th' morning
  as they were welcome o'er night.
BLUNT And yet I warrant he would not touch another
  woman, if he might have her for nothing.
BELVILE That's thy joy, a cheap whore.   50
BLUNT Why, 'adsheartlikins, I love a frank soul: when
  did you ever hear of an honest woman that took a
  man's money? I warrant 'em good ones. But,
  gentlemen, you may be free: you have been kept so
  poor with parliaments and protectors that the little   55
  stock you have is not worth preserving; but I thank
  my stars, I had more grace than to forfeit my estate
  by cavaliering.
BELVILE Methinks only following the court should be
  sufficient to entitle 'em to that.   60
BLUNT 'Adsheartlikins, they know I follow it to do it
  no good, unless they pick a hole in my coat for lending
  you money now and then, which is a greater crime to

25

my conscience, gentlemen, than to the Common-
wealth.   6

Enter Willmore

WILLMORE Ha! Dear Belvile! Noble colonel!

BELVILE Willmore! Welcome ashore, my dear rover!
What happy wind blew us this good fortune?

WILLMORE Let me salute my dear Fred, and then
command me. [*To Frederick*] How is't, honest lad?   70

FREDERICK Faith, sir, the old compliment, infinitely the
better to see my dear mad Willmore again. Prithee,
why cam'st thou ashore? And where's the prince?

WILLMORE He's well, and reigns still lord of the watery
element. I must aboard again within a day or two, and   75
my business ashore was only to enjoy myself a little
this Carnival.

BELVILE Pray know our new friend, sir; he's but bashful,
a raw traveller, but honest, stout, and one of us.

WILLMORE (*embraces Blunt*) That you esteem him gives   80
him an interest here.

BLUNT Your servant, sir.

WILLMORE But well, faith, I'm glad to meet you again
in a warm climate, where the kind sun has its god-like
power still over the wine and women. Love and mirth   85
are my business in Naples, and if I mistake not the
place, here's an excellent market for chapmen of my
humour.

BELVILE See, here be those kind merchants of love you
look for.   90

*Enter several men in masking habits, some playing
on music, others dancing after, women dressed like
courtesans, with papers pinned on their breasts, and
baskets of flowers in their hands*

BLUNT 'Adsheartlikins, what have we here?

FREDERICK Now the game begins.

WILLMORE Fine pretty creatures! May a stranger have
leave to look and love? (*Reads the papers*) What's here:
'Roses for every month'?   95

BLUNT Roses for every month? What means that?

BELVILE They are, or would have you think they're courtesans, who here in Naples are to be hired by the
month.

WILLMORE Kind; and obliging to inform us. [*To a*   100
woman] Pray, where do these roses grow? I would fain
plant some of 'em in a bed of mine.

WOMAN Beware such roses, sir.

WILLMORE A pox of fear: I'll be baked with thee
between a pair of sheets (and that's thy proper still),   105
so I might but strew such roses over me, and under
me. Fair one, would you would give me leave to gather
at your bush this idle month; I would go near to make
somebody smell of it all the year after.

BELVILE And thou hast need of such a remedy, for thou   110
stink'st of tar and ropes' ends, like a dock or pesthouse.

The woman puts herself into the hands of a man,
and [both begin to leave]

WILLMORE Nay, nay, you shall not leave me so.

BELVILE By all means use no violence here.

[Exeunt man and woman]

WILLMORE Death! Just as I was going to be damnably   115
in love, to have her led off! I could pluck that rose
out of his hand, and even kiss the bed the bush grew
in.

FREDERICK No friend to love like a long voyage at sea.

BLUNT Except a nunnery, Fred.   120

WILLMORE Death! But will they not be kind, quickly be
kind? Thou know'st I'm no tame sigher, but a rampant
lion of the forest.

*Advances, from the farther end of the scenes, two
men dressed all over with horns of several sorts,
making grimaces at one another, with papers
pinned on their backs*

BELVILE Oh the fantastical rogues, how they're dressed!
'Tis a satire against the whole sex.   125

WILLMORE Is this a fruit that grows in this warm
country?

BELVILE Yes: 'tis pretty to see these Italians start, swell
and stab, at the word cuckold, and yet stumble at
horns on every threshold.   130

WILLMORE See what's on their back. (*Reads*) 'Flowers of
every night': ah, rogue, and more sweet than roses of
every month! This is a gardener of Adam's own
breeding.

[The two men dressed in horns] dance

BELVILE What think you of those grave people? Is a   135
wake in Essex half so mad or extravagant?

WILLMORE I like their sober grave way: 'tis a kind of legal
authorized fornication, where the men are not chid for't,
nor the women despised, as amongst our dull English;
even the monsieurs want that part of good manners.   140

BELVILE But here in Italy, a monsieur is the humblest
best-bred gentleman: duels are so baffled by bravos,
that an age shows not one but between a Frenchman
and a hangman, who is as much too hard for him on
the Piazza, as they are for a Dutchman on the New   145
Bridge. But see, another crew.

*Enter Florinda, Hellena, and Valeria, dressed like
gipsies; Callis and Stephano, Lucetta, Philippo,
and Sancho in masquerade*

HELLENA Sister, there's your Englishman, and with him
a handsome proper fellow. I'll to him, and instead of
telling him his fortune, try my own.

WILLMORE Gipsies, on my life; sure these will prattle if 150
a man cross their hands.
  [*Willmore*] *goes to Hellena*
Dear, pretty, and I hope young, devil, will you tell an
amorous stranger what luck he's like to have?

HELLENA Have a care how you venture with me, sir, lest
I pick your pocket, which will more vex your English 155
humour, than an Italian fortune will please you.

WILLMORE How the devil cam'st thou to know my
country and humour?

HELLENA The first I guess by a certain forward impudence, which does not displease me at this time; and 160
the loss of your money will vex you, because I hope
you have but very little to lose.

WILLMORE Egad, child, thou'rt i'th' right; it is so little,
I dare not offer it thee for a kindness. But cannot you
divine what other things of more value I have about 165
me, that I would more willingly part with?

HELLENA Indeed no, that's the business of a witch, and
I am but a gipsy yet. Yet, without looking in your
hand, I have a parlous guess 'tis some foolish heart
you mean, an inconstant English heart, as little worth 170
stealing as your purse.

WILLMORE Nay, then thou dost deal with the devil, that's
certain: thou hast guessed as right, as if thou hadst
been one of that number it has languished for. I find
you'll be better acquainted with it; nor can you take 175
it in a better time, for I am come from sea, child, and
Venus not being propitious to me in her own element,
I have a world of love in store. Would you would be
good-natured and take some on't off my hands.

HELLENA Why, I could be inclined that way, but for a 180
foolish vow I am going to make – to die a maid.

WILLMORE Then thou art damned without redemption,

and as I am a good Christian, I ought in charity to
divert so wicked a design; therefore prithee, dear creature, let me know quickly when and where I shall begin   185
to set a helping hand to so good a work.

HELLENA If you should prevail with my tender heart,
as I begin to fear you will, for you have horrible loving
eyes, there will be difficulty in't that you'll hardly
undergo for my sake.   190

WILLMORE Faith, child, I have been bred in dangers, and
wear a sword that has been employed in a worse cause
than for a handsome kind woman. Name the danger;
let it be anything but a long siege, and I'll undertake
it.   195

HELLENA Can you storm?

WILLMORE Oh, most furiously.

HELLENA What think you of a nunnery wall? For he
that wins me, must gain that first.

WILLMORE A nun! Oh how I love thee for't! There's no   200
sinner like a young saint. Nay, now there's no denying
me: the old law had no curse, to a woman, like dying
a maid; witness Jephtha's daughter.

HELLENA A very good text this, if well handled; and I
perceive, Father Captain, you would impose no severe   205
penance on her who were inclined to console herself
before she took orders.

WILLMORE If she be young and handsome.

HELLENA Aye, there's it: but if she be not –

WILLMORE By this hand, child, I have an implicit faith, 210
and dare venture on thee with all faults. Besides, 'tis
more meritorious to leave the world when thou hast
tasted and proved the pleasure on't. Then 'twill be a
virtue in thee, which now will be pure ignorance.

HELLENA I perceive, good Father Captain, you design   215
only to make me fit for heaven. But if, on the contrary,

you should quite divert me from it, and bring me back
to the world again, I should have a new man to seek,
I find; and what a grief that will be. For when I begin,
I fancy I shall love like anything; I never tried yet.   220

WILLMORE Egad, and that's kind. Prithee, dear creature,
give me credit for a heart, for faith I'm a very honest
fellow. Oh, I long to come first to the banquet of love,
and such a swingeing appetite I bring! Oh, I'm impatient. Thy lodging, sweetheart, thy lodging, or I'm a   225
dead man!

HELLENA Why must we be either guilty of fornication
or murder if we converse with you men? And is there
no difference between leave to love me, and leave to
lie with me?   230

WILLMORE Faith, child, they were made to go together.

LUCETTA ([*aside to Sancho,*] *pointing to Blunt*) Are you
sure this is the man?

SANCHO When did I mistake your game?

LUCETTA This is a stranger, I know by his gazing; if he   235
be brisk, he'll venture to follow me, and then, if I
understand my trade, he's mine. He's English, too, and
they say that's a sort of good-natured loving people,
and have generally so kind an opinion of themselves,
that a woman with any wit may flatter 'em into any   240
sort of fool she pleases.

    [*Lucetta*] *often passes by Blunt, and gazes on him;*
    he struts and cocks, and walks and gazes on her

BLUNT [*aside*] 'Tis so, she is taken: I have beauties which
my false glass at home did not discover.

FLORINDA [*aside*] This woman watches me so, I shall get
no opportunity to discover myself to him, and so   245
miss the intent of my coming. ([*To Belvile,*] *looking in
his hand*) But as I was saying, sir, by this line you
should be a lover.

BELVILE I thought how right you guessed: all men are
in love, or pretend to be so. Come, let me go, I'm   250
weary of this fooling.

    *[Belvile] walks away. [Florinda] holds him, he
    strives to get from her*

FLORINDA I will not, till you have confessed whether
the passion that you have vowed Florinda, be true or
false.

BELVILE (*turn[ing] quick towards her*) Florinda!   255

FLORINDA Softly.

BELVILE Thou hast named one will fix me here for ever.

FLORINDA She'll be disappointed, then, who expects
you this night at the garden gate; and if you fail not,
as – (*looks on Callis, who observes them*) let me see the   260
other hand – you will go near to do, she vows to die
or make you happy.

BELVILE What canst thou mean?

FLORINDA That which I say; farewell.

    [Florinda] offers to go

BELVILE Oh, charming sibyl, stay; complete that joy,   265
which as it is will turn into distraction! Where must
I be? At the garden gate? I know it; at night, you say?
I'll sooner forfeit heaven than disobey.

    *Enter Don Pedro and other maskers, and pass over
    the stage*

CALLIS Madam, your brother's here.

FLORINDA Take this to instruct you farther.   270

    [Florinda] gives [Belvile] a letter, and goes off

FREDERICK Have a care, sir, what you promise; this may
be a trap laid by her brother to ruin you.

BELVILE Do not disturb my happiness with doubts.

    [Belvile] opens the letter

WILLMORE [*to Hellena*] My dear pretty creature, a thousand blessings on thee! Still in this habit, you say?   275

And after dinner at this place.

HELLENA Yes, if you will swear to keep your heart, and not bestow it between this and that.

WILLMORE By all the little gods of love, I swear I'll leave it with you, and if you run away with it, those deities 280 of justice will revenge me.

Exeunt all the women [except Lucetta]

FREDERICK Do you know the hand?

BELVILE 'Tis Florinda's.
All blessings fall upon the virtuous maid.

FREDERICK Nay, no idolatry: a sober sacrifice I'll allow 285 you.

BELVILE Oh, friends, the welcom'st news! The softest letter! Nay, you shall all see it; and could you now be serious, I might be made the happiest man the sun shines on! 290

WILLMORE The reason of this mighty joy?

BELVILE See how kindly she invites me to deliver her from the threatened violence of her brother: will you not assist me?

WILLMORE I know not what thou mean'st, but I'll make 295 one at any mischief where a woman's concerned. But she'll be grateful to us for the favour, will she not?

BELVILE How mean you?

WILLMORE How should I mean? Thou know'st there's but one way for a woman to oblige me. 300

BELVILE Do not profane; the maid is nicely virtuous.

WILLMORE Ho, pox, then she's fit for nothing but a husband: let her e'en go, colonel.

FREDERICK Peace, she's the colonel's mistress, sir.

WILLMORE Let her be the devil, if she be thy mistress, 305 I'll serve her. Name the way.

BELVILE Read here this postscript.

[Belvile] gives [Willmore] a letter

WILLMORE (*reads*) 'At ten at night, at the garden gate, of which, if I cannot get the key, I will contrive a way over the wall. Come attended with a friend or two.' — 310 Kind heart, if we three cannot weave a string to let her down a garden wall, 'twere pity but the hangman wove one for us all.

FREDERICK Let her alone for that. Your woman's wit, your fair kind woman, will out-trick a broker or a Jew, 315 and contrive like a Jesuit in chains. But see, Ned Blunt is stolen out after the lure of a damsel.

Exeunt Blunt and Lucetta

BELVILE So, he'll scarce find his way home again, unless we get him cried by the bellman in the market-place, and 'twould sound prettily: 'a lost English boy of 320 thirty'.

FREDERICK I hope 'tis some common crafty sinner, one that will fit him. It may be she'll sell him for Peru; the rogue's sturdy, and would work well in a mine. At least I hope she'll dress him for our mirth: cheat 325 him of all, then have him well-favouredly banged, and turned out naked at midnight.

WILLMORE Prithee, what humour is he of, that you wish him so well?

BELVILE Why, of an English elder brother's humour. 330 Educated in a nursery, with a maid to tend him till fifteen, and lies with his grandmother till he's of age; one that knows no pleasure beyond riding to the next fair, or going up to London with his right worshipful father in parliament time, wearing gay clothes, or 335 making honourable love to his lady mother's laundry-maid; gets drunk at a hunting match, and ten to one then gives some proofs of his prowess. A pox upon him, he's our banker, and has all our cash about him, and if he fail, we are all broke. 340

FREDERICK Oh, let him alone for that matter: he's of a damned stingy quality, that will secure our stock. I know not in what danger it were indeed if the jilt should pretend she's in love with him, for 'tis a kind believing coxcomb; otherwise, if he part with more 345 than a piece of eight, geld him – for which offer he may chance to be beaten, if she be a whore of the first rank.

BELVILE Nay, the rogue will not be easily beaten, he's stout enough. Perhaps, if they talk beyond his capacity, 350 he may chance to exercise his courage upon some of them; else I'm sure they'll find it as difficult to beat as to please him.

WILLMORE 'Tis a lucky devil to light upon so kind a wench! 355

FREDERICK Thou hadst a great deal of talk with thy little gipsy, couldst thou do no good upon her? For mine was hard-hearted.

WILLMORE Hang her, she was some damned honest person of quality, I'm sure, she was so very free and 360 witty. If her face be but answerable to her wit and humour, I would be bound to constancy this month to gain her. In the meantime, have you made no kind acquaintance since you came to town? You do not use to be honest so long, gentlemen. 365

FREDERICK Faith, love has kept us honest: we have been all fired with a beauty newly come to town, the famous Paduana, Angellica Bianca.

WILLMORE What, the mistress of the dead Spanish general? 370

BELVILE Yes, she's now the only adored beauty of all the youth in Naples, who put on all their charms to appear lovely in her sight: their coaches, liveries, and themselves, all gay as on a monarch's birthday, to

attract the eyes of this fair charmer, while she has the   375
pleasure to behold all languish for her that see her.

FREDERICK 'Tis pretty to see with how much love the
men regard her, and how much envy the women.

WILLMORE What gallant has she?

BELVILE None: she's exposed to sale, and four days in   380
the week she's yours – for so much a month.

WILLMORE The very thought of it quenches all manner
of fire in me; yet prithee, let's see her.

BELVILE Let's first to dinner, and after that we'll pass
the day as you please; but at night ye must all be at   385
my devotion.

WILLMORE I will not fail you.

[*Exeunt*]

Act II Scene I

The long street
Enter Belvile and Frederick in masking habits, and
Willmore in his own clothes, with a vizard in his
hand

WILLMORE But why thus disguised and muzzled?

BELVILE Because whatever extravagances we commit in
these faces, our own may not be obliged to answer 'em.

WILLMORE I should have changed my eternal buff too;
but no matter, my little gipsy would not have found   5
me out then; for if she should change hers, it is impossible I should know her, unless I should hear her
prattle. A pox on't, I cannot get her out of my head.
Pray heaven, if ever I do see her again, she prove
damnably ugly, that I may fortify myself against her   10
tongue.

BELVILE Have a care of love, for o'my conscience she
was not of a quality to give thee any hopes.

WILLMORE Pox on 'em, why do they draw a man in then?
She has played with my heart so, that 'twill never lie   15
still, till I have met with some kind wench that will
play the game out with me. Oh for my arms full of
soft, white, kind – woman! such as I fancy Angellica.

BELVILE This is her house, if you were but in stock to
get admittance. They have not dined yet: I perceive   20
the picture is not out.

Enter Blunt

WILLMORE I long to see the shadow of the fair substance;
a man may gaze on that for nothing.

BLUNT Colonel, thy hand – and thine, Fred. I have been
an ass, a deluded fool, a very coxcomb from my birth   25
till this hour, and heartily repent my little faith.

BELVILE What the devil's the matter with thee, Ned?

[BLUNT] Oh, such a mistress, Fred, such a girl!

WILLMORE Ha! Where?

FREDERICK Aye, where?   30

[BLUNT] So fond, so amorous, so toying and so fine;
and all for sheer love, ye rogue! Oh, how she looked
and kissed, and soothed my heart from my bosom; I
cannot think I was awake, and yet methinks I see and
feel her charms still! – Fred, try if she have not left   35
the taste of her balmy kisses upon my lips.

[*Blunt*] *kisses* [*Frederick*]

BELVILE Ha, ha, ha!

WILLMORE Death, man, where is she?

[BLUNT] What a dog was I to stay in dull England so
long! How have I laughed at the colonel when he   40
sighed for love! But now the little archer has revenged
him, and by this one dart, I can guess at all his joys,
which then I took for fancies, mere dreams and fables.
Well, I'm resolved to sell all in Essex, and plant here
forever.   45

BELVILE What a blessing 'tis, thou hast a mistress thou
dar'st boast of; for I know thy humour is rather to
have a proclaimed clap, than a secret amour.

WILLMORE Dost know her name?

BLUNT Her name? No, 'adsheartlikins, what care I for   50
names? She's fair, young, brisk and kind, even to
ravishment; and what a pox care I for knowing her by
any other title?

WILLMORE Didst give her anything?

BLUNT Give her! Ha, ha, ha! Why, she's a person of   55
quality; that's a good one, give her! 'Adsheartlikins,
dost think such creatures are to be bought? Or are we
provided for such a purchase? Give her, quoth ye?
Why, she presented me with this bracelet, for the toy

of a diamond I used to wear. No, gentlemen, Ned 60
Blunt is not everybody. She expects me again tonight.

WILLMORE Egad, that's well; we'll all go.

BLUNT Not a soul: no, gentlemen, you are wits; I am a
dull country rogue, I.

FREDERICK Well, sir, for all your person of quality, I 65
shall be very glad to understand your purse be secure:
'tis our whole estate at present, which we are loth to
hazard in one bottom. Come, sir, unlade.

BLUNT Take the necessary trifle, useless now to me, that
am beloved by such a gentlewoman. 'Adsheartlikins, 70
money! Here, take mine too.

FREDERICK No, keep that to be cozened, that we may
laugh.

WILLMORE Cozened! Death! Would I could meet with
one that would cozen me of all the love I could spare 75
tonight.

FREDERICK Pox, 'tis some common whore, upon my life.

BLUNT A whore! Yes, with such clothes, such jewels,
such a house, such furniture, and so attended! A whore!

BELVILE Why yes, sir, they are whores, though they'll 80
neither entertain you with drinking, swearing, or
bawdry; are whores in all those gay clothes, and right
jewels; are whores with those great houses richly
furnished with velvet beds, store of plate, handsome
attendance, and fine coaches; are whores, and arrant 85
ones.

WILLMORE Pox on't, where do these fine whores live?

BELVILE Where no rogues in office, ycleped constables,
dare give 'em laws, nor the wine-inspired bullies of
the town break their windows; yet they are whores, 90
though this Essex calf believe 'em persons of quality.

BLUNT 'Adsheartlikins, y'are all fools; there are things
about this Essex calf, that shall take with the ladies,

beyond all your wit and parts. This shape and size, gentlemen, are not to be despised; my waist too, toler- 95 ably long, with other inviting signs that shall be name-less.

WILLMORE Egad, I believe he may have met with some person of quality that may be kind to him.

BELVILE Dost thou perceive any such tempting things 100 about him, that should make a fine woman, and of quality, pick him out from all mankind, to throw away her youth and beauty upon; nay, and her dear heart too? No, no, Angellica has raised the price too high.

WILLMORE May she languish for mankind till she die, 105 and be damned for that one sin alone.

> *Enter two bravos [Biskey and Sebastian], and hang up a great picture of Angellica's against the balcony, and two little ones at each side of the door*

BELVILE See there the fair sign to the inn where a man may lodge that's fool enough to give her price.

> *Willmore gazes on the picture*

BLUNT 'Adsheartlikins, gentlemen, what's this?

BELVILE A famous courtesan, that's to be sold. 110

BLUNT How, to be sold! Nay then, I have nothing to say to her. Sold! What impudence is practised in this country! With what order and decency whoring's established here by virtue of the Inquisition! Come, let's begone, I'm sure we're no chapmen for this 115 commodity.

FREDERICK Thou art none, I'm sure, unless thou couldst have her in thy bed at a price of a coach in the street.

WILLMORE How wondrous fair she is. A thousand crowns a month? By heaven, as many kingdoms were 120 too little. A plague of this poverty, of which I ne'er complain but when it hinders my approach to beauty, which virtue ne'er could purchase.

[Willmore] turns from the picture

BLUNT What's this? (*Reads*) 'A thousand crowns a
month'! 'Adsheartlikins, here's a sum! Sure 'tis a   125
mistake. [*To bravo*] Hark you, friend, does she take or
give so much by the month?

FREDERICK A thousand crowns! Why, 'tis a portion for
the Infanta.

BLUNT Hark'ee, friends, won't she trust?   130

BRAVO This is a trade, sir, that cannot live by credit.
Enter Don Pedro in masquerade, followed by Stephano

BELVILE See, here's more company; let's walk off awhile.
Exeunt [Belvile, Willmore, Frederick, and Blunt];
Pedro reads

PEDRO Fetch me a thousand crowns, I never wished to
buy this beauty at an easier rate.
[Pedro] passes off [the stage]. Enter Angellica and
Moretta in the balcony, and draw a silk curtain

ANGELLICA Prithee, what said those fellows to thee?   135

BRAVO Madam, the first were admirers of beauty only,
but no purchasers; they were merry with your price
and picture, laughed at the sum, and so passed off.

ANGELLICA No matter, I'm not displeased with their
rallying; their wonder feeds my vanity, and he that   140
wishes but to buy gives me more pride, than he that
gives my price can make my pleasure.

BRAVO Madam, the last I knew through all his disguises
to be Don Pedro, nephew to the general, and who was
with him in Pamplona.   145

ANGELLICA Don Pedro, my old gallant's nephew! When
his uncle died he left him a vast sum of money; it is
he who was so in love with me at Padua, and who
used to make the general so jealous.

MORETTA Is this he that used to prance before our   150
window, and take such care to show himself an

amorous ass? If I am not mistaken, he is the likeliest man to give your price.

ANGELLICA The man is brave and generous, but of an humour so uneasy and inconstant that the victory 155 over his heart is as soon lost as won: a slave that can add little to the triumph of the conqueror; but inconstancy's the sin of all mankind, therefore I'm resolved that nothing but gold shall charm my heart.

MORETTA I'm glad on't: 'tis only interest that women 160 of our profession ought to consider, though I wonder what has kept you from that general disease of our sex so long, I mean that of being in love.

ANGELLICA A kind, but sullen star under which I had the happiness to be born. Yet I have had no time for 165 love: the bravest and noblest of mankind have purchased my favours at so dear a rate, as if no coin but gold were current with our trade. But here's Don Pedro again; fetch me my lute, for 'tis for him, or Don Antonio the viceroy's son, that I have spread my nets. 170

Enter at one door Don Pedro, Stephano; Don Antonio and Diego [his page] at the other door with people following him in masquerade, anticly attired, some with music. [Angellica closes the curtain. Pedro and Antonio] both go up to the picture

ANTONIO A thousand crowns! Had not the painter flattered her, I should not think it dear.

PEDRO Flattered her! By heaven, he cannot. I have seen the original, nor is there one charm here more than adorns her face and eyes; all this soft and sweet, with 175 a certain languishing air, that no artist can represent.

ANTONIO What I heard of her beauty before had fired my soul, but this confirmation of it has blown it to a flame.

PEDRO Ha!   180

PAGE [*to Antonio*] Sir, I have known you throw away a
    thousand crowns on a worse face, and though you're
    near your marriage, you may venture a little love here;
    Florinda will not miss it.

PEDRO (*aside*) Ha! Florinda! Sure 'tis Antonio.   185

ANTONIO Florinda! name not those distant joys; there's
    not one thought of her will check my passion here.

PEDRO [*aside*] Florinda scorned! And all my hopes
    defeated, of the possession of Angellica!

    A noise of a lute above. Antonio gazes up

Her injuries, by heaven, he shall not boast of.   190

SONG (*to a lute above*)

> When Damon first began to love
> He languished in a soft desire,
> And knew not how the gods to move,
> To lessen or increase his fire:
> For Celia in her charming eyes   195
> Wore all Love's sweets, and all his cruelties.
>
> But as beneath a shade he lay,
> Weaving of flowers for Celia's hair,
> She chanced to lead her flock that way,
> And saw the amorous shepherd there.   200
> She gazed around upon the place,
> And saw the grove (resembling night)
> To all the joys of love invite,
> Whilst guilty smiles and blushes dressed her face.
> At this the bashful youth all transport grew,   205
> And with kind force he taught the virgin how
> To yield what all his sighs could never do.

> *Angellica throws open the curtains, and bows to*
> *Antonio, who pulls off his vizard and bows and*
> *blows up kisses. Pedro, unseen, looks in his face.*
> [*The curtains close*]

ANTONIO By heaven, she's charming fair!

PEDRO 'Tis he, the false Antonio!

ANTONIO (*to the bravo*) Friend, where must I pay my 210
offering of love?

My thousand crowns I mean.

PEDRO That offering I have designed to make,
And yours will come too late.

ANTONIO Prithee begone: I shall grow angry else, 215
And then thou art not safe.

PEDRO My anger may be fatal, sir, as yours,
And he that enters here may prove this truth.

ANTONIO I know not who thou art, but I am sure thou'rt
worth my killing, for aiming at Angellica. 220

> [*Antonio and Pedro*] *draw and fight. Enter*
> *Willmore and Blunt*

BLUNT 'Adsheartlikins, here's fine doings.

WILLMORE Tilting for the wench, I'm sure. – Nay gad,
if that would win her, I have as good a sword as the
best of ye.

> [*Blunt and Willmore*] *draw and part* [*Antonio and*
> *Pedro*]

Put up, put up, and take another time and place, for 225
this is designed for lovers only.

> *They all put up* [*their swords*]

PEDRO We are prevented; dare you meet me tomorrow
on the Molo?

For I've a title to a better quarrel,
That of Florinda, in whose credulous heart, 230
Thou'st made an interest, and destroyed my hopes.

ANTONIO Dare!

I'll meet thee there as early as the day.

PEDRO We will come thus disguised, that whosoever
chance to get the better, he may escape unknown.   235

ANTONIO It shall be so.

    Exeunt Pedro and Stephano

Who should this rival be? unless the English colonel,
of whom I've often heard Don Pedro speak: it must
be he, and time he were removed, who lays a claim
to all my happiness.   240

    Willmore having gazed all this while on the
    picture, pulls down a little one

WILLMORE This posture's loose and negligent,
The sight on't would beget a warm desire
In souls whom impotence and age had chilled.
This must along with me.

BRAVO What means this rudeness, sir? Restore the   245
picture.

ANTONIO [*aside*] Ha! Rudeness committed to the fair
Angellica! –
Restore the picture, sir.

WILLMORE Indeed I will not, sir.   250

ANTONIO By heaven, but you shall.

WILLMORE Nay, do not show your sword: if you do, by
this dear beauty, I will show mine too.

ANTONIO What right can you pretend to't?

WILLMORE That of possession, which I will maintain.   255
You, perhaps, have a thousand crowns to give for the
original.

ANTONIO No matter, sir, you shall restore the picture –
    [*The curtains open;*] *Angellica and Moretta*
    [*appear*] *above*

ANGELLICA Oh, Moretta! What's the matter?

ANTONIO – Or leave your life behind.   260

WILLMORE Death! you lie; I will do neither.

> [*Willmore and Antonio*] *fight; the Spaniards join*
> *with Antonio, Blunt* [*joins with Willmore,*] *laying*
> *on like mad*

ANGELLICA Hold, I command you, if for me you fight.
They leave off and bow

WILLMORE [*aside*] How heavenly fair she is! Ah, plague
of her price.

ANGELLICA You, sir, in buff, you that appear a soldier, 265
that first began this insolence –

WILLMORE 'Tis true, I did so, if you call it insolence for
a man to preserve himself: I saw your charming picture
and was wounded; quite through my soul each pointed
beauty ran; and wanting a thousand crowns to procure 270
my remedy, I laid this little picture to my bosom,
which, if you cannot allow me, I'll resign.

ANGELLICA No, you may keep the trifle.

ANTONIO You shall first ask me leave, and [*flourishing*
his sword] this.   275

> [*They*] *fight again as before. Enter Belvile and*
> *Frederick, who join with the English*

ANGELLICA Hold! Will you ruin me? – Biskey, Sebastian,
part 'em.

> *The Spaniards are beaten off.* [*Exeunt all the men*]

MORETTA Oh madam, we're undone! A pox upon that
rude fellow, he's set on to ruin us: we shall never see
good days, till all these fighting poor rogues are sent 280
to the galleys.

> *Enter Belvile, Blunt, Frederick, and Willmore with*
> *his shirt bloody*

BLUNT 'Adsheartlikins, beat me at this sport, and I'll
ne'er wear sword more.

BELVILE (*to Willmore*) The devil's in thee for a mad
fellow, thou art always one at an unlucky adventure. 285
Come, let's begone whilst we're safe, and remember

these are Spaniards, a sort of people that know how
to revenge an affront.

FREDERICK [*to Willmore*] You bleed! I hope you are not
wounded. 290

WILLMORE Not much: a plague on your dons, if they
fight no better they'll ne'er recover Flanders. What
the devil was't to them that I took down the picture?

BLUNT Took it! 'Adsheartlikins, we'll have the great one
too; 'tis ours by conquest. Prithee, help me up, and 295
I'll pull it down.

ANGELLICA [*to Willmore*] Stay, sir, and ere you affront
me farther, let me know how you durst commit this
outrage. To you I speak sir, for you appear a gentleman.

WILLMORE To me, madam? [*To his companions, taking 300
leave of them*] Gentlemen, your servant.
Belvile stays [Willmore]

BELVILE Is the devil in thee? Dost know the danger of
entering the house of an incensed courtesan?

WILLMORE I thank you for your care, but there are other
matters in hand, there are, though we have no great 305
temptation. Death! let me go.

FREDERICK Yes, to your lodging, if you will; but not in
here. Damn these gay harlots; by this hand, I'll have
as sound and handsome a whore for a patacoon.
Death, man, she'll murder thee. 310

WILLMORE Oh! fear me not. Shall I not venture where
a beauty calls, a lovely charming beauty? For fear of
danger! when, by heaven, there's none so great as to
long for her, whilst I want money to purchase her.

FREDERICK Therefore 'tis loss of time, unless you had 315
the thousand crowns to pay.

WILLMORE It may be she may give a favour; at least I
shall have the pleasure of saluting her when I enter
and when I depart.

BELVILE Pox, she'll as soon lie with thee as kiss thee, 320
and sooner stab than do either. You shall not go.

ANGELLICA Fear not, sir, all I have to wound with is my
eyes.

BLUNT Let him go: 'adsheartlikins, I believe the gentlewoman means well. 325

BELVILE Well, take thy fortune; we'll expect you in the
next street. Farewell, fool, farewell.

WILLMORE 'Bye, colonel.

    [*Willmore*] *goes in*

FREDERICK The rogue's stark mad for a wench.

    Exeunt

Act II Scene II

    A fine chamber

    Enter Willmore, Angellica, and Moretta

ANGELLICA Insolent sir, how durst you pull down my
picture?

WILLMORE Rather, how durst you set it up, to tempt
poor amorous mortals with so much excellence?
which I find you have but too well consulted by the 5
unmerciful price you set upon't. Is all this heaven of
beauty shown to move despair in those that cannot
buy? and can you think th'effects of that despair
should be less extravagant than I have shown?

ANGELLICA I sent for you to ask my pardon, sir, not to 10
aggravate your crime: I thought I should have seen
you at my feet imploring it.

WILLMORE You are deceived; I came to rail at you,
And rail such truths too, as shall let you see
The vanity of that pride, which taught you how 15

To set such price on sin:
For such it is whilst that which is love's due
Is meanly bartered for.

ANGELLICA Ha, ha, ha! Alas, good captain, what pity
'tis your edifying doctrine will do no good upon me. – 20
Moretta! fetch the gentleman a glass, and let him
survey himself, to see what charms he has – (*aside, in
a soft tone*) and guess my business.

MORETTA He knows himself of old: I believe those
breeches and he have been acquainted ever since he 25
was beaten at Worcester.

ANGELLICA Nay, do not abuse the poor creature.

MORETTA Good weather-beaten corporal, will you
march off? We have no need of your doctrine, though
you have of our charity: but at present we have no 30
scraps, we can afford no kindness for God's sake. In
fine, sirrah, the price is too high i'th' mouth for you;
therefore troop, I say.

WILLMORE [*offering money to Moretta*] Here, good fore-
woman of the shop, serve me, and I'll be gone. 35

MORETTA Keep it to pay your laundress (your linen
stinks of the gun room), for here's no selling by
retail.

WILLMORE Thou hast sold plenty of thy stale ware at a
cheap rate. 40

MORETTA Aye, the more silly kind heart I, but this is
an age wherein beauty is at higher rates. In fine, you
know the price of this.

WILLMORE I grant you 'tis here set down, a thousand
crowns a month: pray, how much may come to my 45
share for a pistole? Bawd, take your black lead and
sum it up, that I may have a pistole's worth of this
vain gay thing, and I'll trouble you no more.

MORETTA [*aside*] Pox on him, he'll fret me to death. –

49

Abominable fellow, I tell thee, we only sell by the   5ᵒ
whole piece.

WILLMORE 'Tis very hard, the whole cargo or nothing.
[*To Angellica*] Faith, madam, my stock will not reach
it, I cannot be your chapman. Yet I have countrymen
in town, merchants of love like me: I'll see if they'll   5⁵
put in for a share; we cannot lose much by it, and
what we have no use for, we'll sell upon the Friday's
mart, at 'Who gives more?' I am studying, madam,
how to purchase you, though at present I am unpro-
vided of money.   6ᵒ

ANGELLICA [*aside*] Sure, this from any other man would
anger me; nor shall he know the conquest he has made.
[*To Willmore*] Poor angry man, how I despise this
railing.

WILLMORE Yes, I am poor; but I'm a gentleman,   6⁵
And one that scorns this baseness which you practise.
Poor as I am, I would not sell myself,
No, not to gain your charming high-prized person.
Though I admire you strangely for your beauty,
Yet I contemn your mind.   7ᵒ
And yet I would at any rate enjoy you,
At your own rate, but cannot: see here
The only sum I can command on earth;
I know not where to eat when this is gone.
Yet such a slave I am to love and beauty,   7⁵
This last reserve I'll sacrifice to enjoy you.
Nay, do not frown, I know you're to be bought,
And would be bought by me, by me,
For a mean trifling sum, if I could pay it down:
Which happy knowledge I will still repeat,   8ᵒ
And lay it to my heart; it has a virtue in't,
And soon will cure those wounds your eyes have
    made.

And yet, there's something so divinely powerful there –
Nay, I will gaze, to let you see my strength.
 Holds her, looks on her, and pauses and sighs
By heaven, bright creature, I would not for the world 85
Thy fame were half so fair as is thy face.
 Turns her away from him

ANGELLICA (*aside*) His words go through me to the very
 soul. [*To Willmore*] If you have nothing else to say to
 me –

WILLMORE Yes; you shall hear how infamous you are, 90
For which I do not hate thee,
But that secures my heart, and all the flames it feels
Are but so many lusts;
I know it by their sudden bold intrusion.
The fire's impatient and betrays; 'tis false: 95
For had it been the purer flame of love,
I should have pined and languished at your feet,
Ere found the impudence to have discovered it.
I now dare stand your scorn, and your denial.

MORETTA [*aside*] Sure she's bewitched, that she can 100
 stand thus tamely and hear his saucy railing. – Sirrah,
 will you be gone?

ANGELLICA (*to Moretta*) How dare you take this liberty?
 Withdraw. – Pray tell me, sir, are not you guilty of
 the same mercenary crime? When a lady is proposed 105
 to you for a wife, you never ask how fair, discreet, or
 virtuous she is; but what's her fortune: which if but
 small, you cry 'she will not do my business', and
 basely leave her, though she languish for you. Say, is
 not this as poor? 110

WILLMORE It is a barbarous custom, which I will scorn
 to defend in our sex, and do despise in yours.

ANGELLICA Thou'rt a brave fellow! put up thy gold, and
 know

That were thy fortune large as is thy soul,   115
Thou shouldst not buy my love, couldst thou forget
Those mean effects of vanity
Which set me out to sale,
And as a lover, prize my yielding joys.
Canst thou believe they'll be entirely thine,   120
Without considering they were mercenary?
WILLMORE I cannot tell, I must bethink me first. (*Aside*)
    Ha, death, I'm going to believe her.
ANGELLICA Prithee, confirm that faith; or if thou canst
    not, flatter me a little, 'twill please me from thy mouth. 125
WILLMORE (*aside*) Curse on thy charming tongue! dost
    thou return
    My feigned contempt with so much subtlety?
    [*To Angellica*] Thou'st found the easiest way into my
        heart,
    Though I yet know, that all thou say'st is false.   130
    [*Willmore*] *turn[s] from her in rage*
ANGELLICA By all that's good, 'tis real;
    I never loved before, though oft a mistress.
    Shall my first vows be slighted?
WILLMORE (*aside*) What can she mean?
ANGELLICA (*in an angry tone*) I find you cannot credit me. 135
WILLMORE I know you take me for an arrant ass,
    An ass that may be soothed into belief,
    And then be used at pleasure;
    But, madam, I have been so often cheated
    By perjured, soft, deluding hypocrites,   140
    That I've no faith left for the cozening sex,
    Especially for women of your trade.
ANGELLICA The low esteem you have of me, perhaps
    May bring my heart again:
    For I have pride, that yet surmounts my love.   145
        She turns with pride; he holds her

WILLMORE Throw off this pride, this enemy to bliss,
And show the power of love: 'tis with those arms
I can be only vanquished, made a slave.
ANGELLICA Is all my mighty expectation vanished?
No, I will not hear thee talk: thou hast a charm   150
In every word that draws my heart away;
And all the thousand trophies I designed,
Thou hast undone. Why art thou soft?
Thy looks are bravely rough, and meant for war.
Couldst thou not storm on still?   155
I then perhaps had been as free as thou.
WILLMORE (*aside*) Death, how she throws her fire about
my soul!
—Take heed, fair creature, how you raise my hopes,
Which once assumed pretends to all dominion.   160
There's not a joy thou hast in store
I shall not then command;
For which I'll pay thee back my soul, my life!
Come, let's begin th'account this happy minute!
ANGELLICA And will you pay me then the price I ask?   165
WILLMORE Oh, why dost thou draw me from an awful
worship,
By showing thou art no divinity?
Conceal the fiend, and show me all the angel!
Keep me but ignorant, and I'll be devout   170
And pay my vows for ever at this shrine.
        Kneels and kisses her hand
ANGELLICA The pay I mean, is but thy love for mine.
Can you give that?
WILLMORE Entirely; come, let's withdraw, where I'll
renew my vows, and breathe 'em with such ardour   175
thou shalt not doubt my zeal.
ANGELLICA Thou hast a power too strong to be resisted.
        Exeunt Willmore and Angellica

MORETTA Now, my curse go with you. Is all our project
fallen to this: to love the only enemy to our trade?
Nay, to love such a shameroon; a very beggar, nay, a   180
pirate beggar, whose business is to rifle, and be gone;
a no-purchase, no-pay tatterdemalion, and English
picaroon; a rogue that fights for daily drink, and takes
a pride in being loyally lousy! Oh, I could curse now,
if I durst. This is the fate of most whores.   185
    Trophies, which from believing fops we win,
    Are spoils to those who cozen us again.
[*Exit*]

Act III Scene I

A street
Enter Florinda, Valeria, [and] Hellena, in antic,
different dresses, from what they were in before;
[and] Callis, attending

FLORINDA I wonder what should make my brother in
so ill a humour? I hope he has not found out our
ramble this morning.

HELLENA No: if he had, we should have heard on't at
both ears, and have been mewed up this afternoon;   5
which I would not for the world should have
happened. Hey ho, I'm as sad as a lover's lute.

VALERIA Well, methinks we have learnt this trade of
gipsies as readily as if we had been bred upon the
road to Loretto; and yet I did so fumble, when I told   10
the stranger his fortune, that I was afraid I should have
told my own and yours by mistake. But, methinks,
Hellena has been very serious ever since.

FLORINDA I would give my garters she were in love, to
be revenged upon her for abusing me. – How is't,   15
Hellena?

HELLENA Ah, would I had never seen my mad monsieur!
And yet, for all your laughing, I am not in love; and
yet this small acquaintance, o' my conscience, will
never out of my head.   20

VALERIA Ha, ha, ha; I laugh to think how thou art fitted
with a lover, a fellow that I warrant loves every new
face he sees.

HELLENA Hum, he has not kept his word with me here,
and may be taken up: that thought is not very pleasant 25
to me. What the deuce should this be now, that I feel?

VALERIA What is't like?

HELLENA Nay, the lord knows; but if I should be hanged, I cannot choose but be angry and afraid, when I think that mad fellow should be in love with anybody but me. What to think of myself I know not: would I could meet with some true damned gipsy, that I might know my fortune. 30

VALERIA Know it! why there's nothing so easy: thou wilt love this wandering inconstant, till thou find'st thyself hanged about his neck, and then be as mad to get free again. 35

FLORINDA Yes, Valeria, we shall see her bestride his baggage horse, and follow him to the campaign.

HELLENA So, so, now you are provided for, there's no care taken of poor me. But since you have set my heart a-wishing, I am resolved to know for what; I will not die of the pip, so I will not. 40

FLORINDA Art thou mad to talk so? Who will like thee well enough to have thee, that hears what a mad wench thou art? 45

HELLENA Like me! I don't intend every he that likes me shall have me, but he that I like: I should have stayed in the nunnery still, if I had liked my lady abbess as well as she liked me. No, I came thence not, as my wise brother imagines, to take an eternal farewell of the world, but to love, and to be beloved; and I will be beloved, or I'll get one of your men, so I will. 50

VALERIA Am I put into the number of lovers?

HELLENA You? why, coz, I know thou'rt too good-natured to leave us in any design: thou wouldst venture a cast, though thou comest off a loser, especially with such a gamester. I observed your man, and your willing ear incline that way; and if you are not a lover, 'tis an art soon learnt, that I find. (*Sighs*) 55 60

FLORINDA I wonder how you learned to love so easily.

I had a thousand charms to meet my eyes and ears,
ere I could yield; and 'twas the knowledge of Belvile's
merit, not the surprising person, took my soul. Thou
art too rash, to give a heart at first sight.   65

HELLENA Hang your considering lover; I never thought
beyond the fancy that 'twas a very pretty, idle, silly
kind of pleasure to pass one's time with: to write little
soft nonsensical billets, and with great difficulty and
danger receive answers, in which I shall have my   70
beauty praised, my wit admired (though little or none),
and have the vanity and power to know I am desirable. Then I have the more inclination that way,
because I am to be a nun, and so shall not be suspected
to have any such earthly thoughts about me; but when   75
I walk thus, and sigh thus, they'll think my mind's
upon my monastery, and cry, 'how happy 'tis she's so
resolved'; but not a word of man.

FLORINDA What a mad creature's this!

HELLENA I'll warrant, if my brother hears either of you   80
sigh, he cries gravely, 'I fear you have the indiscretion
to be in love, but take heed of the honour of our
house, and your own unspotted fame', and so he
conjures on till he has laid the soft-winged god in your
hearts, or broke the bird's nest.   85

Enter Belvile, Frederick, and Blunt

But see, here comes your lover; but where's my inconstant? Let's step aside, and we may learn something.

[Hellena, Florinda, Valeria, and Callis] go aside

BELVILE What means this? The picture's taken in.

BLUNT It may be the wench is good-natured, and will
be kind gratis. Your friend's a proper handsome   90
fellow.

BELVILE I rather think she has cut his throat and is fled.
I am mad he should throw himself into dangers; pox

on't, I shall want him, too, at night. Let's knock and
ask for him.   95

HELLENA My heart goes a pit-a-pat, for fear 'tis my man
they talk of.

[The men] knock; Moretta [appears] above

MORETTA What would you have?

BELVILE Tell the stranger that entered here about two
hours ago, that his friends stay here for him.   100

MORETTA A curse upon him for Moretta: would he were
at the devil; but he's coming to you.

[Enter Willmore, from Angellica's house]

HELLENA *[aside]* Aye, aye, 'tis he! Oh, how this vexes
me.

BELVILE And how and how, dear lad, has fortune   105
smiled? Are we to break her windows, or raise up
altars to her, ha?

WILLMORE Does not my fortune sit triumphant on my
brow? Dost not see the little wanton god there all gay
and smiling? Have I not an air about my face and eyes,   110
that distinguish me from the crowd of common
lovers? By heaven, Cupid's quiver has not half so
many darts as her eyes! Oh, such a bona roba! to sleep
in her arms is lying in fresco, all perfumed air about
me.   115

HELLENA *(aside)* Here's fine encouragement for me to
fool on.

WILLMORE Hark'ee, where didst thou purchase that rich
canary we drank today? Tell me, that I may adore the
spigot, and sacrifice to the butt! The juice was divine, 120
into which I must dip my rosary, and then bless all
things that I would have bold or fortunate.

BELVILE Well, sir, let's go take a bottle, and hear the
story of your success.

FREDERICK Would not French wine do better?   125

WILLMORE Damn the hungry balderdash; cheerful sack has a generous virtue in't inspiring a successful confidence, gives eloquence to the tongue, and vigour to the soul, and has in a few hours completed all my hopes and wishes! There's nothing left to raise a new 130 desire in me. Come, let's be gay and wanton; and, gentlemen, study, study what you want, for here are friends that will supply gentlemen. [*Jingles gold*] Hark! what a charming sound they make: 'tis he and she gold whilst here, and shall beget new pleasures every 135 moment.

BLUNT But hark'ee, sir, you are not married, are you?

WILLMORE All the honey of matrimony, but none of the sting, friend.

BLUNT 'Adsheartlikins, thou'rt a fortunate rogue! 140

WILLMORE I am so, sir, let these inform you! Ha, how sweetly they chime! Pox of poverty, it makes a man a slave, makes wit and honour sneak; my soul grew lean and rusty for want of credit.

BLUNT 'Adsheartlikins, this I like well, it looks like my 145 lucky bargain! Oh, how I long for the approach of my squire, that is to conduct me to her house again. Why, here's two provided for.

FREDERICK By this light, y'are happy men.

BLUNT Fortune is pleased to smile on us, gentlemen, to 150 smile on us.

    Enter Sancho and pulls down Blunt by the sleeve.
    They go aside

SANCHO Sir, my lady expects you. She has removed all that might oppose your will and pleasure, and is impatient till you come.

BLUNT Sir, I'll attend you. [*Aside*] Oh, the happiest 155 rogue! I'll take no leave, lest they either dog me, or stay me.

Exit [Blunt] with Sancho

BELVILE But then the little gipsy is forgot?

WILLMORE A mischief on thee for putting her into my thoughts, I had quite forgot her else, and this night's 16 debauch had drunk her quite down.

HELLENA Had it so, good captain!

[Hellena] claps [Willmore] on the back

WILLMORE (*aside*) Ha! I hope she did not hear me.

HELLENA What, afraid of such a champion?

WILLMORE Oh, you're a fine lady of your word, are you 16 not? To make a man languish a whole day –

HELLENA In tedious search of me.

WILLMORE Egad, child, thou'rt in the right: hadst thou seen what a melancholy dog I have been ever since I was a lover, how I have walked the streets like a 17 capuchin, with my hands in my sleeves, faith, sweetheart, thou wouldst pity me.

HELLENA [*aside*] Now, if I should be hanged, I can't be angry with him, he dissembles so heartily. [*To Willmore*] Alas, good captain, what pains you have taken: now 17 were I ungrateful not to reward so true a servant.

WILLMORE Poor soul, that's kindly said, I see thou bearest a conscience. Come then, for a beginning show me thy dear face.

HELLENA I'm afraid, my small acquaintance, you have 18 been staying that swingeing stomach you boasted of this morning: I then remember my little collation would have gone down with you, without the sauce of a handsome face; is your stomach so queasy now?

WILLMORE Faith, long fasting, child, spoils a man's 18 appetite. Yet if you durst treat, I could so lay about me still –

HELLENA And would you fall to, before a priest says grace?

WILLMORE Oh fie, fie, what an old out-of-fashioned thing 190
hast thou named? Thou couldst not dash me more
out of countenance shouldst thou show me an ugly
face.

*Whilst he is seemingly courting Hellena, enter
Angellica, Moretta, Biskey, and Sebastian, all in
masquerade. Angellica sees Willmore and stares*

ANGELLICA Heavens, 'tis he! and passionately fond to
see another woman.   195

MORETTA What could you less expect from such a swag-
gerer?

ANGELLICA Expect? As much as I paid him: a heart
entire,
Which I had pride enough to think whene'er I gave,   200
It would have raised the man above the vulgar,
Made him all soul! and that all soft and constant.

HELLENA You see, captain, how willing I am to be
friends with you (till time and ill luck make us lovers),
and ask you the question first, rather than put your 205
modesty to the blush, by asking me; for alas, I know
you captains are such strict men, and such severe
observers of your vows to chastity, that 'twill be hard
to prevail with your tender conscience to marry a
young willing maid.   210

WILLMORE Do not abuse me, for fear I should take thee
at thy word, and marry thee indeed, which I'm sure
will be revenge sufficient.

HELLENA O' my conscience, that will be our destiny,
because we are both of one humour: I am as incon- 215
stant as you, for I have considered, captain, that a
handsome woman has a great deal to do whilst her
face is good, for then is our harvest-time to gather
friends; and should I in these days of my youth, catch
a fit of foolish constancy, I were undone; 'tis loitering 220

by daylight in our great journey. Therefore, I declare, I'll allow but one year for love, one year for indifference, and one year for hate; and then, go hang yourself: for I profess myself the gay, the kind, and the inconstant. The devil's in't if this won't please you.   225

WILLMORE Oh, most damnably. I have a heart with a hole quite through it too, no prison mine to keep a mistress in.

ANGELLICA (*aside*) Perjured man! how I believe thee now.

HELLENA Well, I see our business as well as humours   230
are alike: yours to cozen as many maids as will trust you, and I as many men as have faith. See if I have not as desperate a lying look, as you can have for the heart of you.

      [*Hellena*] *pulls off her vizard:* [*Willmore*] *starts*
How do you like it, captain?   235

WILLMORE Like it! by heaven, I never saw so much beauty! Oh, the charms of those sprightly black eyes, that strangely fair face, full of smiles and dimples, those soft round melting cherry lips, and small even white teeth! Not to be expressed, but silently adored!   240
[*Hellena replaces her vizard*] Oh, one look more, and strike me dumb, or I shall repeat nothing else till I'm mad.

      He seems to court her to pull off her vizard: she refuses

ANGELLICA I can endure no more; nor is it fit to interrupt him, for if I do, my jealousy has so destroyed   245
my reason, I shall undo him; therefore I'll retire – (*to one of her bravos*) and you, Sebastian, follow that woman, and learn who 'tis – (*to the other bravo*) while you tell the fugitive I would speak to him instantly.

      Exit [*Angellica.*] [*During*] *this* [*time*] *Florinda is talking to Belvile, who stands sullenly. Frederick* [*is*] *courting Valeria*

VALERIA Prithee, dear stranger, be not so sullen, for 250
though you have lost your love, you see my friend
frankly offers you hers to play with in the meantime.

BELVILE Faith, madam, I am sorry I can't play at her
game.

FREDERICK [*to Valeria*] Pray leave your intercession and 255
mind your own affair, they'll better agree apart: he's
a modest sigher in company, but alone no woman
'scapes him.

FLORINDA [*aside*] Sure, he does but rally; yet if it should
be true – I'll tempt him farther. [*To Belvile*] Believe me, 260
noble stranger, I'm no common mistress, and for a
little proof on't, wear this jewel. Nay, take it, sir, 'tis
right, and bills of exchange may sometimes miscarry.

BELVILE Madam, why am I chose out of all mankind
to be the object of your bounty? 265

VALERIA There's another civil question asked.

FREDERICK [*aside*] Pox of's modesty, it spoils his own
markets and hinders mine.

FLORINDA Sir, from my window I have often seen you,
and women of my quality have so few opportunities 270
for love, that we ought to lose none.

FREDERICK Aye, this is something! Here's a woman! [*To
Valeria*] When shall I be blessed with so much kindness from your fair mouth? (*Aside to Belvile*) Take the
jewel, fool. 275

BELVILE You tempt me strangely, madam, every way –

FLORINDA (*aside*) So, if I find him false, my whole repose
is gone.

BELVILE – And but for a vow I've made to a very fair
lady, this goodness had subdued me. 280

FREDERICK [*aside to Belvile*] Pox on't, be kind, in pity to
me be kind, for I am to thrive here but as you treat
her friend.

HELLENA Tell me what you did in yonder house, and
I'll unmask. 28

WILLMORE Yonder house? Oh – I went to – a – to – why,
there's a friend of mine lives there.

HELLENA What, a she or a he friend?

WILLMORE A man, upon honour! a man. A she friend?
no, no, madam, you have done my business, I thank 29c
you.

HELLENA And was't your man friend, that had more
darts in's eyes, than Cupid carries in's whole budget
of arrows?

WILLMORE So – 295

HELLENA 'Ah, such a bona roba! to be in her arms is
lying in fresco, all perfumed air about me.' Was this
your man friend too?

WILLMORE So –

HELLENA That gave you 'the he and the she gold, that 30c
begets young pleasures'?

WILLMORE Well, well, madam, then you see there are
ladies in the world that will not be cruel; there are,
madam, there are.

HELLENA And there be men too, as fine, wild, incon- 305
stant fellows as yourself; there be, captain, there be,
if you go to that now: therefore I'm resolved –

WILLMORE Oh!

HELLENA – To see your face no more –

WILLMORE Oh! 31c

HELLENA – Till tomorrow.

WILLMORE Egad, you frighted me.

HELLENA Nor then neither, unless you'll swear never to
see that lady more.

WILLMORE See her! Why, never to think of womankind 315
again.

HELLENA Kneel, and swear.

[Willmore] kneels; [Hellena] gives him her hand

WILLMORE I do, never to think, to see, to love, nor lie –
with any but thyself.

HELLENA Kiss the book.   320

WILLMORE *(kisses her hand)* Oh, most religiously.

HELLENA *[aside]* Now, what a wicked creature am I, to
damn a proper fellow.

CALLIS *(to Florinda)* Madam, I'll stay no longer, 'tis e'en
dark.   325

FLORINDA *[to Belvile]* However, sir, I'll leave this with
you, that when I'm gone, you may repent the opportunity you have lost by your modesty.

*[Florinda] gives [Belvile] the jewel, which is her
picture, and exit. He gazes after her*

WILLMORE 'Twill be an age till tomorrow, and till then
I will most impatiently expect you. Adieu, my dear   330
pretty angel.

Exeunt all the women

BELVILE Ha! Florinda's picture: 'twas she herself. What
a dull dog was I! I would have given the world for one
minute's discourse with her.

FREDERICK This comes of your modesty! Ah, pox o'   335
your vow, 'twas ten to one but we had lost the jewel
by't.

BELVILE Willmore! The blessed'st opportunity lost!
Florinda, friends, Florinda!

WILLMORE Ah, rogue! Such black eyes, such a face, such   340
a mouth, such teeth – and so much wit!

BELVILE All, all, and a thousand charms besides.

WILLMORE Why, dost thou know her?

BELVILE Know her? Aye, aye, and a pox take me with
all my heart for being modest.   345

WILLMORE But hark'ee, friend of mine, are you my rival?
and have I been only beating the bush all this while?

BELVILE I understand thee not. I'm mad, see here –
    [Belvile] shows the picture
WILLMORE Ha! whose picture's this? 'Tis a fine wench!
FREDERICK The colonel's mistress, sir. 350
WILLMORE Oh, oh, – here. (*Gives the picture back*) I
    thought it had been another prize. Come, come, a
    bottle will set thee right again.
BELVILE I am content to try, and by that time 'twill be
    late enough for our design. 355
WILLMORE Agreed.
        Love does all day the soul's great empire keep,
        But wine at night lulls the soft god asleep.
    Exeunt

Act III Scene II

Lucetta's house
Enter Blunt and Lucetta with a light
LUCETTA Now we are safe and free: no fears of the
    coming home of my old jealous husband, which made
    me a little thoughtful when you came in first, but now
    love is all the business of my soul.
BLUNT I am transported! (*Aside*) Pox on't, that I had but 5
    some fine things to say to her, such as lovers use. I was
    a fool not to learn of Fred a little by heart before I came.
    Something I must say. [*To Lucetta*] 'Adsheartlikins, sweet
    soul! I am not used to compliment, but I'm an honest
    gentleman, and thy humble servant. 10
LUCETTA I have nothing to pay for so great a favour,
    but such a love as cannot but be great, since at first
    sight of that sweet face and shape, it made me your
    absolute captive.

BLUNT (*aside*) Kind heart, how prettily she talks! Egad,   15
I'll show her husband a Spanish trick: send him out
of the world, and marry her; she's damnably in love
with me, and will ne'er mind settlements, and so
there's that saved.

LUCETTA Well, sir, I'll go and undress me, and be with   20
you instantly.

BLUNT Make haste then, for 'adsheartlikins, dear soul,
thou canst not guess at the pain of a longing lover,
when his joys are drawn within the compass of a few
minutes.   25

LUCETTA You speak my sense, and I'll make haste to
prove it.
Exit [Lucetta]

BLUNT 'Tis a rare girl, and this one night's enjoyment
with her, will be worth all the days I ever passed in
Essex. Would she would go with me into England;   30
though to say truth, there's plenty of whores already.
But a pox on 'em, they are such mercenary prodigal
whores, that they want such a one as this, that's free
and generous, to give 'em good examples. Why, what
a house she has, how rich and fine!   35
Enter Sancho

SANCHO Sir, my lady has sent me to conduct you to her
chamber.

BLUNT Sir, I shall be proud to follow.
Exit Sancho
Here's one of her servants too! 'Adsheartlikins, by
this garb and gravity, he might be a justice of peace   40
in Essex, and is but a pimp here.
Exit

Act III Scene III

The scene changes to a chamber with an alcove bed in it, a table, etc. Lucetta in bed
Enter Sancho and Blunt, who takes the candle of Sancho at the door

SANCHO Sir, my commission reaches no farther.

BLUNT Sir, I'll excuse your compliment.

Exit Sancho

– What, in bed, my sweet mistress?

LUCETTA You see, I still out-do you in kindness.

BLUNT And thou shalt see what haste I'll make to quit   5
scores. [*Aside*] Oh, the luckiest rogue!

[Blunt] undresses himself

LUCETTA Should you be false or cruel now!

BLUNT False! 'Adsheartlikins, what dost thou take
me for? A Jew? An insensible heathen? A pox of thy
old jealous husband; an he were dead, egad, sweet   10
soul, it should be none of my fault, if I did not marry
thee.

LUCETTA It never should be mine.

BLUNT Good soul! I'm the fortunatest dog!

LUCETTA Are you not undressed yet?   15

BLUNT As much as my impatience will permit.

Goes towards the bed in his shirt, drawers, etc.

LUCETTA Hold, sir, put out the light, it may betray us
else.

BLUNT Anything; I need no other light, but that of
thine eyes! [*Aside*] 'Adsheartlikins, there I think I   20
had it.

[Blunt] puts out the candle; the bed descends [by means of a trap]; he gropes about to find it

Why – why – where am I got? What, not yet? Where

68

are you, sweetest? – Ah, the rogue's silent now, a pretty
love-trick this: how she'll laugh at me anon! – You
need not, my dear rogue, you need not! I'm all on fire   25
already. Come, come, now call me in pity. – Sure I'm
enchanted! I have been round the chamber, and can
find neither woman, nor bed. I locked the door, I'm
sure she cannot go that way; or if she could, the bed
could not. – Enough, enough, my pretty wanton, do   30
not carry the jest too far. – Ha, betrayed! Dogs!
Rogues! Pimps! Help! help!

    [*Blunt*] *lights on a trap, and is let down. Enter*
    Lucetta, Philippo, and Sancho with a light

PHILIPPO Ha, ha, ha, he's dispatched finely.

LUCETTA Now, sir, had I been coy, we had missed of
this booty.   35

PHILIPPO Nay, when I saw 'twas a substantial fool, I was
mollified; but when you dote upon a serenading
coxcomb, upon a face, fine clothes, and a lute, it makes
me rage.

LUCETTA You know I was never guilty of that folly, my   40
dear Philippo, but with yourself. But come, let's see
what we have got by this.

PHILIPPO A rich coat! Sword and hat; these breeches,
too, are well-lined! See here, a gold watch! a purse –
ha! gold: at least two hundred pistoles! A bunch of   45
diamond rings, and one with the family arms! A gold
box, with a medal of his king, and his lady mother's
picture! These were sacred relics, believe me! See, the
waistband of his breeches have a mine of gold: old
Queen Bess's; we have a quarrel to her ever since   50
eighty-eight, and may therefore justify the theft, the
Inquisition might have committed it.

LUCETTA See, a bracelet of bowed gold! These his sisters
tied about his arm at parting. But well, for all this, I

fear his being a stranger may make a noise and hinder   55
our trade with them hereafter.

PHILIPPO That's our security; he is not only a stranger
to us, but to the country too. The common shore into
which he is descended, thou know'st, conducts him
into another street, which this light will hinder him   60
from ever finding again. He knows neither your name,
nor that of the street where your house is; nay, nor
the way to his own lodgings.

LUCETTA And art not thou an unmerciful rogue, not to
afford him one night for all this? I should not have   65
been such a Jew.

PHILIPPO Blame me not, Lucetta, to keep as much of
thee as I can to myself. Come, that thought makes me
wanton: let's to bed! – Sancho, lock up these.

         This is the fleece which fools do bear,   70
         Designed for witty men to shear.

Exeunt

Act III Scene IV

The scene changes, and discovers Blunt, creeping
out of a common-shore, his face, etc., all dirty

BLUNT (*climbing up*) Oh lord! I am got out at last, and,
which is a miracle, without a clue; and now to damning
and cursing! But if that would ease me, where shall I
begin? with my fortune, myself, or the quean that
cozened me? What a dog was I to believe in woman!   5
Oh, coxcomb! Ignorant conceited coxcomb! to fancy
she could be enamoured with my person, at first sight
enamoured! Oh, I'm a cursed puppy! 'tis plain, fool
was writ upon my forehead! She perceived it; saw the

Essex calf there; for what allurements could there be   10
in this countenance, which I can endure because I'm
acquainted with it? Oh, dull silly dog, to be thus
soothed into a cozening! Had I been drunk, I might
fondly have credited the young quean, but as I was in
my right wits, to be thus cheated confirms it: I am a   15
dull believing English country fop. But my comrades!
Death and the devil, there's the worst of all; then a
ballad will be sung tomorrow on the Prado, to a lousy
tune, of the enchanted 'squire, and the annihilated
damsel; but Fred, that rogue, and the colonel, will   20
abuse me beyond all Christian patience. Had she left
me my clothes, I have a bill of exchange at home,
would have saved my credit, but now all hope is taken
from me. Well, I'll home, if I can find the way, with
this consolation, that I am not the first kind believing   25
coxcomb; but there are, gallants, many such good
natures amongst ye.

> And though you've better arts to hide your
>   follies,
> 'Adsheartlikins, y'are all as arrant cullies.

[*Exit*]

Act III Scene V

The garden in the night
Enter Florinda in an undress, with a key and a
little box

FLORINDA Well, thus far I'm in my way to happiness: I
have got myself free from Callis; my brother too, I
find by yonder light, is got into his cabinet, and thinks
not of me; I have by good fortune got the key of the

garden back-door. I'll open it to prevent Belvile's knocking; a little noise will now alarm my brother. Now am I as fearful as a young thief. (*Unlocks the door*) Hark, what noise is that? Oh, 'twas the wind that played amongst the boughs. Belvile stays long, methinks; it's time. Stay, for fear of a surprise I'll hide these jewels in yonder jessamine.

[*Florinda*] *goes to lay down the box. Enter*
Willmore, drunk

WILLMORE What the devil is become of these fellows, Belvile and Frederick? They promised to stay at the next corner for me, but who the devil knows the corner of a full moon? Now, whereabouts am I? Ha, what have we here, a garden! A very convenient place to sleep in. Ha, what has God sent us here? A female! By this light, a woman! I'm a dog if it be not a very wench!

FLORINDA [*aside*] He's come! – Ha, who's there?

WILLMORE Sweet soul! let me salute thy shoe-string.

FLORINDA [*aside*] 'Tis not my Belvile. Good heavens! I know him not. – Who are you, and from whence come you?

WILLMORE Prithee, prithee, child, not so many hard questions. Let it suffice I am here, child. Come, come kiss me.

FLORINDA Good gods! what luck is mine?

WILLMORE Only good luck child, parlous good luck. Come hither. [*Aside*] 'Tis a delicate shining wench; by this hand, she's perfumed, and smells like any nosegay. – Prithee, dear soul, let's not play the fool, and lose time, precious time; for as Gad shall save me, I'm as honest a fellow as breathes, though I'm a little disguised at present. Come, I say; why, thou mayst be free with me, I'll be very secret. I'll not boast

who 'twas obliged me, not I: for hang me if I know
thy name.

LORINDA Heavens! what a filthy beast is this!

WILLMORE I am so, and thou ought'st the sooner to lie   40
with me for that reason: for look you, child, there will
be no sin in't, because 'twas neither designed nor
premeditated; 'tis pure accident on both sides, that's
a certain thing now. Indeed, should I make love to
you, and vow you fidelity, and swear and lie till you   45
believed and yielded, that were to make it wilful fornication, the crying sin of the nation. Thou art therefore, as thou art a good Christian, obliged in
conscience to deny me nothing. Now, come, be kind
without any more idle prating.   50

LORINDA Oh, I am ruined! – Wicked man, unhand me.

WILLMORE Wicked! Egad, child, a judge, were he young
and vigorous, and saw those eyes of thine, would know
'twas they gave the first blow, the first provocation.
Come, prithee let's lose no time, I say; this is a fine   55
convenient place.

LORINDA Sir, let me go, I conjure you, or I'll call out.

WILLMORE Aye, aye, you were best to call witness to see
how finely you treat me, do.

LORINDA I'll cry murder, rape, or anything, if you do   60
not instantly let me go.

WILLMORE A rape! Come, come, you lie, you baggage,
you lie: what, I'll warrant you would fain have the
world believe now that you are not so forward as I.
No, not you! Why, at this time of night, was your   65
cobweb door set open, dear spider, but to catch flies?
Ha, come, or I shall be damnably angry. Why, what a
coil is here!

LORINDA Sir, can you think –

WILLMORE – That you would do't for nothing? Oh, oh,   70

I find what you would be at. Look here, here's a pistole
for you. Here's a work indeed! Here, take it I say.

FLORINDA For heaven's sake, sir, as you're a gentleman –

WILLMORE So – now, now – she would be wheedling me
for more. – What, you will not take it then, you are
resolved you will not? Come, come, take it, or I'll put
it up again, for look ye, I never give more. Why how
now mistress, are you so high i'th' mouth a pistole
won't down with you? Ha, why, what a work's here!
In good time! Come, no struggling to be gone; but an
y'are good at a dumb wrestle, I'm for ye, look ye, I'm
for ye.

> [*Florinda*] *struggles with* [*Willmore*]. *Enter Belvile
> and Frederick*

BELVILE The door is open. A pox of this mad fellow,
I'm angry that we've lost him; I durst have sworn he
had followed us.

FREDERICK But you were so hasty, colonel, to be gone.

FLORINDA Help, help! Murder! Help! Oh, I am ruined.

BELVILE Ha, sure that's Florinda's voice!

> [*Belvile*] *comes up to* [*Florinda and Willmore*]

A man! – Villain, let go that lady.

> *A noise* [*offstage*]. *Willmore turns and draws,
> Frederick interposes*

FLORINDA [*aside*] Belvile! Heavens, my brother too is
coming, and 'twill be impossible to escape. – Belvile,
I conjure you to walk under my chamber window,
from whence I'll give you some instructions what to
do. This rude man has undone us.

> *Exit* [*Florinda*]

WILLMORE Belvile!

> *Enter Pedro, Stephano, and other servants, with lights*

PEDRO I'm betrayed! Run, Stephano, and see if Florinda
be safe.

*Exit Stephano. [The two groups of men] fight, and
Pedro's party beats [Willmore's party] out*
So, whoe'er they be, all is not well; I'll to Florinda's
chamber.
Going out, [Pedro] meets Stephano [re-entering]

STEPHANO You need not, sir; the poor lady's fast asleep   100
and thinks no harm. I would not awake her, sir, for
fear of frighting her with your danger.

PEDRO I'm glad she's there. – Rascals, how came the
garden door open?

STEPHANO That question comes too late, sir. Some of   105
my fellow servants masquerading, I'll warrant.

PEDRO Masquerading! a lewd custom to debauch our
youth. [*Aside*] There's something more in this than I
imagine.
Exeunt

Act III Scene VI

*The street
Enter Belvile in rage, Frederick holding him, and
Willmore melancholy*

WILLMORE Why, how the devil should I know Florinda?

BELVILE Ah, plague of your ignorance! If it had not
been Florinda, must you be a beast, a brute, a senseless swine?

WILLMORE Well, sir, you see I am endued with patience;   5
I can bear; though egad, y'are very free with me,
methinks. I was in good hopes the quarrel would have
been on my side, for so uncivilly interrupting me.

BELVILE Peace, brute, whilst thou'rt safe. Oh, I'm
distracted.   10

WILLMORE Nay, nay, I'm an unlucky dog, that's certain.

BELVILE Ah, curse upon the star that ruled my birth, or whatsoever other influence that makes me still so wretched!

WILLMORE Thou break'st my heart with these 15 complaints; there is no star in fault, no influence but sack, the cursed sack I drunk.

FREDERICK Why, how the devil came you so drunk?

WILLMORE Why, how the devil came you so sober?

BELVILE A curse upon his thin skull, he was always 20 beforehand that way.

FREDERICK Prithee, dear colonel, forgive him, he's sorry for his fault.

BELVILE He's always so after he has done a mischief. A plague on all such brutes! 25

WILLMORE By this light, I took her for an arrant harlot.

BELVILE Damn your debauched opinion! Tell me, sot, hadst thou so much sense and light about thee to distinguish her woman, and couldst not see something about her face and person, to strike an awful rever- 30 ence into thy soul?

WILLMORE Faith no, I considered her as mere a woman as I could wish.

BELVILE 'Sdeath, I have no patience. – Draw, or I'll kill you. 35

WILLMORE Let that alone till tomorrow, and if I set not all right again, use your pleasure.

BELVILE Tomorrow! damn it,
The spiteful light will lead me to no happiness.
Tomorrow is Antonio's, and perhaps 40
Guides him to my undoing; oh, that I could meet
This rival, this powerful fortunate!

WILLMORE What then?

BELVILE Let thy own reason, or my rage, instruct thee.

WILLMORE I shall be finely informed then, no doubt. 45
   Hear me, colonel, hear me: show me the man and I'll
   do his business.
BELVILE I know him no more than thou, or if I did I
   should not need thy aid.
WILLMORE This you say is Angellica's house; I prom- 50
   ised the kind baggage to lie with her tonight.
      [*Willmore*] *offers to go in. Enter Antonio and his page.*
      Antonio knocks on [*Angellica's door with*] *the hilt*
      of his sword
ANTONIO You paid the thousand crowns I directed?
PAGE To the lady's old woman, sir, I did.
WILLMORE Who the devil have we here?
BELVILE I'll now plant myself under Florinda's window, 55
   and if I find no comfort there, I'll die.
      Exeunt Belvile and Frederick. Enter Moretta
MORETTA Page!
PAGE Here's my lord.
WILLMORE How is this? A picaroon going to board my
   frigate? – Here's one chase gun for you. 60
      Drawing his sword, [*Willmore*] *jostles Antonio,*
      who turns and draws. [*Willmore and Antonio*]
      fight. Antonio falls
MORETTA Oh bless us, we're all undone!
      [*Moretta*] *runs in and shuts the door*
PAGE Help! Murder!
      Belvile returns at the noise of fighting
BELVILE Ha, the mad rogue's engaged in some unlucky
   adventure again.
      Enter two or three masqueraders
MASQUERADER Ha, a man killed! 65
WILLMORE How, a man killed? Then I'll go home to sleep.
      [*Willmore*] *puts up* [*his sword*] *and reels out.*
      Exeunt masqueraders another way

BELVILE Who should it be? Pray heaven the rogue is
    safe, for all my quarrel to him.
        As Belvile is groping about, enter an officer and
        six soldiers
SOLDIER Who's there?
OFFICER So, here's one dispatched. Secure the murderer. 70
BELVILE Do not mistake my charity for murder! I came
    to his assistance.
        Soldiers seize on Belvile
OFFICER That shall be tried, sir. – St Jago, swords drawn
    in the carnival time!
        [Officer] goes to Antonio
ANTONIO Thy hand, prithee. 75
OFFICER Ha, Don Antonio! [*To soldiers*] Look well to
    the villain there. [*To Antonio*] How is it, sir?
ANTONIO I'm hurt.
BELVILE Has my humanity made me a criminal?
OFFICER Away with him. 80
BELVILE What a cursed chance is this!
        Exeunt soldiers with Belvile
ANTONIO [*aside*] This is the man that has set upon me
    twice. (*To the officer*) Carry him to my apartment, till
    you have farther orders from me.
        Exit Antonio, led

Act IV Scene I

A fine room
Discovers Belvile as by dark, alone

BELVILE When shall I be weary of railing on fortune,
who is resolved never to turn with smiles upon me?
Two such defeats in one night none but the devil, and
that mad rogue, could have contrived to have plagued
me with. I am here a prisoner, but where, heaven   5
knows; and if there be murder done, I can soon decide
the fate of a stranger in a nation without mercy; yet
this is nothing to the torture my soul bows with, when
I think of losing my fair, my dear Florinda. Hark, my
door opens: a light; a man, and seems of quality;   10
armed, too! Now shall I die like a dog, without
defence.

Enter Antonio in a night-gown, with a light; his
arm in a scarf, and a sword under his arm. He sets
the candle on the table

ANTONIO Sir, I come to know what injuries I have done
you, that could provoke you to so mean an action as
to attack me basely, without allowing time for my   15
defence.

BELVILE Sir, for a man in my circumstances to plead
innocence, would look like fear: but view me well,
and you will find no marks of coward on me, nor
anything that betrays that brutality you accuse me   20
with.

ANTONIO In vain, sir, you impose upon my sense. You
are not only he who drew on me last night, but
yesterday before the same house, that of Angellica.
Yet there is something in your face and mien   25
That makes me wish I were mistaken.

BELVILE I own I fought today, in the defence of a friend
of mine, with whom you (if you're the same) and your
party were first engaged.
Perhaps you think this crime enough to kill me,   30
But if you do, I cannot fear you'll do it basely.
ANTONIO No, sir, I'll make you fit for a defence with
this.
    [Antonio] gives [Belvile] the sword
BELVILE This gallantry surprises me; nor know I how
to use this present, sir, against a man so brave.   35
ANTONIO You shall not need; for know, I come to snatch
you from a danger that is decreed against you: perhaps
your life, or long imprisonment; and 'twas with so
much courage you offended, I cannot see you
punished.   40
BELVILE How shall I pay this generosity?
ANTONIO It had been safer to have killed another, than
have attempted me. To show your danger, sir, I'll let
you know my quality: and 'tis the viceroy's son, whom
you have wounded.   45
BELVILE The viceroy's son!
   (*Aside*) Death and confusion! was this plague reserved
To complete all the rest? Obliged by him!
The man of all the world I would destroy.
ANTONIO You seem disordered, sir.   50
BELVILE Yes, trust me, sir, I am, and 'tis with pain
That man receives such bounties,
Who wants the power to pay 'em back again.
ANTONIO To gallant spirits 'tis indeed uneasy;
But you may quickly overpay me, sir.   55
BELVILE Then I am well. (*Aside*) Kind heaven! but set
us even,
That I may fight with him and keep my honour safe.
– Oh, I'm impatient, sir, to be discounting

The mighty debt I owe you. Command me quickly.   60

ANTONIO I have a quarrel with a rival, sir,
About the maid we love.

BELVILE (*aside*) Death, 'tis Florinda he means.
That thought destroys my reason,
And I shall kill him.   65

ANTONIO My rival, sir,
Is one has all the virtues man can boast of −

BELVILE (*aside*) Death, who should this be?

[ANTONIO] He challenged me to meet him on the Molo
As soon as day appeared, but last night's quarrel   70
Has made my arm unfit to guide a sword.

BELVILE I apprehend you, sir; you'd have me kill the
man that lays a claim to the maid you speak of. I'll
do't; I'll fly to do't!

ANTONIO Sir, do you know her?   75

BELVILE No, sir, but 'tis enough she is admired by you.

ANTONIO Sir, I shall rob you of the glory on't,
For you must fight under my name and dress.

BELVILE That opinion must be strangely obliging that
makes you think I can personate the brave Antonio,   80
whom I can but strive to imitate.

ANTONIO You say too much to my advantage. Come,
sir, the day appears that calls you forth. Within, sir,
is the habit.
       Exit Antonio

BELVILE Fantastic fortune, thou deceitful light,   85
          That cheats the wearied traveller by night,
          Though on a precipice each step you tread,
          I am resolved to follow where you lead.
       Exit

Act IV Scene II

The Molo
Enter Florinda and Callis in masks, with Stephano

FLORINDA (*aside*) I'm dying with my fears; Belvile's not
coming as I expected under my window, makes me
believe that all those fears are true. [*To Stephano*] Canst
thou not tell with whom my brother fights?

STEPHANO No, madam, they were both in masquerade.
I was by when they challenged one another, and they
had decided the quarrel then, but were prevented by
some cavaliers, which made 'em put it off till now;
but I am sure 'tis about you they fight.

FLORINDA (*aside*) Nay, then 'tis with Belvile, for what   10
other lover have I that dares fight for me? (Except
Antonio, and he is too much in favour with my
brother.) If it be he, for whom shall I direct my prayers
to heaven?

STEPHANO Madam, I must leave you, for if my master   15
see me, I shall be hanged for being your conductor. I
escaped narrowly for the excuse I made for you last
night i'th' garden.

FLORINDA And I'll reward thee for't; prithee, no more.
Exit Stephano. Enter Don Pedro in his masking habit

PEDRO Antonio's late today; the place will fill, and we   20
may be prevented.
[*Pedro*] *walks about*

FLORINDA (*aside*) Antonio? Sure I heard amiss.

PEDRO But who will not excuse a happy lover,
When soft fair arms confine the yielding neck,
And the kind whisper languishingly breathes,   25
'Must you be gone so soon?'
Sure I had dwelt forever on her bosom.

Enter Belvile dressed in Antonio's clothes
But stay, he's here.

FLORINDA [*aside*] 'Tis not Belvile, half my fears are vanished. 30

PEDRO Antonio!

BELVILLE (*aside*) This must be he. [*To Pedro*] You're early, sir; I do not use to be outdone this way.

PEDRO The wretched, sir, are watchful, and 'tis enough you've the advantage of me in Angellica. 35

BELVILE (*aside*) Angellica! Or I've mistook my man, or else Antonio. Can he forget his interest in Florinda, and fight for common prize?

PEDRO Come, sir, you know our terms.

BELVILE (*aside*) By heaven, not I. – No talking, I am 40 ready, sir.

[*Belvile*] *offers to fight. Florinda runs in [between the two men]*

FLORINDA (*to Belvile*) Oh, hold! Whoe'er you be, I do conjure you hold! If you strike here, I die.

PEDRO Florinda!

BELVILE Florinda imploring for my rival! 45

PEDRO Away, this kindness is unseasonable.

[*Pedro*] *puts [Florinda] by. [Belvile and Pedro] fight; [Florinda] runs in just as Belvile disarms Pedro*

FLORINDA Who are you, sir, that dares deny my prayers?

BELVILE Thy prayers destroy him: if thou wouldst preserve him,
Do that thou'rt unacquainted with, and curse him. 50

[*Florinda*] *holds [Belvile]*

FLORINDA By all you hold most dear, by her you love,
I do conjure you, touch him not.

BELVILE By her I love!
See, I obey, and at your feet resign
The useless trophy of my victory. 55

[Belvile] lays his sword at [Florinda's] feet
PEDRO Antonio, you've done enough to prove you love
　Florinda.
BELVILE Love Florinda! Does heaven love adoration,
　prayer, or penitence? Love her! Here, sir, your sword
　again.　　　　　　　　　　　　　　　　　　　　　60
　　　[Belvile] snatches up the sword and gives it [to Pedro]
　Upon this truth I'll fight my life away.
PEDRO No, you've redeemed my sister, and my friend-
　ship.
　　　*[Pedro] gives Florinda [to Belvile]. [Pedro] pulls off
　　　his vizard to show his face, and puts it on again*
BELVILE Don Pedro!
PEDRO Can you resign your claims to other women,　　65
　And give your heart entirely to Florinda?
BELVILE Entire! as dying saints' confessions are!
　I can delay my happiness no longer:
This minute let me make Florinda mine!
PEDRO This minute let it be: no time so proper;　　70
　This night my father will arrive from Rome,
　And possibly may hinder what we purpose.
FLORINDA Oh heavens! This minute!
　　　Enter masqueraders, and pass over
BELVILE *[to Florinda]* Oh, do not ruin me!
PEDRO The place begins to fill, and that we may not be　75
　observed, do you walk off to St Peter's church, where
　I will meet you, and conclude your happiness.
BELVILE I'll meet you there. (*Aside*) If there be no more
　saints' churches in Naples.
FLORINDA Oh stay, sir, and recall your hasty doom!　80
　Alas, I have not yet prepared my heart
　To entertain so strange a guest.
PEDRO Away, this silly modesty is assumed too late.
BELVILE Heaven, madam! what do you do?

FLORINDA Do? Despise the man that lays a tyrant's claim   85
  To what he ought to conquer by submission.
BELVILE You do not know me; move a little this way.
      [Belvile] draws [Florinda] aside
FLORINDA Yes, you may force me even to the altar,
  But not the holy man that offers there
  Shall force me to be thine.   90
      Pedro talks to Callis this while
BELVILE Oh, do not lose so blest an opportunity!
  See, 'tis your Belvile, not Antonio,
  Whom your mistaken scorn and anger ruins.
      [Belvile] pulls off his vizard
FLORINDA Belvile!
  Where was my soul it could not meet thy voice,   95
  And take this knowledge in?
      *As they are talking, enter Willmore, finely dressed,
      and Frederick*
WILLMORE No intelligence! No news of Belvile yet.
  Well, I am the most unlucky rascal in nature. Ha, am
  I deceived, or is it he? Look, Fred, 'tis he, my dear
  Belvile.   100
      *[Willmore] runs and embraces [Belvile]. Belvile's
      vizard falls out [of his] hand*
BELVILE Hell and confusion seize thee!
PEDRO Ha, Belvile! I beg your pardon, sir.
      [Pedro] takes Florinda from [Belvile]
BELVILE Nay, touch her not; she's mine by conquest,
  sir,
  I won her by my sword.   105
WILLMORE Didst thou so? and egad, child, we'll keep
  her by the sword.
      *[Willmore] draws on Pedro. Belvile goes between
      [Willmore and Pedro]*
BELVILE Stand off!

Thou'rt so profanely lewd, so cursed by heaven,
All quarrels thou espousest must be fatal.   110

WILLMORE Nay, an you be so hot, my valour's coy, and
shall be courted when you want it next. (*Puts up his
sword*)

BELVILE (*to Pedro*) You know I ought to claim a victor's
right,
But you're the brother to divine Florinda,   115
To whom I'm such a slave: to purchase her
I durst not hurt the man she holds so dear.

PEDRO 'Twas by Antonio's, not by Belvile's sword
This question should have been decided, sir.
I must confess much to your bravery's due,   120
Both now, and when I met you last in arms:
But I am nicely punctual in my word,
As men of honour ought, and beg your pardon.
For this mistake another time shall clear.
          (*Aside to Florinda as they are going out*)
This was some plot between you and Belvile,   125
But I'll prevent you.
          [*Exeunt Pedro and Florinda.*] Belvile *looks after*
          [*Florinda*], *and begins to walk up and down in
          rage*

WILLMORE Do not be modest now and lose the woman,
but if we shall fetch her back, so.

BELVILE Do not speak to me.

WILLMORE Not speak to you? Egad, I'll speak to you,   130
and will be answered, too.

BELVILE Will you, sir?

WILLMORE I know I've done some mischief, but I'm so
dull a puppy, that I'm the son of a whore if I know
how, or where. Prithee inform my understanding.   135

BELVILE Leave me, I say, and leave me instantly.

WILLMORE I will not leave you in this humour, nor till

I know my crime.
BELVILE Death, I'll tell you, sir!
> *[Belvile] draws and runs at Willmore. Frederick*
> *interposes. [Willmore begins to run] out, Belvile*
> *after him. Enter Angellica, Moretta, and*
> *Sebastian*

ANGELLICA Ha! Sebastian, is not that Willmore? Haste,   140
haste and bring him back.
> *[Exeunt Willmore and Belvile]*

FREDERICK The colonel's mad: I never saw him thus
before. I'll after 'em lest he do some mischief, for I
am sure Willmore will not draw on him.
> *Exit [Frederick]*

ANGELLICA I am all rage! my first desires defeated!   145
For one, for aught he knows, that has
No other merit than her quality,
Her being Don Pedro's sister: he loves her!
I know 'tis so. Dull, dull, insensible;
He will not see me now, though oft invited,   150
And broke his word last night: false perjured man!
He that but yesterday fought for my favours,
And would have made his life a sacrifice
To've gained one night with me,
Must now be hired and courted to my arms.   155
MORETTA I told you what would come on't, but
Moretta's an old doting fool. Why did you give him
five hundred crowns, but to set himself out for other
lovers? You should have kept him poor, if you had
meant to have had any good from him.   160
ANGELLICA Oh, name not such mean trifles; had I given
Him all my youth has earned from sin,
I had not lost a thought, nor sigh upon't.
But I have given him my eternal rest,
My whole repose, my future joys, my heart!   165

My virgin heart, Moretta! Oh, 'tis gone!
Enter Willmore and Sebastian

MORETTA Curse on him, here he comes. How fine she
has made him too.
Angellica turns and walks away

WILLMORE How now, turned shadow?
Fly when I pursue, and follow when I fly? (*Sings*)   170

> *Stay, gentle shadow of my dove,*
>   *And tell me ere I go,*
> *Whether the substance may not prove*
>   *A fleeting thing like you.*

As [Angellica] turns, she looks on [Willmore]
There's a soft kind look remaining yet.   175

ANGELLICA Well, sir, you may be gay: all happiness, all
joys pursue you still; fortune's your slave, and gives
you every hour choice of new hearts and beauties, till
you are cloyed with the repeated bliss, which others
vainly languish for.   180
But know, false man, that I shall be revenged.
[Angellica] turns away in rage

WILLMORE So, gad, there are of those faint-hearted
lovers, whom such a sharp lesson next their hearts,
would make as impotent as fourscore. Pox o' this
whining! My business is to laugh and love; a pox on't,   185
I hate your sullen lover; a man shall lose as much time
to put you in humour now, as would serve to gain a
new woman.

ANGELLICA I scorn to cool that fire I cannot raise,
Or do the drudgery of your virtuous mistress.   190

WILLMORE A virtuous mistress! Death, what a thing
thou hast found out for me! Why, what the devil
should I do with a virtuous woman? A sort of ill-

natured creatures, that take a pride to torment a lover.
Virtue is but an infirmity in woman; a disease that   195
renders even the handsome ungrateful; whilst the ill-
favoured, for want of solicitations and address, only
fancy themselves so. I have lain with a woman of
quality, who has all the while been railing at whores.

ANGELLICA I will not answer for your mistress's virtue,   200
Though she be young enough to know no guilt;
And I could wish you would persuade my heart
'Twas the two hundred thousand crowns you courted.

WILLMORE Two hundred thousand crowns! What
story's this, what trick? What woman? Ha!   205

ANGELLICA How strange you make it. Have you forgot
the creature you entertained on the Piazza last night?

WILLMORE (*aside*) Ha, my gipsy worth two hundred
thousand crowns? Oh, how I long to be with her. Pox,
I knew she was of quality.   210

ANGELLICA False man! I see my ruin in your face.
How many vows you breathed upon my bosom,
Never to be unjust: have you forgot so soon?

WILLMORE Faith no, I was just coming to repeat 'em.
But here's a humour, indeed, would make a man a   215
saint. (*Aside*) Would she would be angry enough to
leave me, and command me not to wait on her.

    Enter Hellena, dressed in man's clothes

HELLENA [*aside*] This must be Angellica, I know it by
her mumping matron here; aye, aye, 'tis she! My mad
captain's with her too, for all his swearing. How this   220
unconstant humour makes me love him!
[*To Moretta*] Pray, good grave gentlewoman, is not this
Angellica?

MORETTA My too young sir, it is. [*Aside*] I hope 'tis one
from Don Antonio.   225

    [*Moretta*] *goes to Angellica*

HELLENA (*aside*) Well, something I'll do to vex him for
this.

ANGELLICA [*to Moretta*] I will not speak with him; am
I in humour to receive a lover?

WILLMORE Not speak with him! Why, I'll begone, and   230
wait your idler minutes. Can I show less obedience to
the thing I love so fondly?
      [*Willmore*] *offers to go*

ANGELLICA A fine excuse, this! Stay.

WILLMORE And hinder your advantage? Should I repay
your bounties so ungratefully?   235

ANGELLICA [*to Hellena*] Come hither, boy – [*to Willmore*]
that I may let you see
How much above the advantages you name
I prize one minute's joy with you.

WILLMORE Oh, you destroy me with this endearment.   240
[*Aside,*] *impatient to be gone*) Death! how shall I get
away? – Madam, 'twill not be fit I should be seen with
you; besides, it will not be convenient; and I've a friend
– that's dangerously sick.

ANGELLICA I see you're impatient; yet you shall stay.   245

WILLMORE (*aside*) And miss my assignation with my
gipsy.
      [*Willmore*] *walks about impatiently. Moretta brings*
      Hellena, who addresses herself to Angellica

HELLENA Madam,
You'll hardly pardon my intrusion
When you shall know my business,   250
And I'm too young to tell my tale with art;
But there must be a wondrous store of goodness,
Where so much beauty dwells.

ANGELLICA A pretty advocate, whoever sent thee.
Prithee proceed. (*To Willmore, who is stealing off*) Nay,   255
sir, you shall not go.

WILLMORE (*aside*) Then I shall lose my dear gipsy forever.
  Pox on't, she stays me out of spite.
[HELLENA] I am related to a lady, madam,
  Young, rich, and nobly born, but has the fate   260
  To be in love with a young English gentleman.
  Strangely she loves him, at first sight she loved him,
  But did adore him when she heard him speak;
  For he, she said, had charms in every word,
  That failed not to surprise, to wound and conquer.   265
WILLMORE (*aside*) Ha! Egad, I hope this concerns me.
ANGELLICA 'Tis my false man he means: would he were
  gone.
This praise will raise his pride, and ruin me. (*To Willmore*)
  Well,   270
  Since you are so impatient to be gone,
  I will release you, sir.
WILLMORE (*aside*) Nay, then I'm sure 'twas me he spoke
  of: this cannot be the effects of kindness in her.
  – No, madam, I've considered better on't,   275
  And will not give you cause of jealousy.
ANGELLICA But, sir, I've – business, that –
WILLMORE This shall not do; I know 'tis but to try me.
ANGELLICA Well, to your story, boy – (*aside*) though
  'twill undo me.   280
HELLENA With this addition to his other beauties,
  He won her unresisting tender heart:
  He vowed, and sighed, and swore he loved her dearly;
  And she believed the cunning flatterer,
  And thought herself the happiest maid alive.   285
  Today was the appointed time by both
  To consummate their bliss;
  The virgin, altar, and the priest were dressed;
  And whilst she languished for th'expected bride-
    groom,

She heard, he paid his broken vows to you. 290

WILLMORE [*aside*] So, this is some dear rogue that's in
love with me, and this way lets me know it; or if it be
not me, she means someone whose place I may supply.

ANGELLICA Now I perceive
The cause of thy impatience to be gone, 295
And all the business of this glorious dress.

WILLMORE Damn the young prater, I know not what he
means.

HELLENA Madam,
In your fair eyes I read too much concern, 300
To tell my farther business.

ANGELLICA Prithee, sweet youth, talk on: thou mayst
perhaps
Raise here a storm that may undo my passion,
And then I'll grant thee anything. 305

HELLENA Madam, 'tis to entreat you (oh unreasonable)
You would not see this stranger;
For if you do, she vows you are undone,
Though nature never made a man so excellent,
And sure he'd been a god, but for inconstancy. 310

WILLMORE (*aside*) Ah, rogue, how finely he's instructed!
'Tis plain: some woman that has seen me *en passant*.

ANGELLICA Oh, I shall burst with jealousy! Do you
know the man you speak of?

HELLENA Yes, madam, he used to be in buff and scarlet. 315

ANGELLICA (*to Willmore*) Thou, false as hell, what canst
thou say to this?

WILLMORE By heaven –

ANGELLICA Hold, do not damn thyself –

HELLENA – Nor hope to be believed. 320
        [*Willmore*] *walks about,* [*Angellica and Hellena*]
        follow

ANGELLICA Oh, perjured man!

Is't thus you pay my generous passion back?

HELLENA Why would you, sir, abuse my lady's faith?

ANGELLICA And use me so inhumanly?

HELLENA A maid so young, so innocent – 325

WILLMORE Ah, young devil.

ANGELLICA Dost thou not know thy life is in my power?

HELLENA Or think my lady cannot be revenged?

WILLMORE (*aside*) So, so, the storm comes finely on.

ANGELLICA Now thou art silent; guilt has struck thee 330
dumb.
Oh, hadst thou still been so, I'd lived in safety.
> [*Angellica*] *turns away and weeps*

WILLMORE (*aside to Hellena*) Sweetheart, the lady's name
and house, quickly: I'm impatient to be with her.
> [*Willmore*] *looks towards Angellica to watch her
> turning, and as she comes towards them he meets her*

HELLENA (*aside*) So, now is he for another woman. 335

WILLMORE The impudent'st young thing in nature; I
cannot persuade him out of his error, madam.

ANGELLICA I know he's in the right, yet thou'st a tongue
That would persuade him to deny his faith.
> *In rage*, [*Angellica*] *walks away*

WILLMORE (*said softly to Hellena*) Her name, her name, 340
dear boy.

HELLENA Have you forgot it, sir?

WILLMORE (*aside*) Oh, I perceive he's not to know I am
a stranger to his lady. [*To Hellena*] Yes, yes, I do know,
but – I have forgot the – 345
> *Angellica turns.* [*Willmore addresses her*]
By heaven, such early confidence I never saw.

ANGELLICA Did I not charge you with this mistress, sir?
Which you denied, though I beheld your perjury.
This little generosity of thine has rendered back my
heart. 350

[Angellica] walks away

WILLMORE *[aside to Hellena]* So, you have made sweet
work here, my little mischief; look your lady be kind
and good-natured now, or I shall have but a cursed
bargain on't.

Angellica turns towards them. [He addresses her]
The rogue's bred up to mischief; art thou so great a   355
fool to credit him?

ANGELLICA Yes, I do, and you in vain impose upon me.
– Come hither, boy, is not this he you spake of?

HELLENA I think it is; I cannot swear, but I vow he has
just such another lying lover's look.   360

Hellena looks in [Willmore's] face; he gazes on her

WILLMORE *[aside]* Ha, do not I know that face? By
heaven, my little gipsy. What a dull dog was I! Had I
but looked that way I'd known her. Are all my hopes
of a new woman banished? *[To Hellena]* Egad, if I do
not fit thee for this, hang me. *[To Angellica]* Madam,   365
I have found out the plot.

HELLENA *[aside]* Oh lord, what does he say? Am I discovered now?

WILLMORE Do you see this young spark here?

HELLENA *[aside]* He'll tell her who I am.   370

WILLMORE Who do you think this is?

HELLENA *[aside]* Aye, aye, he does know me. *[To
Willmore]* Nay, dear captain! I am undone if you
discover me.

WILLMORE *[aside to Hellena]* Nay, nay, no cogging; she   375
shall know what a precious mistress I have.

HELLENA *[aside to Willmore]* Will you be such a devil?

WILLMORE *[aside to Hellena]* Nay, nay, I'll teach you to
spoil sport you will not make. *[To Angellica]* This small
ambassador comes not from a person of quality, as   380
you imagine, and he says; but from a very arrant gipsy,

the talking'st, prating'st, canting'st little animal thou
ever saw'st.

ANGELLICA What news you tell me: that's the thing I   385
mean.

HELLENA (*aside*) Would I were well off the place! If ever
I go a-captain-hunting again –

WILLMORE Mean that thing, that gipsy thing? Thou
mayst as well be jealous of thy monkey or parrot as
of her: a German motion were worth a dozen of her,   390
and a dream were a better enjoyment; a creature of a
constitution fitter for heaven than man.

HELLENA (*aside*) Though I'm sure he lies, yet this vexes
me.

ANGELLICA You are mistaken: she's a Spanish woman   395
Made up of no such dull materials.

WILLMORE Materials! Egad, an she be made of any that
will either dispense or admit of love, I'll be bound to
continence.

HELLENA (*aside to* [*Willmore*]) Unreasonable man, do you   400
think so?

WILLMORE] You may return, my little brazen head, and
tell your lady, that till she be handsome enough to be
beloved, or I dull enough to be religious, there will
be small hopes of me.   405

ANGELLICA Did you not promise, then, to marry her?

WILLMORE Not I, by heaven.

ANGELLICA You cannot undeceive my fears and
torments,
Till you have vowed you will not marry her.

HELLENA (*aside*) If he swears that, he'll be revenged on   410
me indeed for all my rogueries.

ANGELLICA I know what arguments you'll bring against
me, fortune, and honour.

WILLMORE Honour? I tell you, I hate it in your sex;

and those that fancy themselves possessed of that 41
foppery, are the most impertinently troublesome of
all womankind, and will transgress nine command-
ments to keep one: and to satisfy your jealousy, I
swear –

HELLENA (*aside to him*) Oh, no swearing, dear captain. 420

WILLMORE – If it were possible I should ever be inclined
to marry, it should be some kind young sinner; one
that has generosity enough to give a favour handsomely to one that can ask it discreetly; one that has
wit enough to manage an intrigue of love. Oh, how 42
civil such a wench is, to a man that does her the
honour to marry her!

ANGELLICA By heaven, there's no faith in anything he
says.

 Enter Sebastian

SEBASTIAN Madam, Don Antonio – 430

ANGELLICA Come hither.

HELLENA [*aside*] Ha, Antonio! He may be coming hither,
and he'll certainly discover me. I'll therefore retire
without a ceremony.

 Exit Hellena

ANGELLICA I'll see him; get my coach ready. 43

SEBASTIAN It waits you, madam.

WILLMORE [*aside*] This is lucky. [*To Angellica*] What,
madam, now I may be gone, and leave you to the
enjoyment of my rival?

ANGELLICA Dull man, that canst not see how ill, how 440
 poor,
That false dissimulation looks: begone,
And never let me see thy cozening face again,
Lest I relapse and kill thee.

WILLMORE Yes, you can spare me now. Farewell, till
you're in better humour. [*Aside*] I'm glad of this 44

release; now for my gipsy:
For though to worse we change, yet still we find
New joys, new charms, in a new miss that's kind.
    Exit Willmore
ANGELLICA He's gone, and in this ague of my soul
  The shivering fit returns: 450
Oh, with what willing haste he took his leave,
As if the longed-for minute were arrived
Of some blessed assignation.
In vain I have consulted all my charms,
In vain this beauty prized, in vain believed   455
My eyes could kindle any lasting fires;
I had forgot my name, my infamy,
And the reproach that honour lays on those
That dare pretend a sober passion here.
Nice reputation, though it leave behind   460
More virtues than inhabit where that dwells,
Yet that once gone, those virtues shine no more.
Then since I am not fit to be beloved,
I am resolved to think on a revenge
On him that soothed me thus to my undoing.   465
    Exeunt

Act IV Scene III

A street
Enter Florinda and Valeria, in habits different
from what they have been seen in
FLORINDA We're happily escaped, and yet I tremble still.
VALERIA A lover and fear! Why, I am but half an one,
  and yet I have courage for any attempt. Would
  Hellena were here; I would fain have had her as deep

in this mischief as we: she'll fare but ill else, I doubt. 5

FLORINDA She pretended a visit to the Augustine nuns, but I believe some other design carried her out; pray heaven we light on her. Prithee, what didst do with Callis?

VALERIA When I saw no reason would do good on her, 10 I followed her into the wardrobe, and as she was looking for something in a great chest, I toppled her in by the heels, snatched the key of the apartment where you were confined, locked her in, and left her bawling for help. 15

FLORINDA 'Tis well you resolve to follow my fortunes, for thou darest never appear at home again after such an action.

VALERIA That's according as the young stranger and I shall agree. But to our business: I delivered your note 20 to Belvile, when I got out under pretence of going to mass. I found him at his lodging, and believe me it came seasonably; for never was man in so desperate a condition. I told him of your resolution of making your escape today, if your brother would be absent 25 long enough to permit you; if not, to die rather than be Antonio's.

FLORINDA Thou shouldst have told him I was confined to my chamber, upon my brother's suspicion that the business on the Molo was a plot laid between him 30 and I.

VALERIA I said all this, and told him your brother was now gone to his devotion; and he resolves to visit every church till he find him, and not only undeceive him in that, but caress him so as shall delay his return 35 home.

FLORINDA Oh heavens, he's here, and Belvile with him too.

*[Florinda and Valeria] put on their vizards. Enter
Don Pedro, Belvile, [and] Willmore; Belvile and
Don Pedro seeming in serious discourse*

VALERIA Walk boldly by them, and I'll come at distance,
lest he suspect us.   40

*[Florinda] walks by [Don Pedro, Belvile, and
Willmore], and looks back on them*

WILLMORE Ha! A woman, and of an excellent mien.

PEDRO She throws a kind look back on you.

WILLMORE Death, 'tis a likely wench, and that kind look
shall not be cast away: I'll follow her.

BELVILE Prithee, do not.   45

WILLMORE Do not? By heavens, to the antipodes, with
such an invitation.

[Florinda] goes out, and Willmore follows her

BELVILE 'Tis a mad fellow for a wench.

*[Exit Valeria, following Willmore and Florinda.]
Enter Frederick*

FREDERICK Oh colonel, such news!

BELVILE Prithee, what?   50

FREDERICK News that will make you laugh in spite of
fortune.

BELVILE What, Blunt has had some damned trick put
upon him: cheated, banged or clapped?

FREDERICK Cheated, sir; rarely cheated of all but his   55
shirt and drawers. The unconscionable whore, too,
turned him out before consummation, so that,
traversing the streets at midnight, the watch found
him in this fresco, and conducted him home. By
heaven, 'tis such a sight, and yet I durst as well been   60
hanged as laughed at him, or pity him; he beats all
that do but ask him a question, and is in such an
humour!

PEDRO Who is't has met with this ill usage, sir?

BELVILE A friend of ours, whom you must see for 65
mirth's sake. (*Aside*) I'll employ him to give Florinda
time for an escape.

PEDRO What is he?

BELVILE A young countryman of ours, one that has
been educated at so plentiful a rate, he yet ne'er knew 70
the want of money, and 'twill be a great jest to see
how simply he'll look without it; for my part I'll lend
him none, an the rogue know not how to put on a
borrowing face, and ask first; I'll let him see how good
'tis to play our parts whilst I play his. – Prithee, Fred, 75
do you go home and keep him in that posture till we
come.

> *Exeunt [Frederick, Don Pedro, and Belvile]. Enter*
> *Florinda from the farther end of the scene, looking*
> *behind her*

FLORINDA I am followed still. Ha, my brother, too,
advancing this way: good heavens defend me from
being seen by him. 80

> *[Florinda] goes off. Enter Willmore, and after him*
> *Valeria, at a little distance*

WILLMORE Ah, there she sails! She looks back as she
were willing to be boarded; I'll warrant her prize.

> *[Willmore] goes out, Valeria following. Enter*
> *Hellena, just as he goes out, with a page*

HELLENA Ha, is not that my captain that has a woman in
chase? 'Tis not Angellica. – Boy, follow those people at
a distance, and bring me an account where they go in. 85

> *Exit page*

– I'll find his haunts, and plague him everywhere. Ha,
my brother.

> *Belvile, Willmore, [and] Pedro cross the stage.*
> *Hellena runs off*

Act IV Scene IV

Another street
Enter Florinda

FLORINDA What shall I do? My brother now pursues me; will no kind power protect me from his tyranny? Ha, here's a door open; I'll venture in, since nothing can be worse than to fall into his hands; my life and honour are at stake, and my necessity has no choice.   5

[Florinda] goes in. Enter Valeria, and Hellena's
page peeping after Florinda

PAGE Here she went in; I shall remember this house.
Exit page

VALERIA This is Belvile's lodging; she's gone in as readily as if she knew it. Ha, here's that mad fellow again. I dare not venture in; I'll watch my opportunity.

[Exit Valeria.] Enter Willmore, gazing about him

WILLMORE I have lost her hereabouts. Pox on't, she must   10
not 'scape me so.
Goes out

Act IV Scene V

Scene changes to Blunt's chamber; discovers him
sitting on a couch in his shirt and drawers, reading

BLUNT So, now my mind's a little at peace, since I have resolved revenge. A pox on this tailor, though, for not bringing home the clothes I bespoke; and a pox of all poor cavaliers: a man can never keep a spare suit for 'em; and I shall have these rogues come in and find   5
me naked, and then I'm undone; but I'm resolved to

arm myself; the rascals shall not insult over me too much.

Puts on an old rusty sword, and buff belt

Now, how like a morris dancer I am equipped! A fine ladylike whore to cheat me thus, without affording me a kindness for my money! A pox light on her, I shall never be reconciled to the sex more: she has made me as faithless as a physician, as uncharitable as a churchman, and as ill-natured as a poet. Oh, how I'll use all womankind hereafter! What would I give to have one of 'em within my reach now! Any mortal thing in petticoats, kind fortune, send me, and I'll forgive thy last night's malice! Here's a cursed book, too, *A Warning to All Young Travellers*, that can instruct me how to prevent such mischiefs now 'tis too late. Well, 'tis a rare convenient thing to read a little now and then, as well as hawk and hunt.

[Blunt] sits down again and reads. Enter to him Florinda

FLORINDA This house is haunted, sure; 'tis well furnished and no living thing inhabits it. Ha, a man; heavens, how he's attired! Sure 'tis some rope-dancer, or fencing master. I tremble now for fear, and yet I must venture now to speak to him. – Sir, if I may not interrupt your meditations –

[Blunt] starts up and gazes

BLUNT Ha, what's here? Are my wishes granted? And is not that a she creature? 'Adsheartlikins, 'tis! – What wretched thing art thou, ha?

FLORINDA Charitable sir, you've told yourself already what I am: a very wretched maid, forced by a strange unlucky accident, to seek a safety here, and must be ruined, if you do not grant it.

BLUNT Ruined! Is there any ruin so inevitable as that

which now threatens thee? Dost thou know, miserable
woman, into what den of mischiefs thou art fallen,
what abyss of confusion, ha? Dost not see something
in my looks that frights thy guilty soul, and makes   40
thee wish to change that shape of woman for any
humble animal, or devil? For those were safer for thee,
and less mischievous.

FLORINDA Alas, what mean you, sir? I must confess,
your looks have something in 'em makes me fear, but   45
I beseech you, as you seem a gentleman, pity a harmless virgin, that takes your house for sanctuary.

BLUNT Talk on, talk on, and weep too, till my faith
return. Do, flatter me out of my senses again. A harmless virgin with a pox! As much one as t'other, 'ads-   50
heartlikins. Why, what the devil, can I not be safe in
my house for you; not in my chamber? Nay, even being
naked, too, cannot secure me: this is an impudence
greater than has invaded me yet. Come, no resistance.
    [*Blunt*] *pulls* [*Florinda*] *rudely*

FLORINDA Dare you be so cruel?   55

BLUNT Cruel? 'Adsheartlikins, as a galley-slave, or a
Spanish whore. Cruel, yes: I will kiss and beat thee
all over; kiss, and see thee all over; thou shalt lie with
me too, not that I care for the enjoyment, but to let
thee see I have ta'en deliberated malice to thee, and   60
will be revenged on one whore for the sins of another.
I will smile and deceive thee, flatter thee, and beat
thee, kiss and swear, and lie to thee, embrace thee and
rob thee, as she did me; fawn on thee, and strip thee
stark naked, then hang thee out at my window by the   65
heels, with a paper of scurvy verses fastened to thy
breast, in praise of damnable women. Come, come
along.

FLORINDA Alas, sir, must I be sacrificed for the crimes

of the most infamous of my sex? I never understood   70
the sins you name.

BLUNT Do, persuade the fool you love him, or that one
of you can be just or honest; tell me I was not an
easy coxcomb, or any strange impossible tale: it will
be believed sooner than thy false showers or protes-   75
tations. A generation of damned hypocrites! To flatter
my very clothes from my back! Dissembling witches!
Are these the returns you make an honest gentleman,
that trusts, believes, and loves you? But if I be not
even with you – come along, or I shall –   80
    Enter Frederick

FREDERICK Ha, what's here to do?

BLUNT 'Adsheartlikins, Fred, I am glad thou art come,
to be a witness of my dire revenge.

FREDERICK What's this, a person of quality too, who is
upon the ramble to supply the defects of some grave   85
impotent husband?

BLUNT No, this has another pretence: some very unfor-
tunate accident brought her hither, to save a life
pursued by I know not who, or why, and forced to
take sanctuary here at fools' haven. 'Adsheartlikins,   90
to me, of all mankind, for protection? Is the ass to
be cajoled again, think ye? – No, young one, no prayers
or tears shall mitigate my rage; therefore prepare for
both my pleasures of enjoyment and revenge, for I
am resolved to make up my loss here on thy body: 95
I'll take it out in kindness and in beating.

FREDERICK Now, mistress of mine, what do you think
of this?

FLORINDA I think he will not, dares not be so barbarous.

FREDERICK Have a care, Blunt: she fetched a deep sigh;   100
she is enamoured with thy shirt and drawers, she'll
strip thee even of that. There are of her calling such

unconsionable baggages, and such dexterous thieves,
they'll flay a man and he shall ne'er miss his skin,
till he feels the cold. There was a countryman of   105
ours robbed of a row of teeth while he was a-sleeping,
which the jilt made him buy again when he waked.
 – You see, lady, how little reason we have to trust
you.

BLUNT 'Adsheartlikins, why this is most abominable.   110

FLORINDA Some such devils there may be, but by all
that's holy, I am none such; I entered here to save a
life in danger.

BLUNT For no goodness, I'll warrant her.

FREDERICK Faith, damsel, you had e'en confessed the   115
plain truth, for we are fellows not to be caught twice
in the same trap: look on that wreck, a tight vessel
when he set out of haven, well trimmed and laden;
and see how a female picaroon of this island of rogues
has shattered him; and canst thou hope for any mercy?   120

BLUNT No, no, gentlewoman, come along; 'adsheartlikins, we must be better acquainted. – We'll both lie
with her, and then let me alone to bang her.

FREDERICK I'm ready to serve you in matters of revenge
that has a double pleasure in't.   125

BLUNT Well said. – You hear, little one, how you are
condemned by public vote to the bed within; there's
no resisting your destiny, sweetheart.
    [Blunt] pulls [Florinda]

FLORINDA Stay, sir; I have seen you with Belvile, an
English cavalier: for his sake use me kindly; you know   130
him, sir.

BLUNT Belvile, why yes, sweeting, we do know Belvile,
and wish he were with us now; he's a cormorant at
whore and bacon, he'd have a limb or two of thee,
my virgin pullet; but 'tis no matter, we'll leave him   135

the bones to pick.

FLORINDA Sir, if you have any esteem for that Belvile, I conjure you to treat me with more gentleness; he'll thank you for the justice.

FREDERICK Hark'ee, Blunt, I doubt we are mistaken in 140 this matter.

FLORINDA Sir, if you find me not worth Belvile's care, use me as you please; and that you may think I merit better treatment than you threaten, pray take this present. 145

[*Florinda*] *gives* [*Blunt*] *a ring. He looks on it*

BLUNT Hum, a diamond! Why, 'tis a wonderful virtue now that lies in this ring, a mollifying virtue; 'adsheartlikins, there's more persuasive rhetoric in't, than all her sex can utter.

FREDERICK I begin to suspect something; and 'twould 150 anger us vilely to be trussed up for a rape upon a maid of quality, when we only believe we ruffle a harlot.

BLUNT Thou art a credulous fellow, but 'adsheartlikins, I have no faith yet: why, my saint prattled as parlously 155 as this does; she gave me a bracelet too, a devil on her, but I sent my man to sell it today for necessaries, and it proved as counterfeit as her vows of love.

FREDERICK However, let it reprieve her till we see Belvile.

BLUNT That's hard, yet I will grant it. 160

Enter a servant

SERVANT Oh, sir, the colonel is just come in with his new friend and a Spaniard of quality, and talks of having you to dinner with 'em.

BLUNT 'Adsheartlikins, I'm undone; I would not see 'em for the world. Hark'ee, Fred, lock up the wench 165 in your chamber.

FREDERICK Fear nothing, madam; whate'er he threatens,

you are safe whilst in my hands.

Exeunt Frederick and Florinda

BLUNT And, sirrah, upon your life, say I am not at
home, or that I am asleep, or – or anything: away, I'll   170
prevent their coming this way.

[Blunt] locks the door, and exeunt

Act V Scene I

Blunt's chamber
After a great knocking as at his chamber door,
enter Blunt, softly crossing the stage, in his shirt
and drawers as before

[VOICES] (*call within*) Ned, Ned Blunt, Ned Blunt!

BLUNT The rogues are up in arms: 'adsheartlikins, this villainous Frederick has betrayed me; they have heard of my blessed fortune.

[VOICES] (*calling and knocking within*) Ned Blunt, Ned, Ned! 5

BELVILE [*within*] Why, he's dead sir, without dispute dead; he has not been seen today: let's break open the door. – Here, boy –

BLUNT Ha, break open the door? 'Adsheartlikins, that mad fellow will be as good as his word. 10

BELVILE [*within*] Boy, bring something to force the door.
A great noise within, at the door again

BLUNT So, now must I speak in my own defence; I'll try what rhetoric will do. – Hold, hold, what do you mean, gentlemen, what do you mean?

BELVILE (*within*) Oh, rogue, art alive? Prithee open the 15
door and convince us.

BLUNT Yes, I am alive, gentlemen; but at present a little busy.

BELVILE (*within*) How, Blunt grown a man of business?
Come, come, open and let's see this miracle. 20

BLUNT No, no, no, no, gentlemen, 'tis no great business, but – I am – at – my devotion; 'adsheartlikins, will you not allow a man time to pray?

BELVILE (*within*) Turned religious! A greater wonder than the first; therefore open quickly, or we shall 25
unhinge, we shall.

BLUNT This won't do. – Why, hark'ee, colonel, to tell
you the plain truth, I am about a necessary affair of
life: I have a wench with me; you apprehend me? –
The devil's in't if they be so uncivil as to disturb me   30
now.

WILLMORE [*within*] How, a wench! Nay then, we must
enter and partake, no resistance; unless it be your lady
of quality, and then we'll keep our distance.

BLUNT So, the business is out.   35

WILLMORE [*within*] Come, come, lend's more hands to
the door; now heave altogether; so, well done my boys.
     [*Willmore*] *breaks open the door. Enter Belvile,*
     Willmore, Frederick, and Pedro. Blunt looks simply;
     they all laugh at him; he lays his hand on his
     sword, and comes up to Willmore

BLUNT Hark'ee, sir, laugh out your laugh quickly, d'ye
hear, and begone. I shall spoil your sport else, 'adsheartlikins, sir, I shall; the jest has been carried on   40
too long. (*Aside*) A plague upon my tailor.

WILLMORE 'Sdeath, how the whore has dressed him! –
Faith sir, I'm sorry.

BLUNT Are you so, sir? Keep't to yourself then, sir, I
advise you, d'ye hear; for I can as little endure your   45
pity as his mirth. (*Lays his hand on's sword*)

BELVILE Indeed, Willmore, thou wert a little too rough
with Ned Blunt's mistress: call a person of quality
whore? And one so young, so handsome, and so
eloquent! Ha, ha, he.   50

BLUNT Hark'ee, sir, you know me, and know I can be
angry; have a care, for 'adsheartlikins, I can fight too,
I can, sir, do you mark me; no more.

BELVILE Why so peevish, good Ned? Some disappoint-
ments, I'll warrant. What, did the jealous count her   55
husband return just in the nick?

BLUNT Or the devil, sir. (*They laugh*) D'ye laugh? Look
  ye settle me a good sober countenance, and that
  quickly too, or you shall know Ned Blunt is not –

BELVILE – Not everybody, we know that.   6⟨

BLUNT Not an ass to be laughed at, sir.

WILLMORE Unconscionable sinner, to bring a lover so
  near his happiness, a vigorous passionate lover, and
  then not only cheat him of his moveables, but his
  very desires too.   6⟨

BELVILE Ah, sir, a mistress is a trifle with Blunt; he'll
  have a dozen the next time he looks abroad: his eyes
  have charms, not to be resisted; there needs no more
  than to expose that taking person to the view of the
  fair, and he leads 'em all in triumph.   7⟨

PEDRO Sir, though I'm a stranger to you, I am ashamed
  at the rudeness of my nation; and could you learn who
  did it, would assist you to make an example of 'em.

BLUNT Why aye, there's one speaks sense now, and
  handsomely; and let me tell you, gentlemen, I should   7⟨
  not have showed myself like a jack pudding thus to
  have made you mirth, but that I have revenge within
  my power: for know, I have got into my possession a
  female, who had better have fallen under any curse,
  than the ruin I design her. 'Adsheartlikins, she   8⟨
  assaulted me here in my own lodgings, and had doubtless committed a rape upon me, had not this sword
  defended me.

FREDERICK I know not that, but o' my conscience thou
  hadst ravished her, had she not redeemed herself with   8⟨
  a ring; let's see it, Blunt.

  Blunt shows the ring

BELVILE [*aside*] Ha, the ring I gave Florinda, when we
  exchanged our vows. – Hark'ee, Blunt –

  [*Belvile*] *goes to whisper to* [*Blunt*]

WILLMORE No whispering, good colonel, there's a
woman in the case; no whispering.   90

BELVILE [*aside to Blunt*] Hark'ee, fool, be advised, and
conceal both the ring and the story for your reputation's sake; do not let people know what despised
cullies we English are: to be cheated and abused by
one whore, and another rather bribe thee than be kind   95
to thee, is an infamy to our nation.

WILLMORE Come, come, where's the wench? We'll see
her; let her be what she will, we'll see her.

PEDRO Aye, aye, let us see her; I can soon discover
whether she be of quality, or for your diversion.   100

BLUNT She's in Fred's custody.

WILLMORE (*to Frederick*) Come, come, the key.
        [*Frederick*] *gives* [*Willmore*] *the key;* [*Willmore,
        Frederick, Blunt, and Don Pedro*] *are going*

BELVILE [*aside*] Death, what shall I do? – Stay, gentlemen.
– [*Aside*] Yet if I hinder 'em I shall discover all. –
Hold, let's go one at once; give me the key.   105

WILLMORE Nay, hold there, colonel; I'll go first.

FREDERICK Nay, no dispute; Ned and I have the
propriety of her.

WILLMORE Damn propriety; then we'll draw cuts.
        Belvile goes to whisper [*to*] *Willmore*
– Nay, no corruption, good colonel; come, the longest   110
sword carries her.
        *They all draw, forgetting Don Pedro, being as a
        Spaniard, had the longest*

BLUNT I yield up my interest to you, gentlemen, and
that will be revenge sufficient.

WILLMORE (*to Pedro*) The wench is yours. [*Aside*] Pox of
his toledo, I had forgot that.   115

FREDERICK Come, sir, I'll conduct you to the lady.
        Exeunt Frederick and Pedro

BELVILE (*aside*) To hinder him will certainly discover her. (*To Willmore, [who is] walking up and down out of humour*) Dost know, dull beast, what mischief thou hast done? 120

WILLMORE Aye, aye; to trust our fortune to lots! A devil on't, 'twas madness, that's the truth on't.

BELVILE Oh, intolerable sot!
Enter Florinda, running, masked, Pedro after her:
Willmore gazing round her

FLORINDA (*aside*) Good heaven, defend me from discovery. 125

PEDRO 'Tis but in vain to fly me; you're fallen to my lot.

BELVILE (*aside*) Sure she's undiscovered yet, but now I fear there is no way to bring her off.

WILLMORE Why, what a pox, is not this my woman, the 130 same I followed but now?

PEDRO (*talking to Florinda, who walks up and down*) As if I did not know ye, and your business here.

FLORINDA (*aside*) Good heaven, I fear he does indeed.

PEDRO Come, pray be kind; I know you meant to be so 135 when you entered here, for these are proper gentlemen.

WILLMORE But, sir, perhaps the lady will not be imposed upon; she'll choose her man.

PEDRO I am better bred, than not to leave her choice 140 free.
Enter Valeria, and is surprised at sight of Don Pedro

VALERIA (*aside*) Don Pedro here! There's no avoiding him.

FLORINDA (*aside*) Valeria! then I'm undone.

VALERIA (*to Pedro, running to him*) Oh, have I found you, 145 sir? The strangest accident – if I had breath – to tell it.

PEDRO Speak: is Florinda safe? Hellena well?

VALERIA Aye, aye, sir; Florinda – is safe – [aside] from
   any fears of you.   150

PEDRO Why, where's Florinda? Speak.

VALERIA Aye, where indeed sir, I wish I could inform
   you; but to hold you no longer in doubt –

FLORINDA (aside) Oh, what will she say?

VALERIA – She's fled away in the habit – of one of her   155
   pages, sir; but Callis thinks you may retrieve her yet;
   if you make haste away, she'll tell you, sir, the rest –
   (aside) if you can find her out.

PEDRO Dishonourable girl, she has undone my aim. [To
   Belvile] Sir, you see my necessity of leaving you, and   160
   hope you'll pardon it; my sister, I know, will make
   her flight to you; and if she do, I shall expect she
   should be rendered back.

BELVILE I shall consult my love and honour, sir.
      Exit Pedro

FLORINDA (to Valeria) My dear preserver, let me embrace   165
   thee.

WILLMORE What the devil's all this?

BLUNT Mystery, by this light.

VALERIA Come, come, make haste and get yourselves
   married quickly, for your brother will return again.   170

BELVILE I'm so surprised with fears and joys, so amazed
   to find you here in safety, I can scarce persuade my
   heart into a faith of what I see.

WILLMORE Hark'ee, colonel, is this that mistress who
   has cost you so many sighs, and me so many quarrels   175
   with you?

BELVILE It is. (To Florinda) Pray give him the honour of
   your hand.

WILLMORE (kneels and kisses her hand) Thus it must be
   received then; and with it give your pardon too.   180

FLORINDA The friend to Belvile may command me anything.

WILLMORE (*aside*) Death, would I might; 'tis a surprising beauty.

BELVILE Boy, run and fetch a father instantly.   18

Exit page

FREDERICK So, now do I stand like a dog, and have not a syllable to plead my own cause with. By this hand, madam, I was never thoroughly confounded before, nor shall I ever more dare look up with confidence, till you are pleased to pardon me.   19

FLORINDA Sir, I'll be reconciled to you on one condition: that you'll follow the example of your friend, in marrying a maid that does not hate you, and whose fortune, I believe, will not be unwelcome to you.

FREDERICK Madam, had I no inclinations that way, I   19 should obey your kind commands.

BELVILE Who, Fred marry? He has so few inclinations for womankind, that had he been possessed of paradise, he might have continued there to this day, if no crime but love could have disinherited him.   20

FREDERICK Oh, I do not use to boast of my intrigues.

BELVILE Boast? Why, thou dost nothing but boast; and I dare swear, wert thou as innocent from the sin of the grape, as thou art from the apple, thou might'st yet claim that right in Eden which our first parents   20 lost by too much loving.

FREDERICK I wish this lady would think me so modest a man.

VALERIA She would be sorry then, and not like you half so well; and I should be loth to break my word with   21 you, which was that if your friend and mine agreed, it should be a match between you and I. (*Gives him her hand*)

FREDERICK (*kisses her hand*) Bear witness, colonel, 'tis a bargain.

BLUNT (*to Florinda*) I have a pardon to beg too, but 'ads- 215 heartlikins, I am so out of countenance, that I'm a dog if I can say anything to purpose.

FLORINDA Sir, I heartily forgive you all.

BLUNT That's nobly said, sweet lady. – Belvile, prithee present her her ring again; for I find I have not courage 220 to approach her myself.

> [*Blunt*] *gives* [*Belvile*] *the ring;* [*Belvile*] *gives it to Florinda. Enter page*

PAGE Sir, I have brought the father that you sent for.

BELVILE 'Tis well. – And now, my dear Florinda, let's fly to complete that mighty joy we have so long wished and sighed for. – Come, Fred, you'll follow? 225

FREDERICK – Your example, sir: 'twas ever my ambition in war, and must be so in love.

WILLMORE And must not I see this juggling knot tied?

BELVILE No, thou shalt do us better service, and be our guard, lest Don Pedro's sudden return interrupt the 230 ceremony.

WILLMORE Content; I'll secure this pass.

> *Exeunt Belvile, Florinda, Frederick, and Valeria.*
> *Enter page*

PAGE (*to Willmore*) Sir, there's a lady without would speak to you.

WILLMORE Conduct her in; I dare not quit my post. 235

PAGE [*to Blunt*] And sir, your tailor waits you in your chamber.

BLUNT Some comfort yet; I shall not dance naked at the wedding.

> *Exeunt Blunt and page. Enter again the page,*
> *conducting in Angellica in a masking habit and a*
> *vizard. Willmore runs to her*

WILLMORE [*aside*] This can be none but my pretty gipsy.   240
[*To Angellica*] Oh, I see you can follow as well as fly.
Come, confess thyself the most malicious devil in
nature; you think you have done my business with
Angellica.

ANGELLICA Stand off, base villain.   24

> [*Angellica*] *draws a pistol, and holds* [*it*] *to*
> [*Willmore's*] *breast*

WILLMORE [*aside*] Ha, 'tis not she. – Who art thou? and
what's thy business?

ANGELLICA One thou hast injured, and who comes to
kill thee for't.

WILLMORE What the devil canst thou mean?   250

ANGELLICA By all my hopes, to kill thee.

> [*Angellica*] *holds still the pistol to* [*Willmore's*]
> *breast, he going back, she following still*

WILLMORE Prithee, on what acquaintance? For I know
thee not.

ANGELLICA (*pulls off her vizard*) Behold this face, so lost
to thy remembrance,
And then call all thy sins about thy soul,   25
And let 'em die with thee.

WILLMORE Angellica!

ANGELLICA Yes, traitor,
Does not thy guilty blood run shivering through thy
veins?
Hast thou no horror at this sight, that tells thee,   260
Thou hast not long to boast thy shameful conquest?

WILLMORE Faith, no, child; my blood keeps its old ebbs
and flows still, and that usual heat too, that could
oblige thee with a kindness, had I but opportunity.

ANGELLICA Devil! dost wanton with my pain? Have at   26
thy heart.

WILLMORE Hold, dear virago! Hold thy hand a little; I

am not now at leisure to be killed; hold and hear me.
(*Aside*) Death, I think she's in earnest.

NGELLICA (*aside, turning from him*) Oh, if I take not heed, 270
My coward heart will leave me to his mercy.
– What have you, sir, to say? But should I hear thee,
Thou'dst talk away all that is brave about me:
    (*Follows him with the pistol to his breast*)
And I have vowed thy death, by all that's sacred.

ILLMORE Why then, there's an end of a proper hand- 275
some fellow, that might 'a lived to have done good
service yet; that's all I can say to't.

NGELLICA (*pausingly*) Yet, I would give thee – time
for – penitence.

ILLMORE Faith, child, I thank God, I have ever took 280
care to lead a good sober, hopeful life, and am of a religion that teaches me to believe, I shall depart in peace.

NGELLICA So will the devil! tell me,
How many poor believing fools thou hast undone?
How many hearts thou hast betrayed to ruin? 285
Yet these are little mischiefs to the ills
Thou'st taught mine to commit: thou'st taught it love.

ILLMORE Egad, 'twas shrewdly hurt the while.

NGELLICA Love, that has robbed it of its unconcern,
Of all that pride that taught me how to value it. 290
And in its room
A mean submissive passion was conveyed,
That made me humbly bow, which I ne'er did
To anything but heaven.
Thou, perjured man, didst this, and with thy oaths, 295
Which on thy knees thou didst devoutly make,
Softened my yielding heart, and then, I was a slave;
Yet still had been content to've worn my chains,
Worn 'em with vanity and joy forever,
Hadst thou not broke those vows that put them on. 300

'Twas then I was undone.

  All this while follows him with the pistol to his breast

WILLMORE Broke my vows! Why, where hast thou lived?
Amongst the gods? for I never heard of mortal man,
That has not broke a thousand vows.

ANGELLICA Oh, impudence!   30

WILLMORE Angellica, that beauty has been too long
tempting, not to have made a thousand lovers
languish, who, in the amorous fever, no doubt have
sworn like me: did they all die in that faith, still
adoring? I do not think they did.   31

ANGELLICA No, faithless man: had I repaid their vows,
as I did thine, I would have killed the ingrateful that
had abandoned me.

WILLMORE This old general has quite spoiled thee:
nothing makes a woman so vain as being flattered; 31
your old lover ever supplies the defects of age with
intolerable dotage, vast charge, and that which you call
constancy; and attributing all this to your own merits,
you domineer, and throw your favours in's teeth,
upbraiding him still with the defects of age, and 32
cuckold him as often as he deceives your expectations.
But the gay, young, brisk lover, that brings his equal
fires, and can give you dart for dart, you'll find will
be as nice as you sometimes.

ANGELLICA All this thou'st made me know, for which 32
  I hate thee.
Had I remained in innocent security,
I should have thought all men were born my slaves,
And worn my power like lightning in my eyes,
To have destroyed at pleasure when offended:
But when love held the mirror, the undeceiving glass 3.
Reflected all the weakness of my soul, and made me
  know

My richest treasure being lost, my honour,
All the remaining spoil could not be worth
The conqueror's care or value.
Oh, how I fell, like a long worshipped idol, 335
Discovering all the cheat.
Would not the incense and rich sacrifice,
Which blind devotion offered at my altars,
Have fallen to thee?
Why wouldst thou then destroy my fancied power? 340
WILLMORE By heaven thou'rt brave, and I admire thee
      strangely.
I wish I were that dull, that constant thing
Which thou wouldst have, and nature never meant me:
I must, like cheerful birds, sing in all groves,
And perch on every bough, 345
Billing the next kind she that flies to meet me;
Yet, after all, could build my nest with thee,
Thither repairing when I'd loved my round,
And still reserve a tributary flame.
To gain your credit, I'll pay you back your charity, 350
And be obliged for nothing but for love.
      Offers her a purse of gold
ANGELLICA Oh, that thou wert in earnest!
So mean a thought of me
Would turn my rage to scorn, and I should pity thee,
And give thee leave to live; 355
Which for the public safety of our sex,
And my own private injuries, I dare not do.
Prepare: (*follows still, as before*)
I will no more be tempted with replies.
WILLMORE Sure – 360
ANGELLICA Another word will damn thee! I've heard
thee talk too long.
      She follows him with the pistol ready to shoot; he

> *retires still amazed. Enter Don Antonio, his arm in*
> *a scarf, and lays hold on the pistol*

ANTONIO Ha, Angellica!

ANGELLICA Antonio! What devil brought thee hither?

ANTONIO Love and curiosity, seeing your coach at door. 365
Let me disarm you of this unbecoming instrument
of death. (*Takes away the pistol*) Amongst the number
of your slaves, was there not one worthy the honour
to have fought your quarrel? [*To Willmore*] Who are
you, sir, that are so very wretched to merit death from 370
her?

WILLMORE One, sir, that could have made a better end
of an amorous quarrel without you, than with you.

ANTONIO Sure 'tis some rival. Ha! The very man took
down her picture yesterday; the very same that set on 375
me last night; blest opportunity!

> [*Antonio*] *offers to shoot* [*Willmore*]

ANGELLICA Hold, you're mistaken, sir.

ANTONIO By heaven, the very same! – Sir, what pretensions have you to this lady?

WILLMORE Sir, I do not use to be examined, and am ill 380
at all disputes but this.

> [*Willmore*] *draws; Antonio offers to shoot*

ANGELLICA (*to Willmore*) Oh, hold! you see he's armed
with certain death;
– And you, Antonio, I command you hold,
By all the passion you've so lately vowed me.

> *Enter Don Pedro, sees Antonio, and stays*

PEDRO (*aside*) Ha, Antonio! and Angellica! 385

ANTONIO When I refuse obedience to your will,
May you destroy me with your mortal hate.
By all that's holy, I adore you so,
That even my rival, who has charms enough
To make him fall a victim to my jealousy, 390

Shall live, nay and have leave to love on still.

PEDRO (*aside*) What's this I hear?

ANGELLICA (*pointing to Willmore*) Ah thus, 'twas thus, he
    talked, and I believed.

Antonio, yesterday,

I'd not have sold my interest in his heart,   395

For all the sword has won and lost in battle.

[*To Willmore*] But now to show my utmost of
    contempt,

I give thee life, which if thou wouldst preserve,

Live where my eyes may never see thee more;

Live to undo someone whose soul may prove   400

So bravely constant to revenge my love.

    [*Angellica*] *goes out. Antonio follows, but Pedro*
    pulls him back

PEDRO Antonio, stay.

ANTONIO Don Pedro!

PEDRO What coward fear was that prevented thee
From meeting me this morning on the Molo?   405

ANTONIO Meet thee?

PEDRO Yes, me; I was the man that dared thee to't.

ANTONIO Hast thou so often seen me fight in war,
To find no better cause to excuse my absence?
I sent my sword and one to do thee right,   410
Finding myself uncapable to use a sword.

PEDRO But 'twas Florinda's quarrel that we fought,
And you, to show how little you esteemed her,
Sent me your rival, giving him your interest.
But I have found the cause of this affront,   415
And when I meet you fit for the dispute,
I'll tell you my resentment.

ANTONIO I shall be ready, sir, ere long to do you reason.
    Exit Antonio

PEDRO If I could find Florinda, now whilst my anger's

high, I think I should be kind, and give her to Belvile   420
in revenge.

WILLMORE Faith, sir, I know not what you would do,
but I believe the priest within has been so kind.

PEDRO How! My sister married?

WILLMORE I hope by this time he is, and bedded too,   425
or he has not my longings about him.

PEDRO Dares he do this? Does he not fear my power?

WILLMORE Faith, not at all; if you will go in, and thank
him for the favour he has done your sister, so; if not,
sir, my power's greater in this house than yours: I have   430
a damned surly crew here, that will keep you till the
next tide, and then clap you on board for prize. My
ship lies but a league off the Molo, and we shall show
your donship a damned Tramontana rover's trick.

    Enter Belvile

BELVILE [*aside*] This rogue's in some new mischief. Ha,   435
Pedro returned!

PEDRO Colonel Belvile, I hear you have married my
sister?

BELVILE You have heard truth, then, sir.

PEDRO Have I so; then, sir, I wish you joy.   440

BELVILE How!

PEDRO By this embrace I do, and I am glad on't.

BELVILE Are you in earnest?

PEDRO By our long friendship, and my obligations to
thee, I am: the sudden change I'll give you reasons for   445
anon. Come, lead me to my sister, that she may know
I now approve her choice.

    Exit Belvile with Pedro. Willmore goes to follow
    them. Enter Hellena, as before in boy's clothes, and
    pulls him back

WILLMORE [*aside*] Ha, my gipsy! [*To Hellena*] Now, a
thousand blessings on thee for this kindness. Egad,

child, I was e'en in despair of ever seeing thee again; 450
my friends are all provided for within, each man his
kind woman.

ELLENA [*aside*] Ha! I thought they had served me some
such trick!

VILLMORE And I was e'en resolved to go aboard, and 455
condemn myself to my lone cabin, and the thoughts
of thee.

ELLENA And could you have left me behind? Would
you have been so ill-natured?

VILLMORE Why, 'twould have broke my heart, child; 460
but since we are met again, I defy foul weather to part
us.

ELLENA And would you be a faithful friend, now, if a
maid should trust you?

VILLMORE For a friend I cannot promise; thou art of a 465
form so excellent, a face and humour too good for
cold dull friendship; I am parlously afraid of being in
love, child, and you have not forgot how severely you
have used me?

ELLENA That's all one; such usage you must still look 470
for: to find out all your haunts, to rail at you to all
that love you, till I have made you love only me in
your own defence, because nobody else will love.

VILLMORE But hast thou no better quality, to recommend thyself by? 475

ELLENA Faith, none, captain: why, 'twill be the greater
charity to take me for thy mistress. I am a lone child,
a kind of orphan lover; and why I should die a maid,
and in a captain's hands too, I do not understand.

VILLMORE Egad, I was never clawed away with broad- 480
sides from any female before. Thou hast one virtue I
adore, good nature. I hate a coy demure mistress, she's
as troublesome as a colt; I'll break none: no, give me

a mad mistress when mewed, and in flying one I dare
trust upon the wing, that whilst she's kind will come   48
to the lure.

HELLENA Nay, as kind as you will, good captain, whilst
it lasts, but let's lose no time.

WILLMORE My time's as precious to me as thine can
be: therefore, dear creature, since we are so well   49
agreed, let's retire to my chamber, and if ever thou
wert treated with such savoury love! Come, my bed's
prepared for such a guest, all clean and sweet as thy
fair self. I love to steal a dish and a bottle with a
friend, and hate long graces: come, let's retire and fall   49
to.

HELLENA 'Tis but getting my consent, and the business
is soon done: let but old gaffer Hymen and his priest
say amen to't, and I dare lay my mother's daughter
by as proper a fellow as your father's son, without   50
fear or blushing.

WILLMORE Hold, hold, no bug words, child. Priest and
Hymen? Prithee add a hangman to 'em to make up
the consort. No, no, we'll have no vows but love,
child, nor witness but the lover: the kind deity   50
enjoin naught but love and enjoy! Hymen and priest
wait still upon portion, and jointure; love and
beauty have their own ceremonies. Marriage is as
certain a bane to love, as lending money is to friendship: I'll neither ask nor give a vow; though I could   51
be content to turn gipsy, and become a left-handed
bridegroom, to have the pleasure of working that
great miracle of making a maid a mother, if you
durst venture; 'tis upse gipsy that, and if I miss, I'll
lose my labour.   51

HELLENA And if you do not lose, what shall I get? A
cradle full of noise and mischief, with a pack of repen-

tance at my back? Can you teach me to weave incle
to pass my time with? 'Tis upse gipsy that too.

WILLMORE I can teach thee to weave a true love's knot 520
better.

HELLENA So can my dog.

WILLMORE Well, I see we are both upon our guards, and
I see there's no way to conquer good nature, but by
yielding: here, give me thy hand; one kiss and I am thine. 525

HELLENA One kiss! How like my page he speaks. I am
resolved you shall have none, for asking such a
sneaking sum: he that will be satisfied with one kiss,
will never die of that longing. Good friend single-kiss,
is all your talking come to this? A kiss, a caudle! 530
Farewell, captain single-kiss.

    [*Hellena is*] *going out*; [*Willmore*] *stays her*

WILLMORE Nay, if we part so, let me die like a bird upon
a bough, at the sheriff's charge. By heaven, both the
Indies shall not buy thee from me. I adore thy humour
and will marry thee, and we are so of one humour, it 535
must be a bargain. Give me thy hand. (*Kisses her hand*)
And now let the blind ones, love and fortune, do their
worst.

HELLENA Why, God-a-mercy, captain!

WILLMORE But hark'ee: the bargain is now made; but is 540
it not fit we should know each other's names? That
when we have reason to curse one another hereafter,
and people ask me who 'tis I give to the devil, I may
at least be able to tell, what family you came of.

HELLENA Good reason, captain; and where I have cause 545
(as I doubt not but I shall have plentiful), that I may
know at whom to throw my – blessings – I beseech
ye your name.

WILLMORE I am called Robert the constant.

HELLENA A very fine name; pray was it your faulkner 550

or butler that christened you? Do they not use to
whistle when they call you?

WILLMORE I hope you have a better, that a man may
name without crossing himself; you are so merry with
mine.   55?

HELLENA I am called Hellena the inconstant.

Enter Pedro, Belvile, Florinda, Frederick, [and] Valeria

PEDRO Ha, Hellena!

FLORINDA Hellena!

HELLENA The very same. Ha, my brother! Now,
captain, show your love and courage; stand to your   56?
arms, and defend me bravely, or I am lost forever.

PEDRO What's this I hear? False girl, how came you
hither, and what's your business? Speak.

*[Pedro] goes roughly to [Hellena]. [Willmore] puts
himself between [them]*

WILLMORE Hold off, sir, you have leave to parley only.

HELLENA I had e'en as good tell it, as you guess it. Faith,   56?
brother, my business is the same with all living creatures of my age: to love, and be beloved; and here's
the man.

PEDRO Perfidious maid, hast thou deceived me too,
deceived thyself and heaven?   57?

HELLENA 'Tis time enough to make my peace with that;
Be you but kind, let me alone with heaven.

PEDRO Belvile, I did not expect this false play from you.
Wasn't not enough you'd gain Florinda (which I
pardoned) but your lewd friends too must be enriched   57?
with the spoils of a noble family?

BELVILE Faith, sir, I am as much surprised at this as you
can be. Yet, sir, my friends are gentlemen, and ought
to be esteemed for their misfortunes, since they have
the glory to suffer with the best of men and kings: 58?
'tis true, he's a rover of fortune,

Yet a prince, aboard his little wooden world.

EDRO What's this to the maintenance of a woman of her birth and quality?

VILLMORE Faith, sir, I can boast of nothing but a sword 585 which does me right where'er I come, and has defended a worse cause than a woman's; and since I loved her before I either knew her birth or name, I must pursue my resolution, and marry her.

EDRO And is all your holy intent of becoming a nun, 590 debauched into a desire of man?

IELLENA Why, I have considered the matter, brother, and find, the three hundred thousand crowns my uncle left me, and you cannot keep from me, will be better laid out in love than in religion, and turn to as good 595 an account. [*To the others*] Let most voices carry it: for heaven or the captain?

LL (*cry*) A captain! a captain!

IELLENA Look ye sir, 'tis a clear case.

EDRO Oh, I am mad! (*Aside*) If I refuse, my life's in 600 danger. [*To Willmore*] Come, there's one motive induces me.

 [*Don Pedro*] *gives* [*Hellena*] *to* [*Willmore*]
Take her: I shall now be free from fears of her honour; guard it you now, if you can; I have been a slave to't long enough. 605

VILLMORE Faith, sir, I am of a nation that are of opinion a woman's honour is not worth guarding when she has a mind to part with it.

IELLENA Well said, captain.

EDRO (*to Valeria*) This was your plot, mistress, but I 610 hope you have married one that will revenge my quarrel to you.

VALERIA There's no altering destiny, sir.

EDRO Sooner than a woman's will: therefore I forgive

you all, and wish you may get my father's pardon as 61
easily, which I fear.

Enter Blunt dressed in a Spanish habit, looking
very ridiculously; his man adjusting his band

MAN 'Tis very well, sir.

BLUNT Well, sir? 'Adsheartlikins, I tell you 'tis
damnable ill, sir. A Spanish habit, good lord! Could
the devil and my tailor devise no other punishment 62
for me, but the mode of a nation I abominate?

BELVILE What's the matter, Ned?

BLUNT (*turns round*) Pray view me round, and judge.

BELVILE I must confess thou art a kind of an odd figure.

BLUNT In a Spanish habit with a vengeance! I had rather 62
be in the Inquisition for Judaism, than in this doublet
and breeches; a pillory were an easy collar to this,
three handfuls high; and these shoes too, are worse
than the stocks, with the sole an inch shorter than my
foot. In fine, gentlemen, methinks I look altogether 63
like a bag of bays stuffed full of fool's flesh.

BELVILE Methinks 'tis well, and makes thee look *en*
cavalier. Come, sir, settle your face, and salute our
friends. [*Turns to Hellena*] Lady –

BLUNT Ha! (*To Hellena*) Say'st thou so, my little rover? 63
Lady, if you be one, give me leave to kiss your hand,
and tell you, 'adsheartlikins, for all I look so, I am
your humble servant. [*Aside*] A pox of my Spanish
habit.

Music is heard to play

WILLMORE Hark, what's this? 64

Enter page

PAGE Sir, as the custom is, the gay people in masquerade,
who make every man's house their own, are coming up.

Enter several men and women in masking habits,
with music; they put themselves in order and dance

BLUNT 'Adsheartlikins, would 'twere lawful to pull off
their false faces, that I might see if my doxy were not
amongst 'em.   645

BELVILE (*to the maskers*) Ladies and gentlemen, since you
are come so apropos, you must take a small collation
with us.

WILLMORE (*to Hellena*) Whilst we'll to the good man
within, who stays to give us a cast of his office. Have   650
you no trembling at the near approach?

HELLENA No more than you have in an engagement or
a tempest.

WILLMORE Egad, thou'rt a brave girl, and I admire thy
love and courage.   655

    Lead on, no other dangers they can dread,
    Who venture in the storms o'th' marriage bed.
  Exeunt

Epilogue

The banished cavaliers! A roving blade!
A popish carnival! A masquerade!
The devil's in't if this will please the nation,
In these our blessèd times of reformation,
When conventicling is so much in fashion.   5
And yet:
That mutinous tribe less factions do beget,
Than your continual differing in wit;
Your judgement's (as your passion's) a disease:
Nor muse nor miss your appetite can please;   10
You're grown as nice as queasy consciences,
Whose each convulsion, when the spirit moves,
Damns everything that maggot disapproves.
  With canting rule you would the stage refine,
And to dull method all our sense confine.   15
With th'insolence of commonwealths you rule,
Where each gay fop, and politic grave fool
On monarch wit impose, without control.
As for the last, who seldom sees a play,
Unless it be the old Blackfriars way,   20
Shaking his empty noddle o'er bamboo,
He cries, 'Good faith, these plays will never do.
Ah, sir, in my young days, what lofty wit,
What high strained scenes of fighting there were writ:
These are slight airy toys. But tell me, pray,   25
What has the House of Commons done today?'
Then shows his politics, to let you see,
Of state affairs he'll judge as notably,
As he can do of wit and poetry.
The younger sparks, who hither do resort,   30
Cry, 'Pox o' your genteel things, give us more sport;

Damn me, I'm sure 'twill never please the court.'
   Such fops are never pleased, unless the play
Be stuffed with fools, as brisk and dull as they:
Such might the half-crown spare, and in a glass   35
At home, behold a more accomplished ass,
Where they may set their cravats, wigs and faces,
And practise all their buffoonry grimaces;
See how this huff becomes, this dammee stare,
Which they at home may act, because they dare,   40
But must with prudent caution do elsewhere.
Oh, that our Nokes, or Tony Leigh, could show
A fop but half so much to th'life as you.

Postscript

This play had been sooner in print, but for a report about the town (made by some either very malicious or very ignorant) that 'twas *Thomaso* altered; which made the booksellers fear some trouble from the proprietor of that admirable play, which indeed has wit enough to stock a poet, and is not to be pieced or mended by any but the excellent author himself. That I have stolen some hints from it, may be a proof that I valued it more than to pretend to alter it, had I had the dexterity of some poets, who are not more expert in stealing than in the art of concealing, and who even that way out-do the Spartan boys. I might have appropriated all to myself, but I, vainly proud of my judgement, hang out the sign of Angellica (the only stolen object) to give notice where a great part of the wit dwelt; though if the play of *The Novella* were as well worth remembering as *Thomaso*, they might (bating the name) have as well said, I took it from thence. I will only say the plot and business (not to boast on't) is my own: as for the words and characters, I leave the reader to judge and compare 'em with *Thomaso*, to whom I recommend the great entertainment of reading it; though had this succeeded ill, I should have had no need of imploring that justice from the critics, who are naturally so kind to any that pretend to usurp their dominion, especially of our sex, they would doubtless have given me the whole honour on't. Therefore I will only say in English what the famous Virgil does in Latin: I make verses, and others have the fame.

Notes

Technical terms used in these notes are defined in the Glossary, pages 217–221.

sd = stage direction

The prologue

In the 1670s, prologues were usually spoken by female actors, sent forth to negotiate a fresh truce with the audience. Behn is likely to have written this one. By 1677 she was a well-established playwright, yet she disguises her authorship at the very start of her play. How and why does she do this? The prologue takes the argument to the enemy with its accusatory tone and satirical wit. Who is attacked and why? By what means does Behn defend her play? There is a sense of being in a bear pit here; what do you think the response of the audience might have been to the views expressed in this prologue? (See 'Who were the Audience?', page 179.)

Look at the cast list for *The Rover*. Can you decide on the roles these characters will play from what their names suggest to you? What conventions was Behn following in naming her characters?

Rover could mean a pirate, a male flirt, an inconstant lover or a wanderer.

1 **Wits**   belonged to a fashionable, literary set. Their opinions could influence whether a play was a success or failure.
2 **of a different society**   belonging to different professional or social groups.
3 **Rabel's drops**   a well-known patent medicine.
9 **cabal**   secret clique.
10 **hit your humour right**   gives an accurate portrayal of what you are like.
12 **elves**   malicious people.

15 **take** are a success.

16 **censure** judge.

17 **conclave** private meeting.

18 **Catholic** broad-minded.

23 **Bating** except for.

31 Only imitate the kind of writing others can make up as they go along.

33 **lampoon** a vicious, witty and satirical poem that amounted to a character assassination of its subject, often a public figure.

36 **gleanings** leftovers.

42 **debauches** lovers of sensual pleasures.

43 **cits** short for citizens, city-dwellers. The nobility would use this term of contempt when referring to the tradespeople of London.

May-day coaches during the May Day holiday, *cits* would parade in coaches around Hyde Park, imitating their betters. The reference mocks their pretensions.

Act I Scene I

Behn flouts the conventions by opening her play with a scene that is carried by two strong women characters instead of the usual men. She establishes her setting, in Naples during carnival (see 'Carnival', page 193). It is worth thinking about the interconnection of themes: patriarchy (a male-dominated society), militarism and the licence of carnival. From their confined chamber, the voices of her heroines Florinda and Hellena are raised in opposition to the rule of men. Their absent father has sought to control Florinda's future by an arranged marriage. Their brother, Don Pedro, seems to have determined Hellena's destiny, a convent. Rejecting these unappealing options, the women choose new costumes/identities and the chance to *ramble*. The sisters are unusually assertive in their use of language (see 'Language', page 194). They are also very different from one another. Florinda is aware that her beauty and accomplishments should attract a high price in the marriage market and expresses this in conventional terms. She has learned to value her assets within the patriarchal system. She may reject her father's choice of husband in favour of Belvile, but in doing so still upholds the system that exploits her. Hellena's witty resistance suggests that she will be the more challenging of the two with a far more libertine attitude to sex. There is some competitiveness between them, perhaps because they have been treated differently.

The Pamplona 'back story' introduces the important 'rape threat' theme and its association with Florinda. Hellena expresses particular contempt for the colonial trader Don Vincentio. The scene is memorable for Hellena's carefully orchestrated verbal assault on arranged marriage. Her witty tirade is cleverly timed; it steadily increases in vehemence and inventiveness. Don Pedro lacks the linguistic power to return fire. The exchange between brother and sister tells the audience that patriarchal power is going to be strongly contested in this play. But Don Pedro does not shift from Don Vincentio's suit to Don Antonio's because of Hellena's verbal fire; he has already decided that Don Antonio may have Florinda. He, too, intends to disobey his absent father. Leaving instructions for the continuing confinement of the women, he heads off to enjoy the carnival.

13 **to sigh, and sing...** Hellena mocks Florinda's attachment to romantic love.
21 **viceroy** local representative of a distant king; Antonio's father governs Naples in the name of Spain.
27 **my soul** Florinda's claim to possess value beyond her material assets is important in her bid to resist being treated as a commodity by the marriage market.
30 **strangely** strongly.
32 *Inglese* Englishman (Italian term).
34 **gay** high-spirited.
41 **mad** exciting, a term that is also used of Willmore (see I.ii.72).
41–2 **spoil my devotion** wordplay on spoils of war: 'make my

religious devotion into something for himself by plundering it'.
Hellena is the first character to blend religious and sexual
imagery in the play.

43 **proper** handsome, respectable.

44 **humour** temperament.

48–9 **Have I not…** Hellena draws attention to her assets in a way
that bears comparison with the self-promotion of all the
women characters in the play.

54 **fortune** inheritance. Presumably the decision to send Hellena
to a convent is made to save money on a second dowry, to
enrich Florinda and thus increase her chances of making a very
wealthy marriage.
devotee a nun; wordplay suggesting her devotion to worldly
love.

57 **Pamplona** the Spanish and French fought over Pamplona in
northern Spain for many years. Belvile, like other exiled
royalists, would have joined the French cavalry as a mercenary.
He has evidently been part of an invading French force that
captured Don Pedro and his sister Florinda. On leaving the
French army he arrives in Naples, then controlled by Spain. He
has changed sides and is friendly now towards the Spanish.

65 **lover** suitor for marriage.

68 **command from my father** in the absence of his father and
after the death of his uncle, the Spanish general, Don Pedro
assumes control of the family.

71 sd *masking habit* what contrast is Behn drawing between Don
Pedro's words and his deeds in this scene?

75 **ill customs** a criticism of Spanish attitudes towards women
that would have pleased an English audience.

83 **licensed lust** rape of captives allowed by the rules of war.

85 **criminal** as he took Florinda's side against the French.
Belvile's heroics make him seem like a medieval knight.

89–90 **jointure** money or land settled on a wife in return for a
dowry; she could keep it after her husband's death.

98 **Indies** Spain traded in the West Indies in the seventeenth
century; the name would have suggested fabulous wealth to the
audience.

103 **bags** money bags, also wordplay as 'to bag' meant to make
pregnant.

119 **Indian breeding** time Don Vincentio has spent in the Indies.
120 **dog days** July and August, days when the dog star rises; very hot and unhealthy weather.
121 **divertisements** entertainments.
123 **King Sancho** King Sancho ruled Navarre from 905.
129 **coxcomb** foolish, conceited man.
uncase undress.
148 **worse than adultery** it is very radical of Hellena to claim than any marriage might be worse than adultery.
149 *Hôtel de Dieu* medieval hospital for the care of the poor and sick.
156 **Fifty** mocking of Don Vincentio's age, but also wordplay on 'fisty' meaning to fart.
157 **Gambo** colony of the Gambia, West Africa, a slave-trading area.
158 **bell and bauble** the trifles Europeans used to trade with the Africans in exchange for slaves; also wordplay on 'penis' (bauble).
161 **Lent** in the Christian Church, a time for penance and self-denial in preparation for Easter.
170 **grate** latticed window meant to restrict communication between nuns and the outside world.
172 **venture** first of many terms in the play from the semantic field of trading. Behn's use of the language of commerce to describe love and desire will be important in the play's debate about the marriage market (see 'The Marriage Market', page 197).
191 **I ne'er** Why is there a switch from prose to blank verse at this point?
212 **ramble** could mean to look for sexual experience.
220 **habits** costumes.
222 **I'll write a note** the first of many attempts Florinda will make to cast Belvile as the courtly lover to whom she can send secret letters. Behn will question the value of romantic love in the play.
223 **want** lack.

Act I Scene II

The carnival streets of this scene introduce us to the Cavaliers. Their pleasure quest is marred by anxieties amidst an atmosphere of mockery and uncertainty about sex. The emphasis Behn places on looking, reading and interpreting others' bodies indicates the hazards her characters face when social identity becomes unstable in a hypocritical world. Behn contrasts several conventional male perspectives on that 'incompatible' pair, sex and love, before the sisters enter. Disguised as gipsies, Hellena and Florinda are now indistinguishable from the carnival whores who charge for sex. The playful blurring of the distinction between those eternal opposites, virgin and whore, begins in this scene; it is to be a major theme in the play. In their first sparring match, the play's 'gay couple' (see Glossary, page 218) Willmore and Hellena show their strength. Willmore disguises his real nature by adopting religious imagery, and playing holy father to Hellena's escapee nun. Hellena does well to arouse his interest while turning down his sexual advances.

Behn uses anonymous masqueraders to destabilize our certainties about sex and the social order. The 'quality' of the *women dressed like courtesans* is impossible to decipher. Their *papers pinned on their breasts* imply that they are selling sex. At carnival time one cannot be sure; the riddling text, which they have used to re-present themselves, remains open to interpretation. As for the males, their horned figures deride each other in anticipation of the fate that supposedly awaits all men, that of being cheated by their wives.

The hypocritical attitude of the Cavaliers contributes to the uncertainty. Willmore offers to assist Belvile in rescuing Florinda as long as she offers sex – to him and the others! In response Belvile praises Florinda's virtues in religious language. This is enough to change Willmore's mind. Such women are only fit to marry. In the general predatory atmosphere it is ironic that the gullible Blunt is the only male to be snared by a woman, the whore Lucetta. Only Lucetta reads her prey accurately and carries him off. In what other ways does Behn make distinctions between Blunt and the Cavaliers?

Late in the scene we hear word of Angellica, the famed courtesan. Belvile's depiction of her in the language of religious and regal devotion contributes to the prevailing mood of hypocrisy, for Angellica can be reduced to a commodity and sold off piecemeal. What connection can we make between prostitution and marriage through the knowledge that Angellica's dead lover, the Spanish general, was also the uncle of Hellena and Florinda?

This scene has a large number of characters using the forestage to the full. How does Behn group them to achieve the flow and pace required? Look at the transition points between dialogue pairings. How has she captured a carnival mood without using descriptive language?

1 sd **A long street** the painted backdrop is revealed when the side flats are withdrawn (see 'Spectacle and Intimacy: Inside a Restoration Theatre', page 169).

15 **'adsheartlikins** a mild, affectionate oath, this will become a trademark of the character's lack of good taste. Literally, it means 'by God's little heart'.

25 **interest** stake or share.

36 **penitents** a first example of Belvile's expression of courtly love.

42 **hogoes** pungent flavours used in cooking; a first example of sex and food imagery in the play.

49 **if he might** the sense is 'even if...'.

55 **parliaments and protectors** Oliver Cromwell and his son Richard used the title Protector of England from 1653. Successive Parliaments supported the republic against the return of the monarchy.

58 **cavaliering** Blunt, the typical country squire, has not had his estates confiscated like the Cavaliers. His use of the word *grace* may be an intended pun on the spiritual grace claimed by the

Puritans. This may indicate that Behn saw Blunt as a Puritan and the character would have been dressed as such. However, Belvile refers to Blunt as *one of us* (line 79), making the Puritan connection less likely.

61–2 **do it no good** this may suggest that Blunt is a spy for the Parliamentarians.

62 **pick a hole in my coat** find fault with me; this suggests Blunt is an outsider in both camps.

64–5 **Commonwealth** the republican government of 1649–53.

67 **Willmore** his name suggests his dominant characteristic: he wills for more, as women never satisfy him.

73 **prince** the exiled son of Charles I, the future Charles II; the first of many references that associate Willmore with the prince.

79 **honest** often used in restoration plays to mean royalist.

85 **Love** Willmore means sex; love would mean faith towards one woman and must therefore be avoided. Note that the Cavaliers use the terms interchangeably.

87 **chapmen** travelling merchants who buy and sell.

89 **kind** refers to a woman willing to offer sexual favours for nothing.

105 **still** women are likened to roses whose perfume is distilled by being placed in a still and heated. Willmore suggests that the best kind of still is a pair of sheets containing roses like the woman. He would love to be distilled with her into a strong perfume through the heat they will produce in their love-making. This is a ridiculous parody of a courtly conceit, and an example of Willmore's bragging nature.

108 **bush** refers to pubic hair.

111–12 **pesthouse** hospital for plague victims.

114 **no violence** first example of the use of force to settle sexual rivalries between the men.

122 **no tame sigher** *sigher* is a homophone (word that sounds the same but has a different meaning and spelling) for 'sire'. Behn may have intended a pun here, flattering to the king, who would have been addressed as 'sire'.

123 sd **_horns of several sorts_** a sign of the cuckold, a man who has become a laughing stock because his wife is unfaithful.

133 **gardener** the man is a true descendant of Adam since like

him he is a gardener. This man's skill lies in presenting sexually available women, referred to as flowers.

136 **Essex** Blunt comes from Essex. There are many references in the play to Essex as a joke place where people do the unexpected or behave with bad taste. Wakes should be sad occasions and not carnivalesque, as suggested here. Debauchery ought to be a matter of carnivalesque rule-breaking, but in Naples it is offered in a very stately and serious manner.

140 **monsieurs** even the French who are known for their good manners do not offer prostitution in so polite a manner as the inhabitants of Naples do.

142 **baffled by bravos** foiled by hired soldiers, whose presence means that gang brawling rather than honourable duelling between gentlemen is the norm. *Bravos* are hired ruffians, or bodyguards.

144 **hangman** a hangman beat the Frenchman in their contest just as the French beat the Dutch in an incident in 1672–3 at New Bridge. One of many topical references in the play.

146 sd *gipsies* a common euphemism for whores.

169 **parlous** shrewd.

181 **die a maid** wordplay on *die* meaning to have an orgasm, but also an important assertion from Hellena.

196 **storm** take a fortress by violent assault; the 'gay couple' can also flirt using courtly language but in a parodic way. In fact the only 'storming' Willmore succeeds in doing is to enter the courtesan's house at her bidding.

203 **Jephtha's daughter** Jephthah sacrificed his only daughter to God in thanks for a military victory. Before her death her father 'sent her away for two months: and she went with her companions, and bewailed her virginity upon the mountains'. The story can be found in Judges 11:30–40.

205 **Father Captain** Hellena is being sarcastic about Willmore's use of religious argument. She suggests he must belong to a religious order. *Captain* may refer to his swaggering soldier pose, which she also ridicules.

207 **orders** final vows to become a nun.

224 **swingeing** splendid, huge.

232 Notice the change of tone from witty banter to more serious cunning when Lucetta speaks.

234 **game** prey, victim.

235 **I know by his gazing** first use of the gaze to objectify and control another. It is unusual to see a woman using the gaze to take the sexual initiative away from the man. Note the effect it has on Blunt, who foolishly regards himself as physically attractive to her (see also II.i.94).

258 **She'll be disappointed** does Belvile appreciate Florinda's mockery?

265 **sybil** a ridiculous compliment, as Florinda is no prophetess from Greek myth.

275 **habit** why does it matter how Hellena is dressed when they meet again?

314 **Let her alone for that** you can trust her to make the plan work rather than we bungling Cavaliers.

315–16 **broker... Jew... Jesuit** all associated in Behn's day with strong bargaining powers. Jesuits were considered capable of slipping their chains if imprisoned for their faith.

323 **fit** punish him in a way he deserves.
      Peru the Spanish used slave labour in the silver mines of Peru.

324 **the rogue's sturdy** there were laws against sturdy (healthy) beggars in Behn's day.

326 **well-favouredly banged** savagely beaten up.

339 **banker** the Cavaliers have chosen Blunt to look after their funds.

343 **jilt** prostitute.

346 **piece of eight** old Spanish dollar.
      geld castrate; also wordplay on gold?

359 **honest** virtuous.

360 **person of quality** person of high rank or possessing wealth.
      free noble, unrestrained.

361 **her wit** note that it is Hellena's mind and character, evidenced in her language, that makes a lasting impression on Willmore.

368 **Paduana** Padua in northern Italy was famous for its courtesans. As part of the Venetian Republic it was independent from Spanish rule. Angellica Bianca's name suggests both 'angel' and an old English gold coin. This coin was in circulation (like whores) during the restoration, so the correspondences would have been appreciated. The Italian *bianco* means 'white'. The dualism of her name implies that she

is both commodity and divinity. Frederick's announcement of her arrival turns the usually private sphere of sexual relations into public property.

373 **liveries**   servants' uniforms.

374 **monarch's birthday**   new clothes were worn at court to mark the sovereign's birthday.

379 **gallant**   male companion and protector.

380 **exposed to sale**   the passive tense of this verb conceals whether Angellica has decided to sell her body or whether this happens by circumstances outside her control.

385–6 **at my devotion**   attending my worship of Florinda (courtly language).

Act II Scene I

Blunt is revealed as the comic foil to the Cavalier group in this scene. We learn that he is the first to enter a liaison with a whore in Naples. His relationship with Lucetta parodies the love affairs of the more attractive characters, and it also points to some ingrained hypocrisies. Like his companions he can no more distinguish a whore from a woman of quality than he can determine whether the bracelet for which he has exchanged his diamond is valuable or not.

The tone becomes more serious when Angellica's pictures and price are revealed. Her long-anticipated entrance takes the form of a series of stage-managed unveilings. These embody aspects of courtly love and the selling of merchandise. The high price she demands provokes an interesting range of reactions from every one of the male characters – compare them to what you think Angellica's motives might be. We shift from a male perspective on the price of sex in the Blunt episode to a female perspective in Angellica's conversation with Moretta. The fighting and challenge to a duel add a farcical touch while introducing the mistaken identity theme. The men fight readily over access to women and other rivalries.

This makes Willmore's intervention in stealing Angellica's picture all the more individualistic and enterprising. Throughout the scene he is never quite abreast of the Cavaliers' conversation; instead, he hones in on any morsel of dialogue that suggests a woman might be on offer. There is the continuing joke about his lack of cash. To subject a woman to his controlling gaze costs nothing, especially when she has met him halfway by hanging up her image in the marketplace. The satire in this scene lies in the way Behn contrasts the ancient will to fight over women's bodies with the more contemporary economic bargaining being piloted by Blunt and Willmore. The Spaniards Don Pedro and Don Antonio see Angellica's high price as contributing to her mystique. Their instant rivalry is farcical, based entirely on mistaken identity and on ego. While they argue, Willmore's stealing of Angellica's image is the surprising prelude to him being invited into her chamber.

1 **muzzled**   masked, perhaps preventing speech. Why is Willmore the only Cavalier not masked and in his own clothes?

4 **eternal buff**   military coat, of a dull yellow leather. Why would this reference have pleased the audience on the first night of *The Rover*? *Eternal* implies that what is royal cannot be changed or disguised for long.

13 **not of a quality...**   not of low enough rank to be willing to have sex with you.

41 **little archer**   Cupid.

48 **a proclaimed clap**   noticeable signs of gonorrhoea.

50–1 **what care I for names?**   Blunt is not interested in Lucetta's identity. Here and elsewhere Behn takes issue with men who deny women a stable identity.

68 **bottom... unlade**   take the cargo out of the hold, hand over the money.

74 **Cozened**   tricked.

88 **ycleped**   known as; an old-fashioned expression used for comic effect.

91 **Essex calf**   fool; Essex was known for its cattle.

114 **the Inquisition**   body set up by the Roman Catholic Church to try people for witchcraft and heresy.

119–20 **A thousand crowns**   the huge sum almost makes her unattainable, like the Petrarchan lady she wishes to be.

129 **Infanta**   in 1666 the Spanish Infanta had a large dowry on her marriage.

130 **trust**   trust me to pay later.

131 **credit**   letting clients owe her money, but also refers to a reputation for virtue.

140 **rallying**   good-natured joking.

140–2 It is control rather than sex that gives Angellica pleasure. How real is this control?

157 **triumph of the conqueror**   first example of the semantic field of military power, which Angellica uses to resist commodification.

157–8 **inconstancy's the sin of all mankind**   Angellica blames men for her inability to love or feel desire.

160 **interest**   financial gain.

206 **kind force**   an oxymoron (or contradiction in terms), ending this idyllic pastoral poem in a euphemistic depiction of rape. Willmore is shortly to win Angellica by forceful behaviour rather than courtly servitude.

207 sd *throws open the curtains*   audiences would have made the connection between this gesture and that of tragic heroines in plays of the period. The balcony and curtain would suggest the courtly mistress of medieval romance that is an aspect of Angellica's fantasy self.

222 **Tilting**   fighting like a medieval knight on horseback; also carries some sexual connotations.

228 **Molo**   pier or quay.

234 **disguised**   the disguised Don Pedro has identified Don Antonio. Don Antonio could mistake him for a rival suitor to Florinda rather than her brother. The *destroyed hopes* (line 231) are ambiguous. Don Pedro means hopes of Angellica (or perhaps hopes of Florinda marrying Don Antonio); Don Antonio may take them to mean hopes of having Florinda for himself. The virgin/whore duality adds to the comic farce of the scene.

238–9 **it must be he**   Don Antonio wrongly identifies Don Pedro as Belvile.

243 **impotence**   why should a fear of impotence concern

Willmore? Political lampoons of the king linked his impotence
with his failing leadership; this may be the connection Behn is
making here. How has Willmore's reading of the picture
changed from lines 119–123?

255 **That of possession**   Willmore's supreme confidence links him
to Charles II. His high rank allows him to assert ownership
over the picture and all that it implies, despite being penniless.

269 **wounded**   this Petrarchan conceit will appeal to Angellica.
Note how Willmore takes the advantage by blaming his desires
on her beauty. He has revised his motives for taking the picture.
Male rivalry and the desire for a sexual fetish (see Glossary,
page 218) have been replaced by something more romantic.

281 sd *shirt bloody*   why does Behn draw attention to this intimate
aspect of Willmore's body?

291 **dons**   Spaniards, who were famous for their elaborate code of
honour. They would not have taken an insult lightly.

292 **Flanders**   Spain lost Flanders to the French during the
seventeenth century.

295 **ours by conquest**   Blunt sounds a militaristic note that would
have appealed to the audience. Territory, booty, women, and
Anglo-Spanish rivalry are all involved together here.

309 **patacoon**   coin of small value.

318 **saluting**   kissing her.

328 sd *goes in*   an example of Behn's use of doors to quickly relocate
actors. When Willmore returns he is in *a fine chamber* (II.ii).
This would have been indicated by his re-entry through a
different door.

Act II Scene II

By this stage in the play comic convention requires that two pairs
of well-matched lovers will engage in some flirting. It is therefore
surprising to find that this is not part of the immediate plot
development. Instead we have a scene between Willmore and
Angellica that is an uneasy mix of sexual politics and seduction.
Why did Behn expand the courtesan role in this way, compared
to what we find in the source play? Why does Willmore pursue

her instead of Hellena? Compare his seduction strategies with both women.

In a moment of lucidity and truth Angellica makes a telling remark about the hypocrisy of marrying for money. Willmore can only agree with her. What he will not or cannot do is make amends by ignoring Angellica's lost virginity. It is she who makes all the concessions, as she is all too willing to deceive herself for love. She thinks that she can escape stigma by changing a single word; the price of her favours is no longer money but love. It is in this scene that Willmore exercises his full linguistic powers to charm and dissemble. In chameleon-like fashion he uses several registers. With Moretta, who provides an interesting choric role, he is coarse and the invective is fulsome. With Angellica he shifts from the conventional language of unrequited love to vulgar calculations about her body, using the cruel logic of a shareholding economy. The combination of passion and condemnation works. Such is Angellica's desire to reinvent herself that she overcomes her anger at Willmore's insults and gives a selective ear to his libertine and romantic love-making.

Willmore does not need to be masked, nor to brawl like his compatriots. He has all the disguise and power he needs in his language. The courtesan and her woman are both trounced by him and he gets sex for free. Angellica is as much of a gullible fool as Blunt. Like him, but for different reasons, she is one of the play's outsiders.

7 **despair** Willmore's seduction strategy is to suggest that he is an indignant victim of Angellica's powerful beauty.

13 **I came to rail at you** Willmore plays a more subtle game than pretending to be brought to his knees by Angellica's beauty.

26 **Worcester** Cromwell finally defeated Charles II at Worcester in 1651.

28 **corporal** Moretta deliberately gives Willmore a lower rank than captain.

32 **too high i' th' mouth for you** above your rank.

46 **pistole**   Spanish gold coin worth very little. Willmore applies the logic of the marketplace, offering to buy a share of the whole that he cannot afford.
black lead pencil.

58 **mart**   auction. Willmore elaborates on the insulting but logical metaphor.

65 Willmore switches to blank verse, unlike the prose banter he used with Hellena in I.ii. The verse introduces a serious, romantic, elevated tone. His language and gaze combine to overwhelm Angellica.

86 **fame**   reputation; he suggests that he might fall in love with her if she had a better reputation, so it is just as well she does not.

105 **mercenary crime**   Angellica sees through the hypocrisy of the system that condemns her.

116–18 You would not have to buy my love if you could forget that I am a courtesan.

160–2 **dominion... command**   Willmore's royal associations with Charles II are suggested here.

165 **the price I ask**   the price she asks is now love, but her language remains mercenary.

166 **awful**   solemn and reverent.

180 **shameroon**   a trickster.

182 **tatterdemalion**   beggar, in tattered clothes.

183 **picaroon**   pirate.

184 **lousy**   lice infested.

186–7 Moretta is angry at the thought that Angellica's earnings may end up in Willmore's pockets.

Act III Scene I

While Willmore lies in the arms of Angellica, the Spanish sisters and their cousin Valeria experience something of a lull in the hectic pursuit of love. In this scene we learn that Frederick and Valeria are attracted to each other. As they are minor characters the outcome of this attraction is dependent on the fortunes of the main players, as Frederick's impatience with Belvile shows.

The sisters take stock of the situation. They continue their debate about how a woman should conduct herself in love. How does their language express their contrasting views? The scene is played out beneath Angellica's balcony, and she emerges only to find that Willmore has been unfaithful. Her response is to retreat inside, commanding others to act on her behalf. Behn uses contrasting acting areas to suggest that boundaries, real and imagined, curtail women's freedom. Compare Angellica's and Hellena's responses to proof of Willmore's unfaithfulness. How can you account for the differences? Compare also the ways in which all three women use either their face or an image of it in negotiations with their lovers.

Meanwhile we are fast approaching nightfall, when Florinda's self-managed rescue is due to take place. The comic nature of the scene slips into farce. Belvile's supposed devotion to Florinda is such that he fails to recognize her through her disguise, and another opportunity to escape Don Pedro is lost. The scene ends with the Cavalier friends at cross-purposes over who is in pursuit of which sister. The two couples have made new arrangements to meet; one for romantic rescue, the other for sparring.

1 sd *antic*   bizarre; note the number of costume changes Behn assigns to the women (see 'Costume and Masked Disguise', page 190).
   5 **mewed up**   confined; a mew was a cage for hawks.
  10 **Loretto**   there would have been many gipsies on this road as it was a well-known pilgrimage route, and the gipsies would have made money out of the pilgrims.
  25 **taken up**   by a new woman.
  43 **pip**   a mocking term for being lovesick.
  56 **design**   scheme.
  57 **venture a cast**   risk a dice throw, or be willing to be thrown to the ground.
  69 **billets**   billets-doux, love letters.
  84 **conjures on**   appeals to you.
       laid the soft...   until his appeals have increased your

determination to love or destroyed it completely. Cupid is the *soft-winged god*.

106–7 How should the actor deliver this line? In a sentence the Cavaliers' ambivalent attitude to prostitution is summed up; to worship the whore or to menace her with violence? Notice that it is the romantic Belvile who suggests this choice of action.

113 **bona roba** Italian *buona* (good) *roba* (robe/dress), a term used to mean a showy courtesan.

114 **in fresco** in the fresh air.

116–17 How does this line work as an aside? How should the actor deliver it?

120 **spigot** wooden peg of a wine cask.
butt cask.

126 **hungry balderdash** poor mixture of drinks.
sack wine.

135 **beget** the coins are like male and female; when put together they will produce pleasures. The usual exchange of cash for sexual favours has been reversed – Willmore is the paid up-whore.

148 **two provided for** Behn makes the connection between Blunt and Willmore explicit.

171 **capuchin** a friar from a very strict monastic order.

174 **dissembles** pretends.

181 **staying** feeding.

182 **collation** light meal.

188 **fall to** begin (a meal). Hellena asks if Willmore will marry her to fulfil his desire for her.

229 **Perjured** oath-breaking.

236–40 How far does Willmore see the individuality of Hellena's face?

255 **intercession** pleading on another's behalf.

262 **jewel** a locket containing her picture; compare this to Angellica's portrait and Hellena's unmasking of her face in this scene.

263 **bills of exchange** papers with orders to pay a given sum of money on a given date.

284 As the tension mounts in the exchange between Florinda, Belvile and Frederick, Behn shifts attention to Willmore and Hellena. As in I.ii, Behn makes innovative use of the forestage throughout this scene.

317 sd **[Willmore] kneels**   see II.ii.171 for comparison.
  320 **book**   Bible, but Willmore chooses to think this means her hand.
  347 **beating the bush**   servants would beat the bush to scare birds into flight for their masters to shoot down. Willmore mistakenly thinks that he has been arousing Hellena's passion only for Belvile to enjoy.

Act III Scene II

This scene has much topical humour to amuse an English audience. There is the irony of Blunt's view that English whores are meaner than Italian ones, when his 'love affair' is dominated by calculations about cost to himself. Blunt readily accepts the flattering account of his appearance that the audience can see does not bear up to reality. He likens justices of the peace in Essex to pimps and assumes that because Lucetta's house is richly furnished she must be a person of quality, complete with the *old jealous husband* of the sex-comedy genre. (See 'Restoration Comedy as a Genre', page 177.)

  16 **Spanish**   treacherous.
  18 **settlements**   property or money settled on a person before marriage.

Act III Scene III

This scene and the next one offer a rather satisfying gulling of a male character who, though undeserving, seeks to benefit from all the advantages of patriarchy. Women in the audience would enjoy his ritualistic humiliation at the hands of Lucetta. Men in the audience would feel that the Essex calf was not a true Cavalier but a fop who deserved his fate. Why does Behn show Blunt and Lucetta in a bedroom scene? Why does she choose not to show Willmore and Angellica in similar circumstances? What does the late arrival of Philippo add to the scene? Consider his Spanish identity, his control over Lucetta and claims to membership of the ranks of *witty men*.

6 sd **undresses himself** in a period when roles often required women to undress, Behn is unusual in undressing a male character.

28 **I locked the door** one of many instances of men attempting to control the space in which women operate in the play.

45 **two hundred pistoles** the Cavaliers' money.

47 **his king** a medallion with the head of either Charles I or Charles II.

51 **eighty-eight** the Spanish Armada was defeated by the English in 1588; Philippo suggests that stealing Blunt's money, minted in the reign of Elizabeth I, will avenge Spain's defeat.

61 **your name** Blunt's arrogance in not needing to attribute the dignity of a name to his 'true love' will count against him in his argument for 'just' revenge.

Act III Scene IV

Behn intended this to be a 'discovery scene'. She parodies the usual conventions; discoveries were meant to shock, or display a woman's body in a state of undress for the male voyeur. Behn wants her audience to look and laugh at the sight of a man who has been stripped to his underwear. This is an unusual and telling reversal of the way in which the power attributed to the gaze is being used in the play. In the absence of Lucetta's deceitful gaze, Blunt soon realizes the extent of his unattractiveness to women. He has lustily shed his clothing only to be ejected from the house and have his signs of identity and wealth (his mother, his sister, his country's history) appropriated as loot by the Spaniard Philippo. What is there to suggest that a monologue like Blunt's was a set piece in many plays of the period?

2 **without a clue**   a thread that would have guided him out of the maze-like tunnels of the sewer.

4 **quean**   slut.

16 **country fop**   a stock figure of fun among the urbanites in the audience.

29 **cullies**   fools.

Act III Scene V

This scene addresses some well-established serio-comic themes in the play. Mistaken identity, liminal spaces (see Glossary, page 218), and amorous justification for rape are all to be found here. The tone hovers between farce and threat, assisted by the fact that the characters cannot see each other in the dark. Florinda encounters the amorous Willmore instead of the hapless Belvile in the garden. Contemporary critics objected to Florinda's state of undress, which they considered lewd. Were those critics objecting to the fact that the scene was written by a woman? Restoration tragedies regularly featured half-dressed women. Such scenes were mainly gratuitous, exploiting the novelty of the women's physical presence on stage. What the eye could not see – an enactment of rape – salacious language compensated for. Could this scene be Behn's critique of the trend?

A new sexual conquest requires a new type of rhetoric from Willmore: he quotes romantic poetry. He claims that Florinda's anonymity will dissolve the shame of rape and that the law will absolve his guilt. He invokes the specious argument that women invite rape because their beauty is impossible to resist; a Petrarchan conceit is turned against the woman it is meant to praise. In carnival the rule of law is traditionally flouted by exuberant youth, and this convention is echoed here but with sinister implications.

How does Florinda's state of undress square with her initial purpose in the garden? How should Willmore's attempted rape of Florinda be played? As comedy, or is there a darker interpretation? Would Behn's audience have been divided in their responses, depending on their gender? Does the passage of time mean that a modern audience brings a different perspective to the scene? (See 'Modern Critical Approaches', page 203.)

1 sd   *a little box*   the box of jewels may be a symbol of virginity, which is referred to as a jewel of great price in the Bible. It could also be a symbol of the defiant woman. Like Jessica in Shakespeare's *The Merchant of Venice*, Florinda defies her father and brother in her search for love.

4   **the key**   to freedom? Florinda's unlocking of the door admits Willmore, intent upon rape.

19   **wench**   whore. How does Willmore make this judgement of Florinda?

21   **shoe-string**   refers to Robert Herrick's poem, *Delight in Disorder*. He shows nothing of the courtly behaviour the quotation implies.

35   **disguised**   drunk; could also mean not his real, noble self.

36   **I'll be very secret**   Willmore assures Florinda that her reputation will not be damaged by consenting to have sex with him. At this stage of the assault he is trying to seduce her.

40   **I am so...**   Willmore counters Florinda's insult by wit that is either ingenious or ridiculous, depending on your point of view.

51   **unhand me**   remarks like these draw attention to Willmore's use of force.

52–4   **a judge... provocation**   a mix of Petrarchan conceit and appeal to judicial judgement that any force used will be entirely Florinda's fault. Willmore's argument has become subtler in response to Florinda's resistance.

54   **the first blow**   sexual desire is likened here to a chivalric exchange of blows. This justifies Willmore's 'reply' to Florinda's power to attract him. If a man feels desire he is its victim until he can assert his will over the desired object.

66   **door set open**   possession of a key has backfired on Florinda. What does the spider image reveal about Willmore's view of women?

70 **do't for nothing** in the last of Willmore's attempts to
   position Florinda to his advantage, he now makes her role as
   whore blatant by offering to pay her.
88 **Florinda's voice!** Belvile at last recognizes something of
   Florinda's.
91 **impossible to escape** with comic regularity it is once more
   Willmore's sex drive that has ruined the lovers' plan, and it
   takes Florinda's wits to re-schedule the escape plot.

Act III Scene VI

Belvile's condemnation of Willmore as *a beast, a brute, a
senseless swine* echoes that of Florinda in the previous scene
when she exclaims *what a filthy beast is this!* The trauma in the
garden has finally provoked some outrage towards the kind of
behaviour that the comic mood has invited the audience to
tolerate so far. In what ways do the humour and disgrace of the
garden scene rumble on? Is the mood comic or subdued and
anxious? We may dislike Willmore but the other lover, Belvile,
seems an empty echo of true feeling. Willmore curses the wine
he has drunk while Belvile curses his star; neither explanation
redeems the man. Their views collide when Belvile expresses
his disbelief that Willmore could not see Florinda's innate
virtue. This is just the point; in this carnival world patriarchal
values still rule. Women revert to 'type', that is 'whore', when
they have lost male protection and secure identity. Perhaps
Behn uses darkness metaphorically as well as farcically.
Willmore cannot or chooses not to see Florinda in the way
Belvile expects.

The third violent brawl over a woman does have a significant
outcome this time: Belvile is imprisoned by Don Antonio. This
confirms his role as hapless lover and emphasizes Behn's
contempt for the type. It also sets up a case of further mistaken
identity for Act IV. As we expect around Act III of a five-act play,
the plot is at its most complicated at this moment.

30–31 **awful reverence** deep religious respect; Belvile persists in his belief that men can always distinguish virgins from whores. The play works continuously to dispute this view.

40 **Tomorrow is Antonio's** the day when he is to marry Florinda.

82–3 **set upon me twice** Antonio refers to the brawl with Don Pedro outside Angellica's house (see II.i.221). He believes he has fought with *the English colonel* but does not know the name of Belvile. There was a second minor brawl that included Belvile, see II.i.275.

Act IV Scene I

The scene opens with the accident-prone Belvile imprisoned by Don Antonio who, oddly, looks the more vulnerable of the two. Despite the tense situation and confusion, why is it that these men appear to respect each other? Belvile agrees to disguise himself as his rival Don Antonio, who believes that Belvile wounded him when in fact it was Willmore.

12 sd *in a night-gown* Don Antonio cuts a comic figure in this costume, with his arm in a sling and unable to wear his sword.

26 Note the irony – he *is* mistaken.

33 sd *sword* the symbol of manhood passes between two men who barely know each other.

61–2 Is the *rival* Willmore or Don Pedro? Is the *maid* Angellica? Or does Antonio mean Belvile and the *maid* is Florinda?

69 This confirms that Antonio means Don Pedro, whom he mistakenly believes is Belvile. So the *maid* in question could be Florinda or Angellica.

84 **habit** clothes to disguise him as Don Antonio, who will then take credit for Belvile's bravery.

85 **Fantastic fortune** by chance Belvile has the opportunity to duel with Don Pedro for Florinda's hand. This is at last a situation that befits his role of courtly lover. However, the ironies at play undermine his achievement, since he fights as Don Antonio and does not realize that his opponent is to be Don Pedro.

Act IV Scene II

The mistaken identity plot-strand comes to a climax in this scene. Don Pedro is fooled into thinking that Belvile is Don Antonio, while Belvile remains uncertain who his opponent is. One interpretation could be that it is Don Antonio himself. The confusion over the status of the woman they are fighting for is replayed but not resolved. Carnival disguise continues to confound notions of romantic love. It is now Florinda's turn to fail to recognize Belvile, whom she resists marrying as she thinks he is Don Antonio. As the audience has come to expect, success is snatched away from the lovers by the bungling intrusion of Willmore. Florinda is passed like a parcel between the men during an undignified squabble. The farcical confusion gives way to a sombre tone on the entrance of Angellica, who is still in pursuit of Willmore. Her 'scorned mistress' role is ineffectual compared to Hellena's breeches disguise. Nor can she vent her anger by drawing a sword on him as Belvile does. Instead she is forced to plan her revenge alone and without the framework of her balcony/theatre.

The scene closes with a crowd-pleasing use of female disguise. Hellena in the 'breeches part' plans to rebuke Willmore for his arrogant behaviour and warn Angellica off. She may even mean to release Angellica from the grip of a self-destructive passion. If this is the case, cross-dressing places the two women on a supportive footing. Behn is asking her audience to compare Willmore's discomfort to the gulling of Blunt. The final moments of this scene are given to Angellica, one of a number of instances where Behn increases the tragic resonance of this character and asks the audience to sympathize with rather than jeer at the whore's predicament.

1 sd **The Molo** Behn requested a painted scene depicting the Molo specifically for *The Rover*.
    2 **my window** Florinda alternates between being framed within a confined space and being free to roam the streets.

29 **'Tis not Belvile** it is now Florinda's turn not to see through her lover's disguise.

36–7 **or else Antonio** does Don Pedro's reference to Angellica persuade Belvile that Don Pedro is in fact Don Antonio?

96 sd *finely dressed* presumably Willmore has spent some of Angellica's gold coins. Later in the scene she remarks that he seems dressed for his wedding. Perhaps this is the beginning of Willmore's transformation from libertine to husband?

103 **she's mine by conquest** an echo of Blunt's remark about Angellica's picture. The men are comfortable with military solutions to disputes in the marriage market.

161–3 **had I given... nor sigh upon't** if I had given him all the profits earned in my youth from whoring, I would not have given the money a second thought.

166 **My virgin heart** as patriarchy only values the virgin body, Angellica's claim is sentimental and deluded.

177 **fortune's your slave** unlike Belvile who rails at his bad fortune, Willmore is seen as in command of his desires.

179 **cloyed** filled up with.

219 **mumping** sullen.

297 **prater** foolish gossip.

315 **buff and scarlet** flattering to both Willmore and the king.

365 **fit** pay back.

375 **cogging** pleading.

382 **canting'st** most hypocritical.

390 **motion** puppet show.

393–4 **this vexes me** what is there in Willmore's insult that is particularly vexing to Hellena?

399 **continence** reining in my sexual appetite; which Willmore means to be taken as highly unlikely. The audience, though, may start to see the path towards marriage to Hellena.

421–2 Is this a crucial moment in which Willmore concedes that there may be circumstances in which he might agree to marry?

447–8 **find/kind** Willmore's rhyming couplet suggests that the scene concludes on a flippant note, but the soliloquy for Angellica achieves a mood of tragic self-pity.

449 **ague** fever.

457 **name** reputation.

459 **sober** serious and lasting.

460 **Nice** scrupulous.
464 **revenge** the vengeful mistress was a stock character of the restoration stage.

Act IV Scene III

Florinda and Valeria in fresh disguise have escaped from Callis, whom Don Pedro had appointed as their guard. They have become separated from Hellena. Valeria's account of locking Callis up is in keeping with the 'youth turns the tables on authority' theme of carnival. Don Pedro had confined Florinda to her chamber on suspicion of devising the duel on the Molo in collaboration with Belvile. We have a repetition of romantic and sexual themes; Florinda is making yet another assignation with Belvile and Willmore is still on the trail of a wench. Not for the first time he mistakes Florinda for a whore. The misfortunes of Blunt are related. Behn reminds the audience of this character as she needs him as the main narrative agent of the rape threat scene that is to follow. Despite their differences, why would the Cavaliers and Don Pedro be at ease sharing the joke against Blunt?

11 **wardrobe** dressing-room.
19 **young stranger** she means Frederick.
41 **mien** appearance.
56 **drawers** underwear.
58 **watch** night watchmen.
59 **fresco** open air.
74 **borrowing face** face that begs for money.
82 **warrant her prize** guarantee she's a ship I can legally capture under the rules of war.

Act IV Scene IV

Florinda has now become separated from both Hellena and Valeria. Her pursuit of Belvile has left her vulnerable. Even though she enters her lover's house, she does not recognize it as his lodging. Hellena in the meantime has also been moving through the streets alone, but with more security as she is in male disguise. The pace of the action has picked up, with much use of exits and entrances. The door Florinda notices and ventures through leads her into Blunt's chamber in the following scene, another example of Behn's economical use of doors to relocate characters.

Act IV Scene V

Angellica and Blunt, contrasting gulls, seek revenge for being slighted in love. Some eighteenth-century performances of the play cut Blunt's speeches which threaten Florinda with violence and rape. His misogyny would have been too strong for this more sentimental type of theatre. Consider the elements of farce and threat in Blunt's opening monologue.

    Florinda's defence of her honour is very clear. She is in need of protection and as a virgin of quality, is entitled to it. Men know they need to defend the virginity of honourable women to maintain the value of the system. This is why she chooses to buy time by claiming that Belvile will be harmed if she is touched. The reference to a common acquaintance goes some way towards breaking through the perils of anonymity that her disguise has brought her. She is without identity so male logic claims that she is likely to be a whore until proven otherwise. There is another logic working here as well – the one that ends in rape. If a woman can be bought in marriage or prostitution, her value can also be stolen. Considering this point, what is the significance of Florinda's diamond ring?

1 sd   ***discovers him***   the discovery scene had a strong element of visual surprise. Behn directs the audience's gaze upon the physically unattractive figure of Blunt. He is *naked* and *undone* and doing no more than reading. Behn is using this highly dramatic unveiling for parodic effect. Blunt's talk of revenge sits oddly with the comic vulnerability of his state of undress. The stage direction at line 8 refers to him putting on *an old rusty sword, and buff belt.* He is a parody of the good knight who is meant to defend his lady's honour.

  3   **bespoke**   ordered.

  9   **morris dancer**   dressed in white underwear, which adds to Behn's parody of virtue.

28 sd   ***starts up and gazes***   the male gaze holds the victim in its sights.

61   **revenged on one whore for the sins of another**   this is the heart of Blunt's message: all women share the guilt for his humiliation. Therefore any woman can be made to pay for it with her body.

66   **a paper of scurvy verses**   by contrast with the masked women who wrote their own verses and represented themselves in I.ii, Blunt will label Florinda as a whore for the world to gape at. This is the dark side of carnival.

92   **cajoled**   tricked.

111   **Some such devils**   Florinda's defence includes damning other women.

133–4   **cormorant at whore and bacon**   extremely greedy devourer of whores and meat, which he treats alike. This is one of a number of remarks about Belvile that don't match the romantic lover type.

135   **pullet**   young hen.

139   **thank you for the justice**   on what grounds is Florinda making this appeal?

145   **present**   Florinda uses the diamond to indicate that she is a woman of quality under male protection and should be spared. The woman who entered the carnival streets in Act I would not have chosen this path to happiness with Belvile.

151   **trussed up for a rape**   Frederick expresses fear of reprisal from the virgin's high-ranking family should they misjudge the situation.

165   **lock up the wench**   Florinda's usual fate. Blunt closes the

scene by locking an outer door too. Behn uses most of the indoor spaces in the play as places of imprisonment at some stage.

167 **Fear nothing** Frederick has switched from relishing the idea of raping Florinda to this courtly protective idiom. He sees virgin rather than whore in Florinda's diamond.

Act V Scene I

In the play's final scene the revenge plots of Blunt and Angellica are played out unsuccessfully. Blunt acts within a gang, Angellica acts alone. The second of the rape threat scenes is more menacing, more hypocritical and more farcical than the first. Angellica loses her bid for romantic love and freedom from social stigma. The injured Don Antonio easily disarms her of the phallic pistol. She is led tamely away, supposedly into his arms and her fate as courtesan.

Angellica still fantasizes about power rather than equality in her relationship with Willmore. This suggests that Hellena is more suited to him. With her talk of god-like powers, idols and conquerors, the courtesan is trapped in an inflexible set of attitudes. Willmore counters with a simple set of images drawn from nature. Some of his attractiveness to the audience is restored and we are again reminded of the character's association with the king.

Blunt's appearance in a ludicrously exaggerated Spanish costume is a fitting finale for the play's fool. When all disguises are dispensed with, Blunt is forced into one that deceives no one. He fails to resume a stable identity; there will be no pairing into marriage for him. Behn's highly partisan audience would have considered ridiculing Spain while making lucrative and ennobling alliances with its women a very good day's work. Don Pedro expresses some relief at being relieved of responsibility for his sisters' honour. There are burdens for men as well as women under patriarchy.

The scene's main achievement, however, to enable the play to end in the best comic tradition, is Willmore's transformation from rake into faithful lover. He must become the archetypal good catch for the feisty Hellena and her dowry of two hundred thousand crowns. The audience need to feel that Hellena and Willmore are *of one humour* and can benefit equally from marriage. Behn could not completely reform Willmore and retain her credibility as a royalist and libertine advocate. Her solution is a negotiated one: she has three Cavaliers marry three noblewomen. The women bring restored fortune to the Cavaliers' meagre estates. In return the men bring legitimate sexual pleasure to women who have been repressed. How far do you think this summary represents a true sense of a new social order at the end of the play?

7–8 **let's break open the door**   male characters respond to barriers with force.

71–2 **I am ashamed at the rudeness of my nation**   Pedro's apology to Blunt is interesting in the light of what is about to happen.

115 **toledo**   the Spanish fashion was for long swords; the sword is also a phallic joke.

123 sd **Pedro after her**   were Don Pedro to rape Florinda, he would be violating and devaluing his own property. Is this farcical or horrifying?

125 **discovery**   is Florinda fearful of rape or of being found to be disobedient to her brother and father?

180 **give your pardon too**   the first of three pardons granted by Florinda. Why is her forgiveness so immediate?

185 **father**   priest to marry Belvile and Florinda.

203–4 **the sin of the grape**   drunkenness.

228 **juggling**   cheating, as Don Pedro is being deceived.

239 sd **masking habit**   as the plot moves to resolving mistaken identities, Angellica's disguise shows her isolation.

245 sd **pistol**   Angellica wields the male weapon. Unlike the many swords flourished in the course of the action this is a weapon a woman can handle. It is a logical step in her desire for mastery and control.

254 sd **pulls off her vizard**   one of a pattern of unmaskings in the

play. For comparison see Hellena's unmasking to Willmore
(III.i.234) and Belvile's unmasking to Florinda (IV.ii.100).

267 **virago**   warrior woman.

317 **charge**   cost to himself.

324 **nice**   hard to please.

344 **sing in all groves**   serious now, Willmore comes closest to
justifying his behaviour by aligning himself with the natural sex
drive of birds.

351 sd *Offers her a purse of gold*   this is the third time gold has come
between them. The gesture confirms that Angellica's
relationship with Willmore can only be as a commodity bought
for money.

362 sd *his arm in a scarf*   even a wounded man can disarm Angellica,
despite the depth of her grievance. Why is this?

432 **prize**   a prisoner taken in war. Willmore's unabashed show of
military power against the Spaniard works in two ways: Behn
satirizes the way men settle disputes over women when all
farcical mistakes have been exposed, and the underdog English
show of strength over Spain would have pleased her audience.

434 **Tramontana**   a foreign pirate.

478–9 **orphan lover... captain**   typical characters from ballads.

480–1 **clawed away with broadsides**   beaten off by another ship's
guns.

485–6 **come to the lure**   like a bird of prey returning to its trainer
for food, or a woman who will be faithful to a man who can
satisfy her. Note Willmore's return to bird imagery, although
this time the metaphor is taken from hunting rather than
nesting.

492 **savoury**   agreeable.

495 **graces**   prayers or talk before eating.

498 **gaffer**   man.

   Hymen   god of marriage.

511 **left-handed**   fake.

514 **upse gipsy**   like a gipsy.

518 **incle**   thread.

524–5 **conquer... yielding**   can these two words be reconciled?

530 **caudle**   warm drink of gruel and wine given to the sick.

541 **each other's names**   both characters invent names for
themselves after they have agreed to marry. Hellena has been

inconstant in her multiplicity of disguises. She has been *constant* in her pursuit of Willmore, who could be seen as *constant* in his role as serial seducer but *inconstant* to any particular woman.

550–1 **faulkner or butler**   Hellena suggests that Willmore is only likely to be constant to his falconer or his butler because he loves hawking and drinking. The falconer could also suggest his love of prey (women).

554 **crossing**   Willmore remembers that Hellena was destined to be a nun, so he hopes she does not have too holy a name.

560–1 **stand to your arms**   Hellena demands that Willmore throw off his reputation for bungling and become her knight.

576 **spoils of a noble family**   the audience would recall that Charles II's bride was a Portuguese princess. Willmore is also sentimentally likened to the exiled prince in line 582.

594 **you cannot keep from me**   is it really Hellena's fortune that gives her the choice of husband?

604 **slave to't**   how does Behn use Don Pedro's surprising admission here?

616 sd *band* collar.

626 **in the Inquisition for Judaism**   imprisoned by the Catholic Church on suspicion of being a Jew.

631 **bays**   bay leaves used in cooking.

644 **doxy**   whore; he means Lucetta.

647 **apropos**   conveniently.

650 **cast of his office**   a sample of what he does.

652 **engagement**   battle.

657 **storms o'th' marriage bed**   as the play's hero, the final reflection on love and marriage is given to Willmore. The rhyming couplet looks ahead to the risk and storm of marriage and as such is true to the nature of this gay couple, avoiding sentimentality. Marriage, sanctioned by God and law, regulates desire and brings carnival to an end.

Epilogue

The epilogue has a similar hectoring tone to the prologue. What dramatic and political purpose does it have?

5 **conventicling**   illegal meeting of religious dissenters. Behn suggests that Puritans are so fashionable and their opinions so important they won't like her play about Cavaliers in a Catholic setting. She is being sarcastic of course.

7 **That mutinous tribe**   Puritans.

12 **spirit moves**   Puritans claimed to be guided by the holy spirit.

13 **maggot**   someone of strange fancies; theatre audiences are as hard to please as religious dissenters.

14 **canting**   hypocritical.

20 **the old Blackfriars way**   old-fashioned plays like those staged at the theatre at Blackfriars, pulled down in 1655.

21 **o'er bamboo**   over a walking stick.

30 **sparks**   fops who consider themselves wits.

35 **the half-crown spare**   save the money (for a theatre ticket).

39 **dammee**   damn me; Cavaliers and wits were known for their swearing and nicknamed 'Dammes'.

42 **Nokes, or Tony Leigh**   both acted in Behn's plays in the Duke's Company.

Postscript

This is an example of Behn's defence to the charge of plagiarism.

3 *Thomaso*   the source play (see 'The Source Play *Thomaso*', page 182).

12 **Spartan**   said to be clever at hiding what they have done.

13–14 **the sign of Angellica**   a reference that has attracted attention from feminist critics, who see it as Behn's acknowledgement of her need to sell her talents in the marketplace like a whore.

15–16 *The Novella*   Behn admits that she has taken ideas from Richard Brome's comedy of 1632.

17 **bating**   except for.

25 **especially of our sex**   this phrase was added at a later stage. Behn may have decided to make a clear reference to her gender once her authorship of the play became known.

28 **Virgil**   when a work is published anonymously, others may claim it as theirs. Legend suggests that this happened to Virgil.

Interpretations

Spectacle and intimacy: Inside a restoration theatre

Restoration theatres had interiors that were small and intimate. After the wide spaces of the Elizabethan stage, it was a novelty for actors and audience to be so close together. Here are some facts and figures about restoration theatres.

- The Dorset Garden Theatre held about 1200 people.
- A typical stage would have been about 60 feet wide with a depth of 140 feet.
- The forestage jutted out from the curtain line about 20 feet into the pit. This was where most of the play's action took place. As there were doors on either side, characters could indicate a change of scene or time by simply leaving through one door and re-entering at another.
- Most of the scenery movement took place behind the proscenium arch and did not get in the way of the actors.
- The doors from the forestage had balconies above them, providing an upper acting area.
- The theatre's central seating area, the pit, was filled with backless benches. These seats cost about half a crown (two shillings and sixpence).
- Tiered boxes enclosed the pit on three sides. At about four shillings, these seats were the most expensive in the house.
- Ladies tended to favour the boxes, while men were happy with the more intimate atmosphere of the pit.
- There were two galleries at the rear of the auditorium; these held the cheapest seats at a shilling each.
- Plays began at about 3.30 pm and ran for about three hours.

Theatre audiences enjoyed the novelty of representational scenery painted on flats, wings and backdrops. Machines were installed to move the flats into place by means of three or four grooves on each side of the stage floor. The painted wings were arranged on the slant, and were stationary. From the auditorium they appeared to recede upstage towards a vanishing point, creating an illusion of depth. Alternatively, by closing the space between the moveable flats, a shallower stage space could be created. Scene settings could be changed easily by drawing back one pair of flats to reveal another pair behind, and the spaces between the grooves were large enough to allow room for setting furniture and placing actors in tableaux.

Playwrights now had the visual techniques to divide plays into scenes without interrupting the action. Actors no longer needed to move offstage or out of their imaginary location once their dialogue had finished; instead, the scenery moved to relocate them where they stood, thus increasing the pace of the play.

Watching the scene changes became part of the spectacle of theatre. Matching borders, also set in grooves, provided further framing devices. The effect would have been to produce a multi-

The Dorset Garden Theatre, venue of the Duke's Company, held about 1200 people

layered set suggesting depth and perspective; a painted scene on the back wall of the stage added to the illusion of depth. Heavy stage properties, such as Lucetta's bed in III.iii, could be raised through a large, mechanically operated trap-door, in an upstage position. There was a curtain, but it was used only at the start of the play.

The Dorset Garden Theatre was unusual for its time in being able to lighten and darken its acting space; the stage and auditorium were both brightly lit by candles and lamps hanging in chandeliers from the centre of the ceiling and the side walls. In general, unreliable lighting was a good reason for placing the actors on the forestage where their facial expressions could be seen. They could in turn see the audience, which made for some interesting exchanges! Darkness was more reliably suggested through dialogue. The forestage had footlights in a long trough that could be raised or lowered to light the actors. With all this design ingenuity, it is not surprising that spectacle, movement and costume were as vital to the audience's experience of theatre as the dialogue. Looking had become an intense experience.

Plays usually ran for between eight and ten performances, with profits from the third night going to the playwright. The companies operated a repertory system, rotating a large number of plays, finding this the best way to keep audiences coming back on a regular basis. It was not unheard of for actors to lose concentration and slip into lines from the previous night's play!

Activity

Discuss Behn's use of the stage space to explore gender issues in *The Rover*.

Discussion

1   The spaces in which Behn places her characters – either free or confined – emphasize their unequal positions within the patriarchal system. Don Pedro hypocritically confines his sisters to guard their virtue, while he departs for the carnival streets (see I.i.71). The sisters escape. Their decision to *ramble* has its hazards, but serves their purpose better than Angellica's balcony. This

elevated space can be both a vantage point and a confinement. The courtesan avoids the mobility of the carnival streets, preferring to present an illusion of unattainable beauty instead (see II.i.134, 170, 190, 258). When her plans backfire, she lacks the resourcefulness to compete for Willmore's hand. Hellena, by contrast, is quick to mimic the male language and demeanour of the carnival streets.

2 The gull Blunt is the only male character to suffer entrapment in a farcical reversal of a seduction scene. He descends through a trap-door from Lucetta's bedroom into a sewer (see III.iii.32). Behn uses the discovery space to subvert the audience's expectations; instead of a beautiful woman they are surprised to encounter Blunt, the play's least prepossessing character (see III.iv and IV.v). Behn uses sword fights and chases on the forestage to mock male behaviour. The men squabble over women, mistake each other's identity and rely on violence to resolve their differences (see I.ii.114; II.i.220, 261; III.v.97; III.vi.60; IV.ii.41, 107).

3 Florinda is the character most menaced by her decision to enter the carnival streets. Occasionally Behn frames her in a window where she is secure but confined (see I.ii.35). There is much stage business around keys, windows and doors connected with this character. Once she leaves Don Pedro's 'protection', her troubles multiply. She unlocks her garden door to admit her lover and unwittingly lets in the would-be rapist Willmore (see III.v). She is passed like an object from one man to another during a staged duel supposedly for her hand (see IV.ii). Separated from her women friends she stumbles into Blunt's apartment towards the risk of gang rape (see IV.v.29). She is forced to negotiate these spaces alone by constant planning and frenetic movement. By contrast the male characters, usually in a gang, simply step through or break down any barrier they encounter (see V.i.37). Hellena, also separated from female support at the end of the play, fares better as she is in male disguise (see IV.ii.217).

Actors and acting style

Some of London's most famous actors relished their parts in *The Rover*, retaining them for long periods of time. William Smith, a leading actor of the Duke's Company, first played Willmore. As a veteran Cavalier and Stuart loyalist, he brought an authenticity and élan to a character partly meant to be a flattering representation of the king. The part of Hellena was played by Elizabeth Barry, mistress of John Wilmot, the Earl of Rochester. We can see the distinctions between art and life blurring here as parts are played by actors whose real lives resemble those of their characters. This was just the kind of topicality and stylishness that would have made the play a sensation. Note the deliberate echo in the names Wilmot and Willmore. The rise of the celebrity actor had begun.

The roles of Belvile and Florinda were played by Thomas Betterton and his wife Mary. Betterton was usually cast as the rake in Duke's Theatre comedies. There are moments in *The Rover* when one could ask whether the faithful Belvile has a dual nature (beautiful and vile, as suggested by his name?). Angellica was played by the famous beauty Anne Quin, who had a talent for playing passionate characters of tragic stature. Blunt was played by Cave Underhill, who tended to be cast when a comic part required some menace.

Everyone wanted to enjoy the spectacle of seeing women on stage, not least the king, who exercised his royal prerogative by seducing a number of them. Playwrights now had incentives to write great parts for women, and the actors reigned supreme in this new theatre. It was not unknown to cast a play before it was written and then fashion it as a showcase for a particular actor's style. The novelty of the situation gave playwrights excellent opportunities to explore sexual themes with a degree of realism not seen before. A woman writer was at an obvious advantage here in working collaboratively with the women in the company. These were often recruited from the poorer groups in society and wages were low; with its long-established links to prostitution, an acting career seldom attracted 'respectable' women.

For actors who wished to succeed, a substantial period of training lay ahead. Many parts required them to play aristocrats, which meant intensive training in elocution, deportment and fashionable manners. In the late seventeenth century, the upper classes identified themselves by strict codes of etiquette, and these had to be mastered to make the play world believable to the audience.

A realistic acting style was employed for comedies, although a modern audience would not recognize it as such. We expect and value naturalism and psychological realism from actors today. The restoration audience expected a varied and codified range of tones and gestures. Behn's stage directions to her actors in II.ii.52–177 of *The Rover* are an example of the method: the dialogue between Willmore and Angellica, perhaps because neither really understands the other, has a range of asides, changes in tone and formalized gestures and movement.

For an ambitious woman a career on the stage meant there was always the possibility that a wealthy admirer would offer marriage. In reality the offer of becoming someone's mistress was more likely. Men were often invited backstage, and clearly offers of 'protection' were made, even pressed upon women. With judgement and luck, though, a woman perhaps born into poverty could achieve a reasonable degree of autonomy over her life choices.

The 'breeches part' for the female lead was written into many plays of the period. It was a great and enduring favourite with audiences, particularly men. Many playwrights pandered to the desire to see a good deal more of the female lead's body than low-cut bodices afforded. The 'breeches part' meant that Nell Gwyn became famous for her attractive legs as well as her face. Cross-dressing was by no means a new phenomenon on the English stage; Shakespeare had used it to bring complexity to ideas about gender and identity in plays such as *As You Like It*, written about 1598–1600. Restoration playwrights did not match Shakespeare's depth and subtlety; this was not their purpose. The first English women to go on the stage were positioned as sexual objects by male playwrights and audiences. Their presence on stage generally confirmed rather than subverted social prejudices against women.

Nell Gwyn, one of the first English women to gain recognition for her stage performances, especially as one half of the 'gay couple'

One troubling feature of the arrival of women on stage was the fascination with rape plots. They became a major feature of most tragedies written in the years after 1660. A rape plot was cynically seen as a way of presenting a virtuous woman in a lewd and sexualized way; her clothes could be torn and flesh exposed. The aftermath of a rape made for a voyeuristic tableau, the use of the discovery space making the revelation all the more shocking. In the typical comedy plot, a lustful chase with women as the quarry would usually replace the rape plot. Behn is therefore unusual in keeping the threat of rape just below the surface of several scenes in *The Rover*. It is a threat that does not abate until the women are safely aligned to the men they are to marry.

Activity

Read IV.ii and consider whether Behn has subverted the 'breeches part' formula.

Discussion

Male disguise does mean that Hellena can carry out her plan without the threat of assault. She aims to vex Willmore in the style of the 'gay couple' and to wrest him away from her rival. There is nothing new here except for the suggestion that she does manoeuvre Willmore one step closer to marriage by the end of the scene. However, Willmore claims he is anxious to escape Angellica without Hellena's intervention, thus undermining her efforts. Male disguise does not protect her from the humiliation of Willmore's clear desire to quit the presence of both women and seek out the new 'lady' Hellena has created.

Hellena does succeed in releasing Angellica from her self-consuming passion for Willmore. This allows the courtesan's revenge plot to take shape in the play's final scene. There is some serious conversation between the two unlikely female allies, but it is comically upstaged by Willmore's preening. As they warm to their theme, however, their combined verbal assault does amount to a scourging of Willmore in comic style. Whereas Angellica's position is weakened by wearing her heart on her sleeve, Hellena has the advantage of male disguise; she speaks 'on behalf of' a lady who is really herself.

When Willmore's gaze falls upon Hellena's face he does at least recognize her as his gipsy. Hellena can hardly be flattered, as his recognition is of the gipsy mask not the 'real' woman. His stinging verbal insults could be interpreted as 'gay couple' repartee, but there is no reply from Hellena to complete the exchange and make it witty rather than insulting. Power relations in the scene soon shift and Willmore sends a strong message to Hellena that no promise of marriage has been or will be made. However, when the moment of public disavowal comes he equivocates by sending a crucial signal that marriage with the right woman might be possible. The scene is most notable for Willmore's confident unmasking of Hellena and his reductive representation of her as little more than a puppet. If we compare the unmasking to Willmore's earlier appropriation of

Angellica's picture, then Behn is urging her audience to see these women in common cause against the rake's power. This and other moments in the plot when women support each other have no precedent in the source play. Hellena is still dressed as a boy when Willmore agrees to marry her. Is Behn signalling that Hellena's power is like that of a man, since she negotiates her own marriage settlement? Is Behn interested in a further questioning of Willmore's machismo by the subtle suggestion of homosexual desire?

Historical records tell us that cross-dressing was one of the fashionable pastimes at the Stuart court. In Behn's hands, a risqué pastime for the rich becomes a means of exploring women's drive to freedom of choice in the marriage market.

Restoration comedy as a genre

Restoration comedies were written and performed from about 1660 to 1700. The genre is associated with wit, sexual explicitness and intricate plots. These comedies held society, its fads and fashions up to ridicule. Playwrights all had topical and witty things to say about desire, love and the marriage market. Some made comic intrigue their focus, for others it was sex, gulling or cuckoldry.

Comedy of manners was one of the most popular sub-genres. These comedies depicted the fashionable and sophisticated codes of behaviour that were the hallmark of England's upper classes. Appearance and reputation were all; truth and morality came a long way second. The plots typically hinged on characters driven by lust and greed, whose goal was to make the most advantageous match possible through negotiating the marriage market. Their moral disorder was disguised by their cleverness with language and their powers to seduce. This cynical focus on infidelity and gender politics was partly prompted by the arrival of women on the English stage. Women were considered naturally lustful and deceitful, so men 'needed their wits about them'. More seriously, the loss of a sense of natural order and social harmony caused by civil war may have undermined people's faith in personal relationships.

There were usually two character types in the comedy of manners. There were the attractive young aristocrats who understood and could manipulate the codes of acceptable behaviour; pitted against them were the rising middle-class pretenders who wished to appear fashionable and witty but were exposed as fools operating out of their depth.

Behn was not writing to this specific formula; instead, she offers a mixture of styles and moods. Her audience would have recognized Belvile and Florinda as the constant but unexciting pair whose path to true love is thwarted by outside forces. Contrasted to them are the witty, more independent lovers Willmore and Hellena, with time to banter and tease their way to a choice of partner in marriage. Theatre audiences came to refer to such well-matched lovers as 'the gay couple'. The king's mistress Nell Gwyn was the first to play one half of such a couple. Through 'the gay couple' the complexities of commitment could be explored, while the audience could enjoy the spectacle of pleasure deferred. Whatever the lovers' journey, the plots always achieved closure by pairing up the main characters with a reasonable measure of contentment all round. *The Rover* broadly follows the expected conventions in this respect. The difference lies in Behn's questioning of the terms of marriage from a consistently argued female perspective.

Activity

Find examples of Willmore and Hellena acting the 'gay couple' role. How far is Behn successful in using the device as a means of exploring women's choices in the marriage market?

Discussion

You might choose I.ii.147–231. Here, Hellena takes the initiative in their first encounter, singling out Willmore for his handsome appearance. He hints at wanting sex without paying for it. She wishes to explore whether he will be constant in love. The differences based on gender and circumstances are immediately clear. Her virginity seems unassailable, but Willmore uses some very persuasive arguments to talk her out of this position. She counters by revealing her libertine credentials, declaring she has a strong appetite for love. Can Hellena reconcile these contradictory positions? Who or what determines that her virginity remains secure in a play in which her sister's is constantly under threat? She arouses and frustrates male desire yet avoids being punished for this audacity. Hellena uses bawdy to usurp or at least compete for the male position in her encounters with Willmore. This proves to be a successful and temporarily liberating strategy.

In III.i.162–331, it is clear that Hellena sees through Willmore's seductive language, which is just as well as she must resist it if she is to survive with her honour intact. By this second encounter she knows he is serially unfaithful but persists in her bid for nothing less than his undivided love. She moves the debate forward by fashioning herself as inconstant and cynical. It is at this point that she chooses to reveal her face. Her ploy is to suggest her libertine tendencies while maintaining that her virginity remains unassailable, and she chooses to reveal her face when she can use her beauty to best advantage. We do not know whether she is gratified or offended by Willmore's expressions of admiration for what he sees. His lavish praise reduces her to a stock set of features of female excellence. Through exchanges such as these, Behn illustrates the hazards for women who dare to *ramble*.

Who were the audience?

Theatre admission charges were high in relation to income, but this does not seem to have prevented people from most social classes flocking to the theatre. There were aristocrats, fawners on the aristocracy, a substantial middle class and a vocal group of fops and critics. Samuel Pepys's diary condescendingly refers to the large numbers of 'cits', apprentices and 'mean' types seated in the galleries. Only the Puritans stayed away from theatres on principle. As a religious group they were frequently ridiculed in the plays, being portrayed as mercenary hypocrites determined to spoil innocent pleasures.

Audiences were highly sociable, rowdy, even disorderly.

Being seen and socializing with others, including the actors, was more important than paying attention to the play. Pepys refers to frequent scenes of disorder in the playhouses in the 1660s. He also records his dismay at going backstage and experiencing the breaking of theatrical illusion. The female members of the company clearly appeared more beautiful when candle-lit and inaccessible. Other commentators complained about the all-too-obtrusive prostitutes, seeing a chance to do some business, whose voices could be heard above the actors.

Audiences relished the familiar, the tried and tested, in their visits to the theatre. They knew the repertoire, the actors and the best parts. They were not bored by predictable plots and stereotyped characters. Greater familiarity meant a greater level of spectator pleasure. Night scenes of danger and threat, chases, mistaken identity, songs, letters and exhibitions of sword play were all well-loved and expected conventions. We can see Behn employing most of these in *The Rover*.

William Hogarth's print *The Laughing Audience* (1733), though half a century later than Behn's time, shows the audience's liveliness and social variety

Activity

Discuss Behn's use of topical and patriotic referencing.

Discussion

1   Behn intends to flatter the Stuart king and court by presenting the poverty-stricken Cavaliers in a noble light. Willmore's acquaintance with the exiled prince blends fact with fiction (see I.ii.74). His attire is similar to that worn by the prince on his escape from the battle of Worcester (see II.i.4 and II.ii.26). It is seen as right and fitting that the Cavaliers should have their fortunes made by alliances with Spanish noblewomen (see V.i.575, 582).

2   England's long rivalry with Catholic Spain meant that Behn could not fail to strike the right note with her mockery of the Spanish. The Spanish are seen to marry off their women to old men and generally treat them harshly. Abroad they are heartless colonizers, enslavers and spoil takers (see I.i.75, 97, 156). The younger Spaniards, Don Pedro and Don Antonio, are vengeful but inept fighters; the English rout them easily in a just cause. Blunt's claim that Angellica's picture is *ours by conquest* is suitably jingoistic (see II.i.291, 295). Spaniards lend their name to husband-murder, wife-stealing and theft of patriotic relics (see III.ii.16, III.iii.43). This sustained satire concludes with the phallic joke about the length of Spanish swords, their lustful brush with incest and the outlandish nature of their dress (see V.i.115, 123, 616).

3   Behn compares male squabbling over women with larger European disagreements over territory and allegiances. Both women and land can be the objects of conquest. There are brief references to Spanish, Dutch and French territorial disputes (see I.ii.145, II.i.292). At Pamplona only the English Cavalier Belvile shows courtly valour amid the fog of war. The French soldiers threaten rape (see I.i.57, 83).

4   Social snobbery about Essex is not a new phenomenon; Londoners would have enjoyed the portrayal of rural Essex as dull and tasteless. Blunt's behaviour as the Essex calf is the reverse of all that is fashionable (see I.ii.136, 330–340, II.i.44, 91).

5   There is much generalizing banter about sexual attitudes linked to national identity. Englishmen, though lusty, will avoid paying for sex. Women easily make fools of them because of

their immense vanity (see I.ii.239). At least they are not
cuckolds like the Italians (see I.ii.129). The satire at the expense
of the English is predictably gentler than that against their
European rivals.

The source play *Thomaso*

In common with many restoration playwrights, Behn drew on an
existing play for her source material for *The Rover*. Thomas
Killigrew's *Thomaso* was published in 1664. It was a closet drama
(designed for reading rather than performance), in two parts and
ten acts. Its unwieldy length confirms that it was never intended
for the public stage. Behn drew extensively on this source text and
her debt to it is considerable. She used characters, scenes, even
pieces of dialogue from *Thomaso*. But Behn does not plagiarize;
she transforms or subverts the source material into a new
creation. She was, however, being disingenuous when she claimed
that she had merely 'stolen some hints' from *Thomaso* and that
Angellica's sign was 'the only stolen object' from that play (see
postscript to *The Rover*).

In *Thomaso* Killigrew attacks Puritanism and celebrates
patriarchy. Behn exposes the hypocrisy of both value systems in
The Rover. Killigrew's hero is an implausible mix of libertine and
faithful lover, embodying the male virtues of honour and
chivalry in love and war. Behn created the rake Willmore from
this material, making him a free agent, witty and attractive to
women. He is also a self-seeking serial seducer and unreliable
bungler. His behaviour is closely scrutinized, even ridiculed by
Behn, and he is as much the butt of others' wit as he is witty
himself. Behn gives the chivalric side of Thomaso to Belvile, but
then promptly laughs at his inability to make the grade. By this
reshaping she makes the gender relationships in the play more
problematic than in the source play.

Activity

Behn's revision of Angellica's role is an important departure from the source play. She cut the character's scenes, but strengthened her stage presence in those she retained. Analyse one of Angellica's speeches and consider the issues Behn explores through this character.

Discussion

You may have chosen IV.ii.449–465. Here, Behn explores Angellica's humiliation and her motivation for revenge in a blank-verse soliloquy. Her rhetorical flourishes and metaphorical conceits suggest the tragic genre. Angellica likens love to a disease from which she longs to be cured. She expresses her jealousy, anger and misery in a manner that sets a reflective tone in this otherwise fast-paced play. She does not understand why her famed beauty is not enough to keep her lover loyal; when she refers to her charms she speaks in a Petrarchan style, and this self-fashioning as the mistress in a Petrarchan sonnet is an illusion that does not stand up to reality. No amount of Petrarchan conceits will make up for the fact that she lacks chastity. There is no mockery here, rather irony and empathy for her impossible situation.

Against this ideal self-image she places the stark knowledge of her *name* and *infamy*. These are unassailable facts that, under patriarchy, condemn her and offer her no second chance, as virginity cannot be reclaimed. Her *undoing* for which she seeks revenge could refer to her lost virginity, for which she may now blame all men. A more sympathetic interpretation would be that she means her awakening into love. This love is not acknowledged by patriarchy and is therefore the cause of her present misery. By adopting this speech style, Angellica seeks to move herself out of the realm of monetary exchange, but she does not perceive that she has merely substituted one set of linguistic terms for another that is equally restrictive.

Characters

The Rover's characters are English, Spanish and Italian. The English Cavaliers are sharing exile abroad, while the Spanish characters represent a ruling class enjoying the spoils of foreign conquest in Naples. The Italian characters occupy an underworld of criminality and prostitution.

Willmore

Willmore is the familiar rake figure of restoration comedy relocated from London to Naples. He tends to disrupt the plot rather than determine its course, which is unusual for the leading man. He can be open-hearted and loyal, and is a risk taker, quick to take up arms in the service of his friends. He can also be anarchic, self-seeking and menacing to women. Willmore's

Jeremy Irons as Willmore in the Royal Shakespeare Company's production at The Swan Theatre, 1986

promiscuous behaviour is presented as irrational, instinctive and either amusing or exasperating, depending on your point of view. He oscillates between active and passive stances in relation to the women characters. Although much of what he says is clichéd, the strength of his language lies in its variety and flexibility. He can summon the right register, tone and imagery to suit the situation, and it rarely fails him in his drive to control women. His status as hero of the play is severely undermined, however, by scenes where he appears the fool. Behn's fascination with and wary disapproval of the rake figure is evident in this ambiguous representation.

Activity

What does Behn achieve by comparing Willmore and Blunt?

Discussion

Behn juxtaposes scenes featuring these two characters to pose questions about the core attitudes of a libertine when he is without the advantages of a charming tongue and noble blood. In doing so Behn challenges the notion that the rake figure is every woman's fantasy. Examples of comparisons between Willmore and Blunt include the following.

- Both use overblown figurative language which can appear aggressive and pretentious (I.ii.40, 104).
- Both expect to have sex with a whore without paying for the service; both mistake virgins for whores or vice versa (II.i.78, III.v.77, 18).
- Blunt is the object of Lucetta's gaze and is deceived by it (I.ii.241), Willmore uses his gaze to dominate Angellica (II.ii.84) and Hellena (IV.ii.360).
- Willmore emerges from Angellica's bed with her money (III.i.133); Lucetta robs Blunt of all his valuables (III.iii.41). Later, Angellica and Hellena combine forces to gull Willmore (IV.ii.218). Both seek to justify attempted rape; Willmore argues subtly (III.v), while Blunt rages at the entire sex (IV.v). Blunt's loathing for the object of his lusts is more obvious than Willmore's.

- Both change costume towards the end of the play. Willmore's new outfit suggests a readiness for marriage even though it is paid for by a whore's earnings (IV.ii.96). Blunt's clothes reinforce his status as gull (V.i.616).

Hellena

Hellena's libertine desires and contempt for patriarchy are immediately clear to us. Her journey to marriage is conducted through a series of disguises; by costume or reference she is nun, rambler, gipsy, fortune teller, heiress and boy. Her language is as versatile as her costumes. It is unusual for a woman's part to be written with such a variety of registers; she can be bawdy, punning, witty, satirical, argumentative and seductive as the situation demands, and in this she is a match for Willmore. She arouses desire in him and maintains it at a peak by constantly shifting her self-presentation. Clearly it is not enough for a woman to be chaste in word and deed in order to prosper; in this amoral climate, a more active strategy is needed.

Angellica Bianca

Angellica is the sexually transgressive woman who does not see why men should have things all their own way. Some feminist critics have been intrigued by the possible link between Angellica and Aphra Behn. Are their shared initials significant? Like Angellica, Behn had to face the hazard of selling her wares in a fickle marketplace, holding up her 'product' for the speculative gaze of the 'consumer'. Angellica suffers a humiliating defeat in Act V, however, and it doesn't seem likely that Behn would have fully identified with the character's rather short-sighted attitudes and readiness to fall into a trap.

But Angellica is vigorous in her efforts to reposition herself in the sexual marketplace. She brings intrigue and complexity to the stereotype of the courtesan. Why does she fail despite this brilliance? Perhaps the clue lies in that most theatrical of gestures, her use of self-representation in the shape of three pictures. Her pictures idealize and fix her charms. Where Hellena is flexible and pro-active, she is passive and static. She objectifies herself in her bid to turn her main asset, her beauty, into a power base from which she can challenge those who want her to submit to the patriarchal system. Her male clients are at liberty to gaze upon and exploit her image for their own gratification, and she cannot control their responses, which include violent ones.

When she finally appears on stage her appearance can only disappoint after the expectations created by the pictures. Behn may have intended that the pictures should remind her audience of the way women were treated as commodities within the theatre at large. As the king's representative on stage, Willmore is at liberty to help himself to the best and most beautiful of women; this privilege is signalled on stage by his daring theft of

The 'sign of Angellica' in a production at Willamette University, Salem, Oregon

the picture. Behn is reminding her audience that in the worst examples of exploitation in the theatre, women were paraded on stage for male pleasure and could be purchased for sex.

There can be no satisfactory resolution to Angellica's predicament, since the patriarchal system will not allow it. Had she murdered Willmore the law would have punished her by death. Such a fate confirms the negative stereotype of the tragic, self-sacrificing heroine. Instead she curses Willmore, retains her dignity and departs to resume the role of courtesan, the only one open to her. For the play to achieve its happy ending she has to be absent from the stage, as her strong feelings cannot be soothed away. Her departure contributes to the uneasy truce with which the play closes.

Activity

What does Behn achieve by blurring the distinctions between Hellena and Angellica?

Discussion

- Both characters express and act upon strong desires. The convent girl is the worldly pragmatist, whereas the whore is unusually romantic (see I.i.141 and II.ii.87).
- Both have financial support from the same man. Hellena inherits her fortune from her uncle, the Spanish general who was Angellica's lover. This ensures that however badly Willmore behaves towards the two women, he cannot lose: Angellica rewards him with the general's money and he can expect to pocket Hellena's inheritance on marrying her.
- Both Hellena and Angellica understand the value of their beauty; they display it or withhold it strategically. Sound financial considerations help Willmore choose between the two, even though the hard facts are disguised in the comic game of chase. The virgin with the fortune can bargain well in a marriage market in which the reformed courtesan has no stake.
- Money aside, Willmore clearly admires Hellena's mix of sexual potential and cerebral wit compared to Angellica's emotional fire.
- Angellica has lost her desire by turning her body into a commodity

(see II.i.140, 158). When she falls in love with Willmore she can only express her awakened desire in terms of the Petrarchan mistress, finding it impossible to let go of her need for dominance. This fantasy positions Willmore in a subservient role as her lover (see IV.ii.152, 161). By contrast, Hellena offers equality in any possible relationship with him.

Belvile and Florinda

This pair of faithful lovers provides the norm for romantic relationships in the play. Behn takes a fresh look at this stereotypical yet popular pairing. Belvile has heroic attributes; his gallantry towards Florinda at Pamplona is a typical motif of heroic drama, and his change of allegiance from France to Spain is highly appropriate in a courtly lover who puts his mistress first. Audiences would have read the action as being in tune with the sentiments of his prince, the exiled Charles II who, in time of war, when French support was withdrawn, negotiated a treaty with Spain in 1656.

However, like his comrade Willmore, Belvile is presented as unreliable and flawed. He makes a poor showing of defending Florinda's honour and securing her hand in marriage during a carnival atmosphere that should have made it easy to dare all for love. Florinda is unusually active in seeking him out and plotting to achieve his supposed protection.

Belvile can talk about violence as naturally as he can talk about undying love. If *The Rover* were a true romantic comedy, Belvile would be the main focus of attention, but he constantly loses ground to his subordinate in rank, Willmore. He fails to control Willmore's lust, which is as much a threat to women as that shown by the French soldiers at Pamplona.

Activity

Discuss the way Behn contrasts courtly language with comic mishap in Belvile's role in *The Rover*.

Discussion

- Behn mocks the mismatch between this Cavalier colonel's language and actions throughout the play. Whereas the 'gay couple' communicate with each other intensively and exclusively, Belvile has little to say to Florinda directly. This is a courtship of messages, assignations and misunderstood linguistic and visual clues.

- Belvile's language is threadbare and clichéd. His desire is fed by letters, and by being thwarted and separated from the loved object. He uses religious imagery to suggest his adoration and honourable intentions towards Florinda (see I.ii.36, 284, 301, 386).

- He talks of love in absolute terms yet fails to recognize Florinda on several occasions (see I.ii.250 and III.i.332). Belvile finally recognizes her cries for help from the garden where he is meant to have met with her (see III.v.88). He responds to this series of mishaps by playing the woeful lover who passively curses his fate (see III.vi.12).

- His desire to fight for Florinda's hand in the role of valiant knight is undermined by the mistaken-identity plot. Florinda fails to recognize him as her rescuer because he is disguised as his enemy Don Antonio. His attempt at duelling is foiled by a farcical series of mishaps that leave him enraged and helpless (see IV.ii.101). Florinda's final rescue from the threat of gang rape is achieved by Valeria, when her quick thinking diverts Don Pedro's attention. It is this minor female character who hastens them to their marriage (see V.i.155, 170).

Costume and masked disguise

In *The Rover* costume is not linked to social class but to wider issues of interpretation and power. Behn orders costume changes for her heroines whenever a change of scene allows. For Angellica there are fewer changes, emphasizing her lack of options.

The rake figure was usually elegant, fastidious and urban. By contrast, Willmore's costume attracts comment because of its ordinariness, its smell, and its associations with the docks and the sea; it bears witness to his adventures with the prince. His innate aristocratic breeding means he is a match for the Spanish nobles, however, despite his humble clothing. In II.i.289 Frederick draws attention to his bloody shirt. The spectacle of his blood seems intimate and physical in this world of disguise. To the periwigged men in the audience, the king included, Willmore's natural and rough appearance must have been striking and attractive.

With the exception of Willmore, Behn's characters are often masked – carnival requires it. The intrigue and mistaken-identity plot work through the light-hearted confusion of the mask. Masking enables a character to look at others without being identified or seduced by an exchange of looks. The look in its overt and concentrated form becomes a *gaze*, a word Behn uses several times in her stage directions. This is linked to desire and the will to dominate. When our attention is drawn to the gaze, the different points of view of the two sexes are emphasized. Hellena avoids Willmore's controlling gaze by masking herself.

In the 1660s, respectable women started to wear masks when they attended the theatre, and the fashion caught on quickly. Women enjoyed the freedom of movement that disguise afforded them; without a mask a woman's reputation might be compromised in such a public and notorious place. However, prostitutes soon caught on to the fashion and started to solicit for customers from behind masks at the playhouses. In an ironic reversal, respectable women with masks began to be mistaken for prostitutes and had to abandon the practice. The subversive potential of the masked woman had become clear.

Seventeenth-century audiences were sophisticated in reading the meaning of masks. At a simple level they offer anonymity and freedom of speech and movement: masked characters can gull others while maintaining a strong tactical position for themselves. But the mask may signal an obvious hypocrisy and therefore render the wearer harmless to all but the most foolish. The mask may also conceal a truth that could be threatened by a hostile environment.

Activity

Make notes for an essay on costume, gazing, and masking in *The Rover*.

Discussion

- We first notice the mask in Don Pedro's preparations for carnival (I.i.71). Willmore's subtle language is a different kind of mask. His only costume change emphasizes his nobility and is therefore not a disguise (IV.ii.96).
- In I.ii masqueraders signify who they are by papers pinned to their breasts (see I.ii.90). If they are whores, at least they control their representation to prospective clients.
- The same scene shows Hellena's freedom through disguise, which contrasts with Blunt's fantasy of male control where the masked woman (Florinda) is cast as a whore, having no say in her representation (see IV.v.29, 57). Also, Willmore's justification of rape, based on interpreting Florinda's state of undress (see III.v) is relevant.
- The Lucetta/Blunt plot strand explores gaze reversal (see I.ii.235, 241). The two Blunt discovery scenes show Behn directing the audience's gaze and making them aware of its objectifying power at the same time (see III.iv and IV.v).
- For Willmore's masterly use of the gaze to subdue Angellica see II.i.108, 241 and II.ii.84.
- Good contrasts to these scenes are Hellena's decision to unmask herself when it suits her, and the response this provokes in Willmore (see III.i.235, 243 and IV.ii.361).
- For comic variations on these motifs refer to Willmore's clumsy unmasking of Belvile before Don Pedro (see IV.ii.100), and Don Antonio and Blunt in states of undress (see III.iii.7, III.iv.1, IV.i.12, and V.i.1).
- Angellica uses the mask rarely. When she does it is too late to empower her to settle her grievances with Willmore (see V.i.239, 254).

• **Willmore is unable to 'fix' Hellena's image because of her many disguises. Florinda's vulnerability is marked by her state of undress, something that we do not see in Hellena's costuming (see I.ii.147, IV.ii.217 and V.i.447).**

Carnival

Carnival time was enjoyed as a short feast before the observance of Lent in Catholic Europe. The tradition of Lent was associated with a period of penance, self-control and abstinence lasting 40 days and nights. At the end of this period Christ's resurrection was celebrated at Easter. Seventeenth-century Catholics abstained from eating meat and having sexual intercourse during Lent. Puritan rule was not unlike a prolonged period of Lent following the English Civil War.

Carnival, by contrast, celebrated free and self-indulgent behaviour. It meant liberation from the restrictions of social class, gender and morality. The desires of the flesh could be fully indulged, and the privileges of rank and power could be challenged by those with the courage and desire to do so.

Carnival mixes social classes, genders and nationalities and the streets are its proper setting. Many of Behn's characters are displaced outsiders taking advantage of the temporary suspension of rules. Naples itself is displaced as an Italian city under Spanish rule, but apart from some scattered references to the contemporary political situation, there is a rather non-specific feel to the location, although Italians were renowned for their pre-Lenten carnivals.

From the very start of the play when Don Pedro dons his masking habit in front of his sisters, even interior scenes seem to be invaded by a carnival atmosphere. Time and place are in flux; energy and movement set the tone. The play's energetic pace is supported by its brief references to passing time. Speed is of the essence. In keeping with the comic genre, the characters hasten towards love or humiliation at a reckless pace. The references to time usually refer to yesterday or tomorrow, and they point to a very concentrated framework for the action.

Characters from the 'high' and 'low' comic styles are mixed, and serious themes can deepen the mood as the plot lines intertwine. Some critics have argued that the carnival setting marks only a temporary departure from the status quo; Behn allows her characters a 'holiday' from the patriarchal system in a space where unconventional behaviour is acceptable (presumably to those who wield real power); *The Rover* can therefore never be truly subversive.

Language

Behn is interested in the way characters use language to exercise power over others while disguising themselves. She gives them dialogue that parodies familiar styles, mocks pretensions and dissembles about the truth. Her main characters are given distinctive registers and emotional tones. She suggests the spontaneity and energy of colloquial speech by mixing plain speaking with simple metaphorical references to everyday matters such as food and trading.

Behn writes in prose for the most part, switching to blank verse to suggest intimate revelation or dramatic intensity. Behn gives Hellena a number of lines that Killigrew had originally written for men in the source play. The dialogue in I.i proves that a woman can carry an important scene; here Behn uses Hellena to show that the centre of the play will be female guile rather than rakish wit.

Hellena's use of expletives is very unusual for a woman of her social class in the seventeenth century. Words like *death* and *pox* would have sounded far bolder and more shocking to her audience than they appear to modern ears. Hellena curses well: *Hang me* suggests the pirate rather than the noblewoman. She makes strong sexual references and puns, such as hoping that a suitably attractive man will *spoil [her] devotion*. A man she certainly intends to ensnare, *though I ask first*. There is a boldness, clarity and immediacy to phrases such as these. She can employ the prestige forms of rhetoric too, notably in relation to boasting of her physical charms. She highlights their importance wittily through a series of inversions of adjective–noun word order in this example: *A humour gay? A beauty passable? A vigour desirable?* (I.i.49–50).

She can be colloquial, using expressions that shock with their punning barbs: *increase her bags* leaves little to the imagination in the context. She blurs the distinction between religious and sexual experience with expressions such as: *I'll have a saint of my own to pray to shortly, if I like any that dares venture on me* (I.i.171–2).

Here is a woman using language to resist the will of a father and brother. It is typical of the way wit is relied upon as women's first line of defence. With word choices such as *venture* she takes the argument to the enemy, appropriating the language of commerce and risk, making it her own. There is a degree of deliberate suggestiveness in her language, with her call to *ramble* invoking a libertine desire usually associated with male characters. The fact that her virginity remains non-negotiable despite her 'loose' tongue marks her out as one of the play's most skilful strategists.

Willmore's dialogue is the most versatile of all. Its one constant is the tension between his changing modes of speech and the concealed motives of his sub-text. In common with all the Cavaliers, he uses the words *love* and *sex* interchangeably to suit his seduction strategy. Behn does not condemn his hypocrisy; her view seems to be that women must match him word for word, with the language of seduction being a necessary weapon in the mating game. Witty expression is not an indicator of truth, and there is no sense that an innate nobility of character shows itself naturally in a character's words. When Willmore makes remarks of a moral or passionate nature, for example, this is all part of his seduction plan: the sentiments are customized to work well with the particular woman he is addressing.

A comparison between the ways he addresses Hellena and Angellica illustrates the point. When women play Willmore at his own game, as Hellena does, it is questionable how far they are allowing themselves to be compromised. They risk more than he does since they do not have social power to fall back on. Hellena is at least better equipped than Florinda, whose language is full of earnest wishing and pleading. Such terms confirm her dependence on male protection.

Activity

Examine Behn's use of these semantic fields in *The Rover*:

1 nature, birds
2 cooking, eating
3 religion and sex
4 mercantile economy, trading.

Discussion

1 Willmore's use of natural imagery to represent his sex drive confirms his view that it is instinctive and irresistible. His tone becomes more humble and soothing compared to when he promotes his libertinism through bawdy (see III.i.347 and V.i.344, 484).
2 Images of cooking and eating explore male sexual appetite and its desire to 'consume' women's bodies. These images can be grotesque and ill-conceived, such as Blunt's talk of roasting and hogoes (I.ii.40) and his depiction of Belvile's appetite for women (IV.v.133). Food imagery can also be flirtatious and combative from the lips of the 'gay couple' (see I.ii.223, III.i.180 and V.i.494, 530). Hellena's verbal skill in exchanges like these means she avoids being 'eaten' by the voracious Willmore.
3 Male and female characters use religious imagery differently. For Willmore it is a means of sanctioning sexual licence (see I.ii.182 and II.ii.166). Hellena uses it to legitimize her desire for Willmore (see I.i.41, 171 and III.i.207, 317). In a major exchange when they first meet, Hellena counters his use of religious language word for word (I.ii.180). Angellica is represented by the Cavaliers as the object of a somewhat cynical male devotion, one that can easily

turn to desecration if thwarted (see I.ii.371). She in turn uses religious imagery to construct an unattainable image of herself.

4 Mercantile imagery locates the play within the context of England's growing wealth and sea power in the late seventeenth century. The economic system had undergone modernization to cope with the expansion in overseas trade. Coins had replaced barter and exchange as a means of trading. Men could now invest in commodities and shipping by buying shares and joining with others in part ownership of a company. Metaphor produces a correspondence between human beings, their bodies and a trading system that turns them into commodities to buy and sell. Such figurative language comes naturally to the play's male characters since they have the advantage when it comes to trading in sex (see I.ii.85 and II.i.107–131, 165). The play's 'back story', the siege of Pamplona and its associations with military prowess, gives way to the commerce of the streets. Women fare no better from this shift of emphasis in the way men run things. Willmore mounts a challenge to Angellica's strategy of pricing herself so highly as to be beyond most men's pockets. She wishes to be on the same footing as a wife, who is sole property of her husband. His logic is that he can purchase a part of the whole, or sell off shares in her to his comrades (see II.ii.71 and III.i.133).

The marriage market

Under seventeenth-century law a husband's rights in all matters domestic and economic were fully recognized at the expense of his wife's. Women had virtually no control over their property; rather a woman was her husband's property. In return for the surrender of her rights, a wife could expect the lifelong protection of her husband as long as she maintained her honour.

Libertine rakes such as Willmore took a different view. They saw the safeguarding of women's chastity as an obstacle to their pursuit of the pleasures of sexual freedom. Why should free will and the sex drive be reined in to serve the interests of property? Fidelity in marriage served only to safeguard the family bloodline by guaranteeing that any heirs born were legitimate sons and daughters. Such arrangements only benefited the ruling classes with land and property to pass on down the family line, the libertine argument maintained.

This is not a wholly liberated viewpoint; rather, it is a male viewpoint. Behn regretted that women were prevented from embracing libertine values in the same way as men. The risks were many: pregnancy, loss of honour and marriage prospects, and disinheritance. Women's opinions on the matter were neither sought nor tolerated. A woman's chastity, and her reputation for chastity referred to as her honour, were all that mattered in the marriage market; an economic value was thus placed upon a human one. Behn tackled the subject of arranged marriage in 11 of her plays; she understood what was at stake for women, turned into commodities to answer the needs of others.

The dilemma faced by Hellena in her search for a husband illustrates the pitfalls of the marriage market. Hellena chooses to enter into a marriage with Willmore knowing of his promiscuous and charlatan behaviour. Is this a comment on her character, on her choices, or on marriage itself? Behn wants her audience to see that if a monetary value is set upon virginity, marriage and prostitution are two sides of one coin.

In his negotiations with virgins and whores Willmore cleverly avoids taking part in the exchange economy that dominates the streets, even though he spends a lot of time talking about it. He has no money to pay with, yet the system rewards him with the love, bodies and money of the play's two most desirable women.

The play's historical context throws some light on the matter. The real marriage market of the restoration period had been altered by the social upheavals and uncertainties of war. The returning Cavalier exiles were largely of aristocratic stock, but some of them failed to recover the property and land that had been confiscated by Parliament. They found themselves in the novel position of being noblemen without estates. This made possible previously unlikely matches between noblemen and daughters of the newly enriched bourgeoisie, which sharpened competition for wives and placed an additional value on chastity. At the same time the place within the family of the wife and mother was being redefined. The family was becoming recognized as a sphere separate from that of public affairs, occupied by men. A small measure of autonomy, or at least a place where one might have opinions, was taking shape.

Behn provides space in the parallel world of carnival to show women outside both the bourgeois and libertine systems. Women seem to try on roles. Some they have not chosen, like that of nun, whore or domesticated woman; these they toy with and parody. Women tend to be more financially secure than men prior to making marriage contracts, and the connections between the women are significant; even women who are not acquainted seem to speak with one voice and work towards shared goals.

Sex and the body politic

Writers have often represented the human body as an analogy for the political state, or vice versa. Many correspondences can be found between them. The health of the state can be understood in terms of a healthy body whose parts work for the common good. Feminists have seen the threat of violence against women as a sign of 'sickness' in the body politic, because if one section of society is badly treated on grounds of sexual difference then the state has a malaise and will not prosper.

Behn daringly asks her audience to link Willmore's treatment of women to the king's guardianship of the state. In II.i Willmore is twice asked to *restore* Angellica's picture and trade fairly in the sexual marketplace. His refusal to do so, his exploitation of women's bodies and destruction of their feelings are signs of his lack of a truly royal nature.

Behn's challenge to her audience is to ask them to re-examine their hypocritical attitudes. Angellica seeks to provoke a price war for possession of her body. This will satisfy her desire to dominate, a desire that disguises her self-alienation. The duplication of her picture from a single object to three reminds us that commodification denies a person's uniqueness and identity. She can be multiply reproduced, diminished to a numerical sum that can be divided up and resold. A succession of male characters approach her picture, and transforming it into a sum of money comes naturally to them, as does repeatedly exchanging views on the worth of the sum.

A London courtesan, in an engraving by Pierce Tempest after Marcellus Laroon, about 1688

Behn's comic take on rape in the theatre could be interpreted as an attempt to present it as something other than pandering to voyeurs. The issues a modern audience may have with Behn's approach would not have presented themselves as such to a seventeenth-century audience. Physiological theories current at the time held that women could only become pregnant if they felt pleasure during intercourse; this meant that any pregnancy, even one resulting from a rape, was evidence that the woman had consented and enjoyed the experience. Whatever the motives and feelings involved, legal documents of the time show that rape brought dishonour to a woman's family and she was blamed for the disgrace. Despite her libertine sympathies, Behn saw that sexual desire could not be freed from its political and social context.

Activity

Discuss Behn's use of the virgin/whore duality in IV.ii.

Discussion

- Florinda has ventured onto the streets in search of Belvile, who as usual has failed to turn up. The audience knows that her mask will destabilize her identity. Florinda never acknowledges this risk, even though she is presented with plenty of evidence that it is the case. The men's treatment of her oscillates between aggression and respect, which suggests that her status changes according to the men's antagonisms towards each other. She knows that Don Pedro is due to meet an opponent to duel on the Molo, but the antagonists were masked when the duel was arranged so no one can be certain who will fight or the identity of the woman they are fighting about. Florinda assumes it is Belvile and that she is the cause. This would suit her romantic fiction nicely, but the joke is on all the participants and on patriarchy itself.
- Belvile is disguised as Don Antonio because he owes him a debt of honour. This debt dishonours his loyalty to Florinda, as Don Antonio is his rival for her hand. Don Antonio believes that Belvile is in fact Willmore and therefore a rival for the favours of Angellica, when in fact his real rival is Don Pedro; it is not only women who are nameless or assigned the wrong identity in this play. Belvile assumes the duel is about Florinda as she is the only woman he is interested in, but to the audience he is no more than the comic parody of a knight, setting forth to fight with himself on behalf of his main rival in love. At every turn his honour is compromised. Why should he allow his noble nature to disguise itself as the openly promiscuous Don Antonio?

- The audience knows that Don Antonio is committed to a duel with Don Pedro over Angellica, and that Don Pedro is the man to whom he may become related if Florinda marries him. The characters remain unclear whether they are fighting over Florinda's virtue and safeguarding it for one man, her future husband (yet to be decided), or whether they are fighting for Angellica, who is *common prize* and the property of a succession of men.
- Much energy is expended defending a woman the combatants cannot name or recognize. Identities refuse to stay fixed for men or women as the patriarchal system fails to withstand the disruptive forces of carnival. Behn comically undermines the smugness of masculine valour in its attempts to uphold the virgin/whore duality in this scene.

The critical background

Theatre critics attacked Behn's writing because of her gender, her strong sexual themes and her use of source plays. In 1683 the poet Robert Gould published his *Satyrical Epistle* in which he refers to Behn as a jilt (whore), making the now infamous claim that women who write for money must be prostitutes. In reply Behn published many prefaces to her plays which defended her writing and her right to publish bawdy material. The preface to her play *The Lucky Chance* (1686) is a good example. Modern critics have disagreed strongly over what Gould meant and whether it mattered.

As the performance history of *The Rover* shows, it was much in demand in theatre repertoires for most of the late seventeenth and eighteenth centuries. As tastes and the moral climate changed it was intermittently edited to make it acceptable. By the beginning of the nineteenth century the play was no longer in performance.

At the height of the Victorian era we can see one or two critics returning to the attack on the woman playwright with the 'unwomanly' imagination. The approach taken is that of regret that a great talent was allowed to become dissolute.

It was in universities in the late nineteenth to mid-twentieth centuries that the notion of the 'canon' of English literature was shaped. Academics drawing up their reading lists for students exercised great influence over the nation's sense of which writing was of value and worthy of the highest critical regard. As a woman at the margins writing plays in an era that was always going to be regarded as inferior to the Elizabethans, what chance did Behn stand of being included in that canon? With the development of feminist literary theory in the late twentieth century, however, Behn's work was taken up and examined in new ways.

Modern critical approaches

Feminist and new historicist approaches to *The Rover* have led the revival of interest in Behn's writing in the late twentieth century and beyond. What follows is a summary of some of the main approaches, and information on the source material.

Helen Burke, in her essay *The Cavalier Myth in The Rover*, suggests that Behn's reluctance to acknowledge authorship of *The Rover* stemmed from the way she parodied the source play. Behn's relationship with Killigrew and the royal circle might have suffered had her satire on Cavalier values given offence. Burke considers the satire timely, since the theatre was responding to the political failures and sexual scandals that had rocked the Stuart court in the 1670s. Burke argues that to a certain extent Behn does offer a flattering celebration of royalist and male libertine morality, and that these were in tension with Behn's concerns over the ill-treatment of women. This is why Behn complicates gender relations in the play and leaves Angellica in an unsatisfactory state in V.i. With her mockery of male antics, there is room in the play to foreground the aspirations and voices of the female characters. The space and respect afforded them was unusual in the genre.

Burke concludes her essay with a discussion of the 'double reading' implied in the play's ending. Florinda's acknowledgement of Valeria's role in saving her from gang rape could be interpreted as pointing to a new political order in which women take the initiative through mutual support. By contrast, the Cavaliers force Don Pedro into accepting the marriages of his sisters by a show of strength that is unanswerably primitive in nature.

You can read the full version of *The Cavalier Myth in The Rover* in *The Cambridge Companion to Aphra Behn*, edited by Derek Hughes and Janet Todd (see 'Further Reading').

Anita Pacheco, in her essay *Rape and the Female Subject in Aphra Behn's The Rover*, refers to seventeenth-century rape law to discuss Behn's use of the rape-threat theme. Pacheco asks why any challenge to the patriarchal order made by women characters exposes them to the threat of rape. She explores how men justify their assaults on women, focusing on the contrasting female types Florinda and Angellica. She traces changes in the understanding of rape in English law. Rape shifts from being seen as a property violation against male family members to the sexual violation of a woman against her will. Such a change had radical implications and was very unlikely to have been simple and uncontested. If a wrong done to a woman was no longer seen as a wrong done to her extended family, she could lose male protection.

Pacheco's view is that Behn's play can be read as a struggle over the definition of rape. The essay presents a subtle analysis of Florinda's attempts to define her independence within the limited opportunities that patriarchy offers to women. The contradictions in her position are exposed. The essay then offers an analysis of III.v, providing a critique of male justification of rape. Clothing, body language, speech, violence, consent and guilt are all examined. Pacheco's discussion of Angellica's language considers the courtesan's attempt to turn her beauty, her only asset, into an alternative form of power. The play's examination of the psychology of the courtesan asks serious questions about a woman's quest for self-determination in a society that can only see her as unchaste.

Pacheco's essay does justice to the modernity and complexity of Behn's sympathy for the woman whose sexuality attracts many men but who can feel no desire herself. The essay concludes by asking why Hellena's position is successful in pursuing libertine desire while avoiding the threat of rape that plagues the other women in the play.

You can read the full version of *Rape and the Female Subject in Aphra Behn's The Rover* by Anita Pacheco in *English Literary History* 65 (1998) – see 'Further Reading'.

Julie Nash's essay *'The sight on't would beget a warm desire': Visual Pleasure in Aphra Behn's The Rover*, draws on feminist film theory to explore audience pleasure and the 'gendered gaze' in *The Rover*. Nash explores the theory that the active male gaze objectifies the passive female body for its own controlling pleasure. How far the audience's experience in the theatre is comparable to that in the cinema is open to question. Film selects and intensifies the spectator's experience of the objects to be viewed in a way that theatre cannot. Compared to the multiple viewpoints in Elizabethan theatres, the 'tennis court' shape of the restoration stage with its depth perspective did concentrate the viewing experience more than in previous periods, however.

Nash shows how Behn aligns the audience with Willmore's attempts to use his gaze to control Angellica and Hellena (with varying success). For the male audience this may be an unproblematic position. Nash asks whether women in the audience can adopt any position other than that of a male spectator.

She argues that both Angellica and Lucetta offer negative role models for women. She is more interested in what happens when Hellena takes control of the gaze for her own ends; through Hellena, Behn offers some degree of release from the opposing positions of active male and passive female. Hellena's gipsy disguise links her to prostitution, but only on a visual level. She refutes the charge through her wit and assertiveness about her virginity. She will choose from among those who *venture* upon her and her sole criterion will not be price but *liking*. Just as she teases Willmore verbally, she uses her gaze to look upon him without humiliating him. For most of their encounters she has the advantage of being able to see his face when he cannot see hers.

Nash uses Angellica's picture to explore the analogy between the theatre and prostitution; the audience pays to enjoy a few hours of visual pleasure, which is not unlike the pleasure the Cavaliers gain from the courtesan's pictures.

You can read the full version of *'The sight on't would beget a warm desire': Visual Pleasure in Aphra Behn's The Rover* by Julie Nash in *Restoration: Studies in English Literary Culture* (see 'Further Reading').

Essay Questions

1 What insights can be gained from comparing Willmore and Blunt in *The Rover*?

2 'The evidence that Willmore is a fool and a seducer cannot be reconciled with the claim that he is innately noble and heroic.' How far do you find these views helpful in your understanding of Willmore in *The Rover*?

3 Trace Willmore's journey from resistance to acceptance of marriage and consider how convincing you find the transformation.

4 What issues would a feminist approach to Angellica's pictures raise for a modern audience of *The Rover*?

5 'Whatever the value of her opinions and the depth of her feelings, Angellica is, in the end, a victim.' Is this a fair assessment of Angellica in *The Rover*?

6 Discuss Behn's presentation of the language and actions of Belvile in *The Rover*.

7 'Behn's female characters have complex desires and conflicted motives.' Discuss.

8 What types of suitor are represented by Don Vincentio, Don Antonio and Belvile to a woman like Florinda?

9 What clues are there that Willmore and Hellena might be a compatible couple? What kind of courtship do they embark on compared to that of Florinda and Belvile?

10 'Behn's world is one where the strong dominate the weak and women are the losers.' Discuss the representation of two female characters from *The Rover* in the light of this comment.

11 How might an appreciation of the forms and conventions of restoration theatre inform our understanding of the characters of Blunt and Angellica in *The Rover*?

12 Discuss Behn's handling of the rape-threat theme in *The Rover*.

13 Discuss Behn's use of dramatic tension and humour to explore male/female relationships in *The Rover*.

14 Discuss Behn's use of the language of love and the language of commerce in *The Rover*.

15 'A comic surface with serious intent.' Discuss Behn's use of comic techniques in *The Rover*.

16 Discuss Behn's use of gendered space and boundaries in *The Rover*.

17 How far and in what ways does *The Rover* explore the light and dark sides of carnival?

18 How important is the mask and costume to your understanding of *The Rover*'s serio-comic concerns?

19 How successful is Behn in presenting her audience with evidence of the hypocrisy of the virgin/whore duality in *The Rover*?

20 Consider Behn's handling of concerns about male and female identity in *The Rover*.

Chronology

Aphra Behn's life

c. 1640   Born at Harbledown, near Canterbury in Kent; her father, Bartholomew Johnson, was a barber or innkeeper, her mother Elizabeth a wet-nurse.

1663   Behn's father appointed lieutenant-general to the English colony of Surinam. He dies on the outward voyage to the colony. Behn completes the journey and stays in Surinam for about two months.

1666   Behn travels to Antwerp as a spy in the service of Charles II.

1667   Behn returns to England with debts that may have landed her in prison.

1669   By this time Behn had begun her writing career.

1670   *The Forced Marriage*, her first play, performed.

1673   *The Dutch Lover*, her third play, published.

c. 1674–5   Behn begins a long-term relationship with lawyer John Hoyle.

1677   *The Rover* performed.

1680   *The Second Part of the Rover* performed.

1682   The Duke's Company takes over the King's Company, forming the United Company.

1684   Behn publishes a collection of poetry.

1686   Behn returns to the theatre with *The Lucky Chance*.

1687   Behn's popular farce *The Emperor of the Moon* performed.

1688   Behn writes *Oroonoko*, drawing on her experiences in Surinam in her youth. Behn writes the novel *Love Letters between a Nobleman and his Sister* during the political upheavals of the end of Charles II's reign and the beginning of James II's.

1689   Behn dies 16 April, two months into the reign of William III and Mary. She is buried in Westminster Abbey.

Key historical events

1649	Charles I beheaded and the Commonwealth proclaimed.
1651	Charles II defeated by Cromwell at the battle of Worcester; Charles escapes to the Continent where he lives mainly in Paris.
1653	Cromwell becomes Lord Protector until his death in 1658.
1661	King Charles II crowned; royalist supporters of the king are given back their confiscated lands on their return from exile.
1662	King Charles II marries Catherine of Braganza.
1665	The Great Plague in London.
1666	The Great Fire of London.
1685	Death of Charles II; accession of his brother James II. Monmouth, Charles's illegitimate son, stages a rebellion in a bid to take the throne in the name of Protestantism.
1688	The 'Glorious Revolution' sees James II deposed and exiled. Protestant rule in England is secured under William of Orange. William and his wife Mary, daughter of James II, are invited to come to England and assume the throne as constitutional monarchs.
1689	William and Mary crowned in Westminster Abbey.

The Rover's performance and publishing history

- First performed March 1677.
- First quarto edition published 1677; the only one printed in Behn's lifetime, so the only authoritative text.
- Publication of the third issue adds 'written by Mrs A Behn' to the title page. Copies of three issues of the first quarto still exist; they were all published during 1677 and differ only in theatre page.
- From seventeenth-century stage records (incomplete) we can see that the play was revived at least four times in the 1680s and several times in the 1690s.
- In 1703 it was revived at Drury Lane and is recorded as being performed every year except 1719 until 1743, or even 1750.
- The play was altered from time to time during the eighteenth century to suit contemporary notions of acceptable taste.
- The play's last recorded production in London was in 1790, by this time much altered to avoid charges of immorality.
- From about 1790 it was dropped altogether until the 1970s saw a revival of interest in Behn's work.
- In 1986 the Royal Shakespeare Company performed the play, directed by John Barton at the Swan Theatre, Stratford upon Avon.
- The NXT New Cross Theatre staged a production in 1991.
- In 1994 an experimental modern version directed by Jules Wright for the Women's Playhouse Trust was staged; this production was a collaboration between the WPT and the Open University/BBC.
- Any Internet search today will reveal that the play is still regularly performed in the US and in British universities. The play has fared less well on the English stage since the late twentieth century. Neither subsidized nor commercial companies have been attracted to the play in recent years.

Further Reading

Biography

Maureen Duffy, *The Passionate Shepherdess: Aphra Behn 1640–1689* (Weidenfeld & Nicholson, 1977)

Angeline Goreau, *Reconstructing Aphra: A Social Biography of Aphra Behn* (Dial Press, 1980)

Janet Todd, *The Secret Life of Aphra Behn* (Andre Deutsch, 1996)

Claire Tomalin, *Samuel Pepys: The Unequalled Self* (Penguin, 2003) Useful for a historical, social and cultural account of the restoration period

Critical books

Richard W. Bevis, *English Drama: Restoration and Eighteenth Century, 1660–1789* (Longman Literature in English Series, 1988)

Susan Carlson, *Cannibalizing and Carnivalizing: Reviving Aphra Behn's 'The Rover'* (*Theatre Journal*, Vol. 47, No. 4, Eighteenth Century Representations, Dec. 1995, 517–539)

Elin Diamond, *Gestus and Signature in Aphra Behn's The Rover* (*English Literary History*, Vol. 56, No. 3, Autumn 1989, 519–541)

John Donohue (ed.), *The Cambridge History of British Theatre, Volume 2 – 1660 to 1895* (Cambridge University Press, 2004)

John Franceschina, *Shadow and Substance in Aphra Behn's The Rover: The Semiotics of Restoration Performance* (*Restoration: Studies in English Literary Culture 1600–1700*, 1995, Vol. 19, pt. 1, 29–42)

Elaine Hobby, *No Stolen Object, but Her Own: Aphra Behn's Rover and Thomas Killigrew's Thomaso* (*Women's Writing*, Vol. 6, No. 1, 1999)

Elizabeth Howe, *The First English Actresses: Women and Drama 1660–1700* (Cambridge University Press, 1992)

Derek Hughes, *The Theatre of Aphra Behn* (Palgrave Macmillan, 2001)

Derek Hughes, *The Masked Woman Revealed: or, the Prostitute and the Playwright in Aphra Behn Criticism* (*Women's Writing*, Vol. 7, No. 2, 2000)

Derek Hughes and Janet Todd (eds.), *The Cambridge Companion to Aphra Behn* (Cambridge University Press, 2004)

Julie Nash, 'The sight on't would beget a warm desire': Visual Pleasure in Aphra Behn's The Rover (*Restoration: Studies in English Literary Culture 1600–1700*, 1994, Vol. 18, pt. 2, 77–87)

W.R. Owen and Lizbeth Goodman (eds.), *Shakespeare, Aphra Behn and the Canon* (Open University, 1996)

Anita Pacheco, *Rape and the Female Subject in Aphra Behn's The Rover* (*English Literary History*, Vol. 65, No. 2, 1998, 323–345)

Stephen Szilagyi, *The Sexual Politics of Behn's Rover: After Patriarchy* (*Studies in Philology*, Chapel Hill, Fall 1998, Vol. 95, Issue 4)

Katy Thomas, *Liberation through Façade: The Role of Masquerade in Aphra Behn's The Rover* (*Emagazine*, English and Media Centre, September 2005)

Janet Todd (ed.), *Aphra Behn: Contemporary Critical Essays* (New Casebooks, Macmillan 1999)

Videos and DVDs

BBC drama in four parts: *Charles II, the Power and the Passion*, 2003; includes a historical documentary about the period

Stage Beauty, directed by Richard Eyre, 2004; film about Edward Kynaston (1643–1712), leading actor in the King's Company (Behn could only have used him in her plays after the two companies merged)

The Libertine, directed by Laurence Dunmore, 2005; film about the life and times of John Wilmot, Earl of Rochester

The Rover, Open University Video, 1996; a multi-racial company
of actors place particular emphasis on a colonial theme in
this production

Websites

The Aphra Behn Society
http://prometheus.cc.emory.edu/behn/caywoodtour.html

The Aphra Behn page (a starting point that links to other
websites on Behn)
http://www.lit-arts.net/Behn

Website with a variety of resources and essays on Behn
http://www.sukipot.com/angellica

On-line text of the play, free for non-commercial use
http://drama.eserver.org/plays/17th_century/rover/

Restoration theatre website
http://www.st-andrews.ac.uk/~www_se/murray/Restoration/
Front.html

Glossary

Literary and cultural terms

analogy an extended comparison which assists in understanding two things

bawdy humour with sexual content that is meant to shock

canon a body of literature that academics consider most worthy of critical praise and attention

closet drama a text that has the shape of a play, but is intended for private reading rather than performance in a public theatre

commodification the act of turning a person or value into a commodity that has a market price and can therefore be exchanged for money

conceit a form of simile, often extended and elaborated upon; it can suggest a surprising and witty comparison between two unlike things

courtly love term originating in the Middle Ages, probably first appearing in the poetry of the troubadours of southern France. Courtly love is based on the idea that the strong feelings a man may feel for a woman will ennoble him. This love will be experienced as a Platonic, even spiritual experience. In the Middle Ages, marriages among the nobility were made for dynastic and financial reasons. Courtly love provided an alternative way into emotional and sexual relationships between men and women; as such it always carried the risk that it would become adulterous. The male lover cannot be a husband, so constantly needs to renew proof of his total worship of the woman. To do this he may engage in single combat, battle or quests, all of which follow the ideals of chivalric codes of honour

euphemism a use of language to refer to something frightening, violent or taboo, in a way that disguises its disturbing features

feminist criticism a major contributor to literary debate since the 1960s, feminism asserts that gender and in particular women's inferior status under a patriarchal (male-dominated) system are significant features in the writing and interpretation of literary texts.

Feminism asserts that male-dominated ways of perceiving and structuring reality are designed into the social order. As literary texts represent aspects of that society, attitudes and values that cast women as inferior to men can be found in them. The purpose of feminist criticism is to uncover and challenge such ideologies

fetish   object representing something desired; Angellica's pictures function as fetishes as they stand in for her absent body and become the focus of Willmore's sexual arousal

fop   in drama, a foolish male character who is obsessed with his appearance; one who pretends to the manners and style of a social class he does not belong to by birth

gay couple   in comic drama, the term refers to a pair of clever, witty lovers. They seem to act independently of family and other social constraints. They use verbal sparring to test each other's character and faithfulness with a view to eventual marriage

gulling   making a fool of a character in a ritualistic way, usually a character the audience will enjoy seeing humiliated

irony   an effect that occurs when a character says one thing and means another, or says something that can be contrasted to his or her context and a wider significance uncovered by the audience. The irony may or may not be intentional

juxtaposition   the placing of two or more features in a text next to each other for the purposes of contrast or comparison

liminal   related to thresholds or boundaries. When a character is in a liminal state, he or she is uncertain about how to act and identity becomes unstable. There is both risk and potential in the liminal state

metaphor   a figure of speech where two unlike things are yoked together in a process that implies that one thing is the other. This assumption is meant to be read imaginatively rather than literally. Metaphors communicate many meanings that are difficult to express literally

new historicism   the study of a literary text that seeks to understand the effect of its historical context on its meaning. Critics will research original documents in painstaking detail, paying attention to what writers exclude as well as include in their writing

oxymoron   a figure of speech that juxtaposes two apparently contradictory terms

parody   an imitation of a literary style or genre that mocks its conventions through exaggeration and/or exaggerated seriousness

patriarchy   any social, economic or political system structured in such a way that it favours men over women. Its value system will support the idea that such inequality is natural and just

patron   in the past, writers earned very little from their art. They needed a rich patron to provide for them. A patron would usually be aristocratic, certainly very wealthy. They would be people of acknowledged good taste and might influence the writer's work

Petrarchan   a term that describes the style and subject matter of the fourteenth-century Italian poet, Petrarch. He is best known for his sonnets, in which he uses elaborate conceits written in memory of an idealized woman. His poetry concentrates on the effects of his unrequited passion on his emotions, mood and state of mind. His poetry was a major influence on European writers from the sixteenth century onwards

plagiarism   the practice of taking ideas and language from a fellow artist and disguising them as one's own. This is not the same as openly incorporating other writers' ideas or using earlier work as source material

register   a style of language used for a specific purpose; it can be a type, like a political register; a mood, like an emotional or comic register; or relate to the social class of the speaker

repartee   a succession of rapid and witty replies in a dialogue between characters, especially one that turns an insult against the originator

rhetorical language   highly patterned language that seeks to create special effects through repetition and figures of speech; speech intended to persuade the listener to accept the speaker's point of view

satire   writing that ridicules people, behaviour or values in a comic manner with a view to reforming or changing them. This implies there is a strong moral attitude in the satirist

semantic field   a group of words defined by similarities in meaning; words that work together in a text to suggest a common theme

simile   a comparison between two things that have a number of points in common. The reader sees and understands more thoroughly by appreciating those similarities. The words 'like' or 'as' indicate a simile rather than a metaphor

wit   language used in an intellectually stimulating and novel way. Such language would be elegant, structured and subtle. The means of expressing a clever idea will be as important as the idea itself

Historical terms

bourgeoisie   the middle-class majority, whose values are seen as unadventurous and restrictive

coterie   a small, privileged group of people who associate with one another

interregnum   literally, 'between reigns'; the period from 1649 to 1660, which was a period of republican government under the leadership of Oliver Cromwell and his son Richard. It occurred after the execution of Charles I and before the restoration to the throne of his son, Charles II

libertine   term used to describe highly self-interested people who are sexually promiscuous. They reject traditional morality and religious teaching. Usually associated with aristocratic males of the Stuart court

Puritan   a member of a group of English Protestants who in the sixteenth and seventeenth centuries advocated strict religious discipline along with simplification of the ceremonies and creeds of the Church of England. Seventeenth-century Puritans were involved in commerce and saw Parliament as a place to further their interests against royal privilege

rake   an abbreviation of 'rake-hell', used commonly in the seventeenth-century to describe someone who is utterly immoral, debauched and dissolute

restoration   the period 1660–1700 as a whole, but more specifically the return of a constitutional monarchy in 1660 under Charles II

royalist   a supporter of government by monarchy; a soldier who fought for Charles I during the English Civil War, also referred to as a Cavalier

Tory   not to be confused with members of the modern-day Conservative Party, Tories sat in Parliament in opposition to the Whigs. They defended traditional political and social institutions against the forces of democratization or reform. They supported the Stuart monarchy

Whig   political party in opposition to the Tories, they were pro-Parliamentarian and had Puritan beliefs

Appendix 1

Aphra Behn's London

Westminster Abbey

Behn is buried in the cloisters.
Tube: Westminster

Theatres

The Dorset Garden Theatre was demolished in 1709. It was situated on the Thames at Whitefriars. Until 1989 the City of London School used the site as a playground.
Tube: St Paul's

Theatre Royal Drury Lane: Catherine Street, London WC2B 5JF. Built in 1633 and rebuilt three more times on the same site. The first building was burnt down in 1672; Nell Gwyn appeared here before she became the king's mistress and retired from the stage. Sir Christopher Wren re-built the theatre and it was opened in 1674 in the presence of the king. Lacking space and fashionable extras, it was demolished in 1719. The present building dates from 1812.
Tube: Covent Garden

The Royal Opera House Covent Garden is the third theatre on the present site. It was a playhouse before becoming an Opera House from 1728.
Tube: Covent Garden

Paintings

Paintings from the period on view at the National Portrait Gallery, Trafalgar Square:
Room 5 Charles I and Civil War
Room 6 Science and Arts in the Seventeenth Century (the

engraving of Aphra Behn can be found in a glass case in this
room)
Room 7 Charles II: The Restoration of the Monarchy
Room 8 The Later Stuarts
Room 9 The Kit-Cat Club
Tube: Leicester Square

Buildings

Buildings erected in London during the restoration period:

The Banqueting House, Whitehall Palace, was built for King
James I between 1619 and 1622. It is all that remains of the royal
palace, which was destroyed by fire in 1698. It was originally built
for state ceremonials, plays and masques. The ceiling paintings
are the work of Sir Peter Paul Rubens and are a magnificent
statement of the Stuart dynasty's belief in the divine right of
kings. King Charles I was executed outside the building on 30
January 1649. It was here that Charles II was received by both
Houses of Parliament in 1660 after his triumphal procession
through London. During the restoration the hall was much in
demand for occasions of state and visits from foreign dignitaries.
Tube: Westminster

The Monument, designed by Sir Christopher Wren and Dr
Robert Hooke to commemorate the Great Fire of London of
1666, was built in 1677, the year of *The Rover*'s first performance.
Tube: Monument

St Paul's Cathedral was built by Sir Christopher Wren between
1675 and 1710. It is the best example of English baroque
architecture in the country. It replaced Old St Paul's, which was
destroyed in the Great Fire of London in 1666.
Tube: St Paul's

Hyde Park was in existence for hundreds of years before the restoration period but both Charles I and II developed it during their reigns. Charles I created a circular track called the Ring where members of the royal court could drive their carriages. In 1637 the park was opened to the public. Behn refers to the May Day rides in the park in the prologue to *The Rover*. You can still find evidence on the east side of the park of earthworks built to defend the city of Westminster from royalist attacks during the civil war. In 1660 most evidence of warfare was cleared and Hyde Park became a royal park again. King Charles II restocked it with deer and encircled it with a brick wall. It became the scene of splendid courtly carriage rides, and of course the 'cits' also returned.

Tube: Hyde Park Corner

Appendix 2

Ideas for studying the play in the classroom

1 Buy, hire or make some masks and use them when acting out scenes where masking matters.

2 Write a sentence for each character that sums up their type. Students could choose a character each and bring in a single item of clothing or prop that they think helps identify that character. Use the items for easy identification of characters while acting out the play.

3 Research the restoration theatre and use the information to sketch out a theatre interior, labelling the parts.

4 Write a 60–90-second version of the play to familiarize yourself with the plot; present your version to the class. This could take the form of a ballad, puppet show, mime, or magazine gossip column.

5 Try 'hot seating'; after reading or acting a scene, students who have taken the main parts could sit on a panel and, keeping in role, answer questions on their motivation, feelings and behaviour.

6 Try gender switching; swap male for female parts and vice versa. Discuss how the scenes play differently.

7 Try writing an additional scene, rewriting an existing one or adapting a scene for a contemporary context. The on-line text can be used for easy cutting and pasting to a Word document, which can then be re-drafted for these exercises.

8 Take on the role of casting director; create a collage featuring actors you would cast for the play.

9 Try voice recognition; select chunks of dialogue that you think reveal contrasts in character through style and expression. Type them into a Word document and ask other

students to match the dialogue to the characters and justify their decisions.

10 Dictionary exercise: track these words though Act I Scene II, showing their meaning for the characters and situation. If you have access to an on-line dictionary such as the Oxford English Dictionary you can also check their meaning for a seventeenth-century audience.

- interest, trade, chapmen, value, merchants, venture, exposed to sale, commodity, credit
- kind/a kindness, honest, bush, game
- Father Captain, be at my devotion, Jephtha's daughter.

11 Find out about Samuel Pepys and his interest in restoration theatre. Read some of his diary entries about the theatre (available on the Internet). Write a diary entry in the manner of Pepys describing a visit to the Dorset Garden Theatre to see *The Rover*.

12 Use digital cameras and a simple software package such as Word to create a cartoon strip of Act IV Scene II lines 1–139. Photograph each other in role, then add speech bubbles to explore the comic instability of disguise and mistaken identity that leads to the duelling on the Molo. It will also help you explore the degree of anarchy Behn brings to the play at this point.

13 Using an on-line text of *The Rover*, track Behn's use of a particular word, theme or motif. When you have the page on the screen click on Edit, then Find on the top tool bar. Type in the word you are researching and the computer will highlight it each time it is used in the text.

14 Research a history of prostitution. Find out about how it has been policed and how attitudes to it have evolved in the past (be selective!). Consider also current debates about what constitutes rape in UK law. Discuss the relevance of Behn's sexual politics in the light of your research.

Appendix 3

Comparative texts

Behn's presentation of gender relationships can be compared with these scenes from Shakespeare and Ben Jonson.

Gender disguise

A scene from *As You Like It*, William Shakespeare (1598/1600)
Act III Scene III from line 268 (Rosalind: I will speak to him like a saucy lackey) to the end of the scene

The trials of marriage and treatment of wives

A husband who is willing to prostitute his wife for gain, in a scene from the comedy *Volpone*, Ben Jonson (1605)
Act III Scene VII

The suspicious husband

The tragedy *Othello*, William Shakespeare (1602–4)
Act IV Scene II

The gay couple

An early example of the gay couple in the comedy *Much Ado About Nothing*, William Shakespeare (1598)
Act I Scene I lines 105–131 (Beatrice: I wonder that you will still be talking... *to* Beatrice: You always end with a jade's trick. I know you of old.)
Act II Scene I lines 114–255 (Beatrice: Will you not tell me who told you so? *to* Benedick: I cannot endure my Lady Tongue.)